Valiant and Wise

by

Laura Strickland

Hearts of Caledonia, Book Two

Valiant and Wise

Cover Art by *Diana Carlile*

The Wild Rose Press, Inc.
PO Box 708
Adams Basin, NY 14410-0708
Visit us at www.thewildrosepress.com

Publishing History
First Tea Rose Edition, 2018
Print ISBN 978-1-5092-2243-8
Digital ISBN 978-1-5092-2244-5

Hearts of Caledonia, Book Two
Published in the United States of America

"Me?" She jerked up her gaze and once more met his. Barely a whisper separated them, and Verica lost her breath at what she saw in his eyes.

Another smile quirked his lips and warmed his gaze. "Do you not need your wounds tended? Will you take off your clothing, also, for me?"

Quite an improper suggestion, even under the circumstances. But the soft mischief in his voice lent no offense; instead Verica felt a stir of titillation.

With the native honesty that marked most of her utterances, she said, "I might."

His fingers rose and cupped the back of her head. Gently—so very gently—he drew her to him. Their lips met.

A caress. A whisper. Verica had never been kissed this way, by lips so warm they wooed, coaxed, and persuaded. Tentatively he tasted her, decided he liked the flavor, and dove deeper.

Verica had a sudden flashback to one of Morirex's kisses—swift and brutal, teeth clashing on teeth, the taste of blood. The pain of invasion accompanied by the overwhelming subjugation of her body. Hard-learned experience told her a man took what he wanted without asking.

But Wick map Radoc's lips asked. They sought, thrilled, and comforted. His fingers slid lower and caressed her cheek, the calloused thumb stroking lightly like the touch of a butterfly, and Verica's entire body melted.

Dedication

Books by Laura Strickland
available from The Wild Rose Press, Inc.

Dead Handsome: A Buffalo Steampunk Adventure
Off Kilter: A Buffalo Steampunk Adventure
Sheer Madness: A Buffalo Steampunk Adventure
Steel Kisses: A Buffalo Steampunk Adventure
Tough Prospect: A Buffalo Steampunk Adventure
~*~
Devil Black
His Wicked Highland Ways
Honor Bound: A Highland Adventure
The White Gull (part of the Lobster Cove Series)
Forged by Love (sequel to *The White Gull*)
Words and Dreams (sequel to *Forged by Love*)
The Hiring Fair (part of the Help Wanted Series)
Awake on Garland Street
Stars in the Morning (part of the Landmarks Series)
~*~
The Guardians of Sherwood Trilogy:
Daughter of Sherwood
Champion of Sherwood
Lord of Sherwood
~*~
Short Stories:
Mrs. Claus and the Viking Ship
The Tenth Suitor
Christmastime on Donner's Mountain
Ask Me (part of the Candy Hearts Series)
~*~
Hearts of Caledonia Series:
Loyal and True
Valiant and Wise

Caledonian hearts are loyal and true.
Caledonian hearts are valiant and wise.
Caledonian hearts are noble and blessed.

Laura Strickland

A word about the Picts and the Caledonii

Dear Reader,

Not a great deal is known about the Picts, certainly not as much as we might wish. They left few written records, which makes research for even a work of romantic fiction challenging. One thing we do know is that they did not call themselves "Picts." That appellation was leveled by the Romans and stemmed from the pictures (tattoos) they wore on their skin, so numerous they were often referred to as "blue men."

At the time of my story, Celtic clans had moved into western Scotland from Ireland and settled the kingdom of Dal Riada. The north and east of Scotland, a vast territory, was still controlled by tribes loosely gathered under the name "Caledonii." Beneath this name there existed sub-tribes, and I have called that of my hero the "Epidii." Predictably, conflict arose between the Gaels and the Caledonii, who contested for land. Later, as legend has it, they would be united under Kenneth MacAlpin, but before then a considerable amount of fighting and displacement must have ensued.

The language of the Picts/Caledonii has not survived except in place names and some given names inscribed on stones. Research tells us it was closely related to ancient Welsh, and I have chosen to give my characters names with an ancient Briton/Welsh flavor. Since this is in fact a work of romantic fiction, I hope you will join me in imagining the details of Caledonian life, including what they may have called their gods—and how they might have proved themselves to be valiant.

Laura Strickland

Chapter One

The region of the Moray Firth, Scotland, Early Winter 754 AD

Wick map Radoc ran like a stag before the hunter; he ran for his life. Breath surged in his lungs, searing like fire, and sweat drenched his body despite the chill air of the morning. He leaped over hillocks and rivulets, wove his way between the trunks of trees, and dodged low-hanging branches. Yet still his pursuers grew ever closer, behind.

He longed to look back, wanted desperately to steal one glance over his shoulder, but did not dare. A single check in his stride, one stumble, and he might be lost. Then he would be slain here in this stretch of Caledonian forest and lie beneath the dawn sky, never to experience another morning.

Dead. Like his mother, his father—like his friends, so many he'd lost count.

Upon that thought, his toe caught a root or stone and he nearly went flying. A howl rose from his pursuers even as he spread his arms in a wild bid to regain his balance and pelted on. By the goddess, that cry meant they had him in clear sight just as he had them within hearing.

Where had they picked up his trail? Must have been when he crossed that icy stream just south of the

Moray. He hadn't seen them—he who, as acting war chief of his tribe, the Epidii, should know better. He, who fancied himself a half-decent tracker in his own right. Fool—he'd been distracted, thinking of the past.

One such mistake, as he well knew, could shatter a life, a world.

He caught his breath with a great whoop and, straining every muscle, started up an incline and into a thicker stand of trees. The Gaels—and he had no doubt they were Gaelic warriors, probably a hunting party— exclaimed once more and came on. This made a deadly hunt, and no mistake. Mortal enemies, as he'd learned, did not give up the pursuit and, above all things, these men were his enemies.

A terrible grimace contorted his features as he bared his teeth, seeking more air to fuel his burning muscles. At least they'd been forced to abandon their infernal chariots, the ones with the blades fitted to the wheels, blades that could cut a man to pieces where he stood—no room to maneuver them here among the trees. They ran just like Wick, but in a pack—five? Six?—like hounds behind the hart, and the question, the question remained…

How far could this hart run?

A second rivulet appeared before him—nay, not a rivulet but a stream. He checked involuntarily—too wide to leap?—and nearly tumbled in. Gasping, legs weak as boiled sinew, he turned.

And saw them.

They materialized like an evil dream, one of those awful night visions that had plagued Wick since his parents' deaths. They'd spread out behind him, each finding a separate path through the trees, like a woven fishing net; it would, he saw instantly, do him no good to cut to one side or the other. Their gaudy clothing looked shockingly bright in the clear morning light—reds and yellows, garish banners that proclaimed their bold confidence—and their hair flew like tattered flags.

Wick spun again and faced the stream. Better to break himself on the rocks there than be taken prisoner. He knew what his enemies did to captured tribesmen such as he.

Utterly at bay, he closed his eyes and whispered a frantic prayer.

Goddess, please—lend me the strength I lack. Lend it to me and I will devote what remains of my life to you.

A missile carved the air at his shoulder; another sailed near his ear. At least one of his pursuers had paused long enough to use his sling. Desperate strength came to Wick from nowhere—from everywhere—and filled him to the brim.

He leaped the stream.

Even at that glorious moment, part of him wondered how. It would have made a fearsome feat for a man running at full tilt, impossible from a dead start. Yet he soared over the chasm effortlessly as if lifted from beneath.

He landed without so much as a stagger and heard cries of wonder behind him. Another missile flew but fell short, splashing into the water. He bounded on, weaving a path through the trees, the breath now coming easy and deep in his lungs.

Would his pursuers continue to follow? He could hear their voices still, yet soon those sounds fell away behind. Swiftly, swiftly Wick ran.

A mist rose around him, streaming up from the damp ground, from the rock itself, and filling the gaps between the trees. Wick's feet pounded the ground hard. Yet looking down through the swirls of fog, he saw his feet were no longer *feet*. Instead, hooves struck the sodden leaves and loam. His neck stretched out as he leaped and ran; he felt a great weight on his head.

Ah, and he no longer ran alone. A herd of deer—other deer?—ran around him, half hidden by the mist. Wild music possessed him, a song that rushed through his blood the way the wind rushed past his ears, impossible to contain. For the first time in ready memory, joy touched him, rough and sweet. He no longer ran to escape but for the sheer pleasure of it.

Nothing could touch him. No one could harm him.

He recognized the tune pounding through him in time with his hoof beats, one of those his mother used to sing while sitting by the fire at night, or during one of her sacred rituals.

But how could that be? Her voice had fallen silent, never to be raised again. She lay far behind Wick, in her grave.

Yet her song, by some miracle, lived on.

****

The magic faded slowly, step by step. The mist dissolved around Wick, and the phantom herd of deer with it. Once more pleading for breath, he collapsed face down in the bare leaf mold, his lungs working like bellows. What had happened to him back there? That wild and impossible chase must have been a dream, a waking vision born of pure desperation. For here, on the frosty ground, he once more found himself inhabiting the form of a man. His own clothing covered his limbs—brown deer-hide leggings and tunic, not unlike the coat of a deer—and his pack still weighted his back.

Madness, and miracle. Cheek pressed against the cold ground, waiting for his breath and heartbeat to calm, he thought about it as clearly as he could. It might well have been a Vision. Yet he had, yes, called upon the goddess for help. And as his mother had taught him, those who called with an earnest heart might expect an answer. But why, of all the men in the world, should the great goddess help Wick map Radoc?

He, who did not deserve such assistance.

He flopped onto his back and stared at the sky, debating truth and fancy. If it were true...what of the promise he'd given the goddess in return for his life? That he would devote what remained of it to her. His features contorted in a fierce scowl.

A poor bargain on the goddess's part.

He struggled to his feet, fighting against the ache of overworked muscles. Swaying, he stood wondering whence he was bound. Away, or toward? Running from a past he had no hope of evading or toward a future he did not want to embrace?

Better perhaps to have let the Gaels catch him. But he could not do that—he had been raised by a woman who believed far too deeply in the sacred fabric of life and by a man who refused to give up no matter the challenge he faced. A bitter smile twisted his lips; he gathered up his few possessions—a spear, a long knife, and the slim hide pack he'd brought from home—and moved on, northeastward.

As he went, the bright morning faded and clouds once more gathered, moving in from the west. He knew this land and loved it to his very bones. Yet now it felt as torn and uncertain as his own spirit.

He gazed ahead through the trees, listening to the silence. Caledonia, land of endless trees, wore her cloak of shaggy green and brown frosted with snow like the goddess herself. He wondered suddenly whether swearing his service to the goddess differed any from swearing it to Caledonia. This he had always done. From the age of sixteen, when his father, Radoc, suffered a crippling injury at the hands of the Gaels, Wick had stepped up and filled the place.

And now he fled. Fled those who loved and needed him. Fled his own failure.

Oh, he might make excuses. He might tell himself he went to make connections with his father's allies farther north, who also fought against the Gaels.

In his heart he knew he lied.

What happened when a strong man broke? He had no frame of reference for it, having only his father's staunch example before him.

A soft tendril of air touched his cheek; it felt almost like the touch of a chilly hand and sent a shiver down his spine. He thought he heard his mother's voice. *You live not for yourself but for she who has spared your life.*

A poor bargain, indeed.

****

A curious thing, that a man walking alone should no longer feel quite alone. Wick kept thinking he felt others around him, unseen—the previously imagined herd of deer, perhaps, or his parents. Did they accompany him in spirit? It could not be; were his father, Radoc, here even in spirit, he would harangue

Wick, tell him to go back home, take up his duties, and act like the chief he'd been raised to be.

But, Father, he repeated the lie, *I go to seek an alliance for the tribe.*

Yet even if he believed the fabrication, he had yet to come upon anything but ruined settlements. He'd met with no bands of Caledonii warriors or scouts, not even the remnants of a fleeing tribe. Combined with the Gaelic presence, it made him wonder if he'd trekked too far west.

Direct me, Father.

But it was his mother's voice he heard again. *Go on, son, where She directs...*

Late in the afternoon he stumbled upon the remnants of yet another Caledonii settlement. By then the rain had resumed, icy pricks of moisture that flayed the skin of his face and found their way through the folds of his clothing. The scent of burning came to him first, damped down by the wet, and closed his throat tight. A reek all too familiar, one that hit him in the gut like memory, it smelled not only of torched wood but scorched flesh.

The settlement appeared ghostly, a scene conjured from dark imaginings. Bodies lay everywhere, bloodied and broken, some half-burnt. In the clearing between the huts lay a wrecked chariot on its side, its bright paint darkened by rain. This tribe, probably the Taranos, he figured, had tried to fight back, just like Wick's own tribe.

His eyes narrowed on the scene; they had failed. Dwelling after dwelling lay burned. Many a tribe member lay staring sightlessly at the sky.

Vomit rose to the back of Wick's throat, and he

had to gulp deep breaths of air in order to beat it back. He whispered another prayer to the goddess, this one without much faith behind it. Where had the goddess been when these folk needed her—when they called to her, screamed and cried and begged?

For Wick knew they had begged; he'd lived through just such an attack as this. And where were the Gaels now? Why did they so seldom occupy the land they conquered? Another violent shiver traveled up his spine, and he had the sudden conviction someone watched him from under cover.

The Gaels would return. One thing he had learned, and that the hard way—they always returned.

Chapter Two

Wick tramped blindly on through the waning afternoon, contemplating a stark truth. Any hope he'd had, when leaving his home, of enlisting the Taranos to assist the Epidii had now evaporated.

The Gaels had spread faster and farther this season than he'd ever imagined. Here in the north, so near the Moray Firth, he'd thought to find the Caledonia of old, that of which his father and grandfathers once spoke—a land of virgin forest and breathtaking beauty, wild and free.

Instead he encountered only death. The sickness assailed him once more as he thought of the settlement behind him, and a thick haze invaded his mind.

He must remain alert. A warrior who failed to pay attention courted his own death—how many times had he heard that from his father's lips? He'd heard it each time he stood guard or sent men to fight or defend the settlement. After his father's terrible injury, that had been his duty: defending the settlement.

Failing to defend the settlement.

Fiercely, he tried to push that thought away. It refused to go. His father, slain. His mother, Essa, so full of magic and beauty...silenced forever. His young brother, Taloc, sorely injured.

He gave a harsh laugh and stopped walking in mid stride, frozen in place. The endless forest swayed overhead, the branches gathering great armfuls of clouds from which to squeeze more rain. He barely noticed, far too focused within.

Most of his tribe, loyal to his father, had expected Wick to go on leading after Radoc's death. But there existed those who, no doubt perceiving Wick's inherent weakness, spoke for choosing a new and stronger leader instead. Wick's own friend, Brude, coveted the place.

So Wick had left it to him—Brude the strong, Brude the confident, he who had no apparent doubt of himself and whose world had not come apart all around him.

Let Wick's sister, Barta, who had always wanted to be a warrior, contest Brude for the place of chief. He, Wick, turned his back squarely upon it.

He jerked back into motion even as the rain drove down harder, beating at him.

But could he? Could a man ever truly turn his back on what he loved?

****

"Mistress, we believe the Gaels mean to attack again at first light. Our scouts have seen them preparing to mobilize."

The man who delivered the warning to Verica looked wild with despair. Blood ran down one side of his face from a deep cut above his eyebrow, and all his knuckles had been laid open. That did not keep him from clutching a long knife so tightly Verica doubted he'd be able to leave go of it if he tried.

And why do you bring this news to me? She longed to speak the words, to be free of the demands that surrounded her, yet she could not. Because she knew the answer—there was no one else to carry the weight of responsibility and answer those demands.

Once, she'd been an ordinary Caerena tribeswoman, a young wife whose biggest concern remained pleasing her husband. Then the Caledonian tribes to their west had fallen, encouraging the Gaels to move in south of the Moray Firth. Inevitably, battle by battle, the Gaels crept northward until, this ripe autumn, the Caerena found themselves in a fight for their very existence.

She scowled at Motius and shot a hard-eyed glare at his fellow warrior, Cintus, who also sidled up to her. A haze of burning hung over the settlement, and she could hear the groans of the wounded. Groans and weeping.

Striving to close her ears against both, she asked Motius, "How many of our warriors fell? How many remain who are able to fight?"

The two men exchanged glances before Motius answered, "Nearly half a score have fallen. How many can still fight? I am not certain."

"How many remain, then, who are uninjured?"

"Uninjured?" Motius repeated and stole a second look at his companion. "I dare say none."

None. The shock of hearing that went through Verica like a death cry; she fought to keep from revealing her dismay. "How many do you think will be able to take their feet and hold a weapon?"

Motius turned his head and ran his gaze over the smoky settlement as if counting, and Verica saw he'd lost an ear.

By all that's holy—he has lost an ear and yet he still stands.

She muttered a curse even as a wave of compassion

15

swamped her. She could not show the compassion, not if they needs must face another attack at dawn. No softness, not now.

"Perhaps three score and ten."

So few. And each man in some way hampered.

Verica drew a breath. This next battle, then, might well be the one that finished them. What would happen after? They'd heard terrifying stories from refugees of other tribes, of what befell the Caledonii at the hands of the Gaels. Slaughter. Capture. Rape and slavery.

What must she do? Fight or flee? Both men stared at her, awaiting some profound pronouncement, wisdom she did not possess.

What would her husband, Morirex, have done? The war chief of tribe Caerena, Morirex had been a strong man and a dauntless, canny fighter. He'd possessed a hard kind of intelligence.

Yet he'd fallen. Not three months since, at the height of the season's fighting, he'd taken a terrible injury and bled to death, just as had their chief, Ammin, months before.

The Caerena might have stopped battling then, given up and surrendered to what seemed inevitable. But Cunarda, widow of the chief, had come to Verica, weeping.

"I have three daughters, nearly grown." Ammin's eldest child, a son, had died in battle even before his father. "I must keep them from rape and capture. Will you lead us, Mistress Verica?"

"Me?"

"Help us battle on. Teach my daughters to fight at your side, as you fought at Morirex's. I would rather see them die with weapons in their hands than be used in rut by those filthy beasts." Cunarda palmed her wet cheeks. "Winter is coming. If we can but hold out till then, the Gaels should fall back. They always have, before."

"Battle is not easy for a woman." Verica should know. The only reason she'd taken up arms had been in an effort to win her husband's approval.

Not his love; all too swiftly had she learned she had no hope of that.

Now she blinked at the stifling haze hanging over the settlement and struggled to think. Since complying with Cunarda's wishes and assuming leadership, Verica had seen one of the chief's daughters fall in the fighting. The two who remained were decent fighters. But she had grown fond of them and did not want to risk their lives.

What would their father, Ammin, have done? Morirex, she did not doubt, would have chosen to battle on.

She looked at her men. "Round up everyone who can still hold a weapon. The rest—especially mothers with children—we will send into the forest. Mistress Cunarda will lead them. The rest of us will lay a trap here."

"Trap?" Motius's forehead furrowed in a frown.

Verica smiled grimly. "A small welcoming party for the Gaels."

Both men nodded. The second man, Cintus, swept Verica with a look. "What of you, Mistress? Are you badly wounded?" He grimaced and added, "It would be miraculous, were you not."

Without a word, Verica held out her hands which, covered by hacks and cuts, showed red to the wrists. A slice to her right arm—now covered by a ragged sleeve—had been hastily bound. She would not speak of the gash to her back, just beside one shoulder blade, concealed by her shredded tunic and her long, black hair.

Cintus pressed, demonstrating real concern, "But you will still lead us? You are able to fight?"

A rueful smile curled Verica's lips. "I will stand beside you," she assured them grimly.

They exchanged yet another look and left her; she sought to take stock of her condition.

She felt depleted, beaten, and inexpressibly discouraged. To face another battle she would need strength, and she could not imagine from whence it might come. She'd given up praying, had lost faith in asking for what would not come. Far too often, in the past, had she prayed hard and gone without answer.

She'd cried to the goddess while lying beside her new husband on the night following her handfasting. She'd pleaded when she realized he was beyond pleasing, at least by her, Verica. Belief had seeped away from her like water from a leaky vessel.

Now when she might wish for some solace, she found only emptiness and the remnants of stubborn strength. That, and fear so bright she dared not contemplate it. All might be lost in the next battle. Quite possibly nothing she did would be enough to save them.

Nothing she did had ever been enough.

Maybe, she thought wearily, it was wrong to stand. Perhaps they should all flee into the forest along with Cunarda. It would solve nothing, but at least some of them might survive.

She spoke then, not to the goddess but to herself, "What we need is saving. We need someone valiant and wise."

It was not surprising that she heard no reply.

Chapter Three

Wick awakened from his dream when the first snowflake touched his cheek and lay looking up at the lead-gray sky. As so often when he emerged from sleep, he had little grip on reality. His body seemed to belong to someone else, and he could seldom remember where he'd lain down the night before.

Now snowflakes fell dizzyingly, adding to his sense of disorientation. Snow—the first of the season. The sight filled his heart with both hope and dread.

His mother had always greeted the first snow with joy. A holy woman, possessed of both deep faith and wisdom, she'd marked it as a significant point in the turning of the year, the great wheel of seasons by which the Caledonii lived.

Quite apart from that, it usually signaled an end to the attacks launched so relentlessly by the Gaels. After the snows, they tended to fall back to territory they'd seized earlier in the season.

Winter, thus, meant respite. In this case it also meant Wick needed to find shelter somewhere.

He climbed to his feet and shook his body the way a hound might. He must stop wandering aimlessly and choose a direction. Find one of his father's old allies— if any still existed. Else he would die out here, and no one among his tribe would ever learn what had befallen him.

He did not wish that grief, that uncertainty, on those he loved.

He recalled the dream from which he'd just awakened—in it he'd once more run with the deer, swift and sure, the wind rushing past like a river. His heart beat a wild tattoo in his chest, and he could feel life pump through him with every leaping stride.

The herd ran together in magical unity, hooves pounding a concerted rhythm. Up ahead Wick saw the leader—no stag, this, but a graceful hind whose hide glowed silver-white in a haze of magic.

As if Wick's thoughts snagged her attention, she paused on a rise and looked back at him. Her sides heaved, and steam rose from her flanks. Her gaze connected with his, and a spear of awareness pricked him to the heart.

Just a dream, he thought now, but he didn't believe that. Had his mother not told him there were dreams, and dreams? Some meant nothing. Others—the ones that focused the dreamer's emotions to such a wondrous degree—came from the gods.

He must, then, not disregard this dream. Despite the snow, despite the cold that struck him to the bone.

Despite his despair.

Only when he stooped beside the nearby stream to fill his water skin did he see the tracks that dotted the softened earth—deer tracks, a myriad of them.

Had the passing of a herd in the night prompted his dream? Had he heard them in the gray light before he woke?

Or was this a sign?

The tracks leaped the narrow stream and led northeastward. With new resolution, Wick followed.

****

"Snow." Verica whispered the word as she stepped from her shelter into the dawning. It fell in broad, sweeping swaths, the flakes big as a baby's fist, dizzying to the eyes.

A miracle.

But would it keep the Gaels at bay?

Mayhap not. Just because the wolves from the west usually left off battling at the arrival of winter didn't mean they would this time. They must know they held the Caerena pinned to the wall, teetering on the brink of defeat.

Had Verica been in their leader's position, she would have pressed on—instinctively—to provide the finishing blow. Strange how she'd developed an ability for this, she who at the start had only raised a spear in an effort to win the favor of a man.

But strength came with the ability. And they needed every shred of strength they could muster.

She turned her gaze on the girl who stood beside her. Hectia, second daughter of their felled chief, Ammin, looked ridiculously lovely to be so loaded down with weapons. Yet she stood firm, the terror in her eyes well banked.

"Mistress Verica, what does it mean? Is it a sign?"

Verica drew a breath of the searing cold air and wondered. "Perhaps." Or possibly only a breather, a chance for her people to lick their extensive wounds and gain a measure of rest before having to fight again.

She wished she knew.

The girl turned her head and gazed into Verica's eyes. "What about our trap?"

Verica struggled to think with a mind so weighted

down by weariness that the effort felt like wading through mud. What to do? If they kept to the plan she and her advisors had formulated overnight, feigned they had abandoned the settlement while ringing it round, waiting for the Gaels to arrive, they might well freeze in their places.

Yet if they complacently hunkered down and waited for the storm to pass, they might all be slain.

Hectia said, "The snow falls so thick, if it comes to a fight I am not sure I could tell friend from foe."

A truth. Was the foul weather to the Caerena's advantage, though, or that of the Gaels?

A figure, white against white, suddenly loomed through the snow. It resolved itself into that of one of their youngest warriors, named Nactovus. Not surprising—wherever Hectia was, Nactovus would not be far behind.

Verica could see that the young man fancied himself in love with the girl and was eager to prove his worth in her eyes. She knew the signs all too well.

Now, though, as he appeared through the snow, she saw he bore a terrible injury, a knife slash across his face that had barely scabbed over.

The lad should not be on his feet. But his dark gaze sought out first Hectia and then Verica.

"Mistress Verica, the others ask if we should take our places despite the storm."

Storm. He had spoken the word. Was that truly what fate had sent? Dared she let down her guard?

Verica pressed her lips together. Ignoring Nactovus's question, she very gently touched his face. "You need to get this tended."

His eyes burned. "I am well enough," he declared

starkly.

Verica tried to keep from showing sympathy. As a woman she felt it; as leader of a tribe on its knees, she had no room to display any perceived weakness.

"Then," she told the boy in a flat voice, "go gather the others. We will meet at the chief's house."

His eyes widened. "Meet? Now? But—"

"Where is Ivomagus?" Despite Verica's loss of faith, the shaman, in many ways, made her best ally.

"I do not know, Mistress. At prayers?" Nactovus hazarded.

No doubt. Ivomagus possessed sincere devotion and a genuinely holy heart.

"Hectia, go with Nactovus. Gather everyone." Together they would try to decide what should be done. The decision might well dictate their survival.

The heavy snow dampened sound and lent a curious feeling of isolation. Voices seemed muffled and distance difficult to judge; fighting in such weather could well prove disastrous.

As could standing still. They would never see the Gaels coming.

Verica thought of the folk who remained beneath the Caerena banners. Aged men and women; many widows, most with children. A good number of those were close to Hectia and Nactovus in age, willing to fight but not particularly able, though Hectia and her sister, Smerta, did not do badly. Every remaining warrior injured.

If only someone, far wiser than she, could tell her what to do. No assistance came; the snow just fell faster, spreading a thick blanket.

Slowly Verica walked toward the chief's house.

Chapter Four

"I say we fight."

No surprise there, Verica thought ruefully, eyeing the face of the speaker. Segovax—one of her young cousins—always chose bloodshed and would kill a Gael whenever he could, whether or not the act proved hazardous.

Now, despite the wind howling outside the chief's house, his face shone with sweat. And the wound at his shoulder, earned in yesterday's battle, continued to ooze red through its bandages.

Despair once more touched Verica's heart, a sickeningly familiar sensation. She ran her gaze over the faces of her other advisors—woefully few in number—which included their slain chief's wife, Cunarda, and the tribe's shaman, Ivomagus.

Cunarda looked worried, as well she might. Some of the others avoided Verica's gaze. Ivomagus met it steadily, seeking a connection.

A tall man, and thin with it, Ivomagus had eyes a clear, light shade of brown in a heavily tattooed face. He wore his dark hair long—longer even than most of their warriors—and braided. Young to be holy leader of a tribe, he'd still been in training when their former elder was cut down. Like so many of them, he'd been forced to step into a place for which he hadn't been prepared.

But no one could question Ivomagus's honesty or his devotion. And despite the slightly uncomfortable relationship between them, Verica found herself looking to him often.

Like now.

Their gazes met, and he lifted his brows.

"What say the gods?" Verica asked. In her heart she might scoff at such a question. But given the trouble that now beset them, many among the Caerena believed they must have done something to anger their gods sorely, bringing this ordeal upon their heads.

If she, Verica, wanted to earn their support and agreement, she must allow room for such belief, and their need for assurance.

"The gods," Ivomagus pronounced, "advise caution. Signs say we should hold our hands for the time being."

Verica grunted softly.

Segovax immediately protested. "It is a course for cowards."

"And," one of the other warriors, Derux, took up the argument swiftly, "an impetuous battle is a course toward death."

Again Verica looked at Ivomagus. "How strong are the signs?"

Something flickered in his eyes. "Strong."

"Perhaps," another of the men suggested, "the signs but pertain to the weather. Perhaps we should hold our hands during the storm." He cocked his head. "Just listen to it!"

Despite the thick walls of the chief's dwelling, dug in half underground, the howl of the wind came to their ears, sharp and wild.

Cunarda shifted uneasily and laid her arm around Smerta's shoulders.

"And if the Gaels decide to attack despite the storm?" Segovax asked with an edge.

"Then," said Motius, "we let the weather deal with them and clean up the remains after."

Verica glanced again at Ivomagus, asking a question with her eyes. Ultimately the responsibility for the decision—faulty or otherwise—fell to her.

"If the Gaels hold back from attacking because of the storm," Ivomagus posed, "we have no need for the planned trap. Yes?"

Verica nodded decisively. Ultimately, postponing the setting of the trap solved nothing, but it did buy them a bit of time and a chance for their wounds to close over.

"We will stand down for the duration of the storm. But keep your weapons close to hand. If it comes to a defensive fight..." Her voice died away, and all the faces in the chamber tensed. The worst of their defeats had come during such defensive battles, hand-to-hand fighting in doorways and at hearthstones. The Gaels could not be permitted access to the settlement, save in a trap such as they'd planned.

"Before we disperse," Cunarda asked, "will you, Master Ivomagus, please speak a blessing?"

He did, his head bowed and his narrow-palmed, blue-flecked hand raised. Afterwards the others filed out. Ivomagus lingered.

"A word in private, Mistress Verica," he requested softly.

She eyed him askance. "Have you Seen something more?"

The light again filled his eyes. "I have Seen many things. One in particular pertains to you."

Verica went hot and cold in turns. Her own death? Ivomagus, honest to the core, had been known to warn others of such an approaching event. Nothing so shook a warrior in battle.

And if she, Verica, were doomed to perish in the next fight? She shivered before lifting her chin; at least then she would have some rest.

"What is it?"

Ivomagus touched her shoulder lightly. Cunarda shot them a curious look as they stepped away to a corner of the room.

Fear gnawing sharply at her heart, Verica demanded, "Ivomagus?"

He hesitated a moment as if marshaling his thoughts, or seeking the best way to impart bad news.

"Someone comes."

The last thing Verica expected him to say. Her eyes widened. "Someone?"

"Or something. It is difficult to tell. But"— Ivomagus seemed to anticipate her reaction—"it was a true Vision, the sort I cannot hope to deny."

"Someone or something? Explain." Verica had no time or energy for fancy. Yet despite her own lack of faith she found it impossible to doubt this man.

Ivomagus wetted his lips. "A man, but not a man. Possibly a man in animal form. He may be our savior— or mayhap only your savior. I cannot tell."

"That is madness."

"I know. That's why I held back from telling you in front of the others. Yet the Vision has now visited me not once but three times. I had to bring you the warning."

"Why would you suppose that this person—a stranger, you say?"

"A stranger."

"Comes for me?"

"He carries a Vision of you, in turn, in his eyes."

Verica's throat closed. She sought to dismiss the news as nonsense. "We imagine all kinds of things and dream all sorts of dreams when pressed." She herself had been dreaming she ran with a herd of deer. In her heart, she believed the persistent dream evinced her desire to escape all her responsibilities, to cut and flee.

"So we do." Ivomagus's gaze remained steady. "As I say, I can tell the difference. The stranger comes for you, and he may take the form of the god himself."

"What?"

"The god, in his guise as the horned one."

"And he comes to help us?" A likely story. "How?"

"That I do not know. A great warrior, perhaps? One to relieve you of your perilous place?"

And did she, Verica, wish to be relieved of her place? Only in a thousand ways. She'd stepped into it over Morirex's dead body, the day he died of his battle wounds. Now she carried a weight she could barely support. But did she want a stranger coming to take that place from her?

"Mistress Verica," Ivomagus said, "it is wrong for you to be leading this tribe. You are a beautiful woman and should be cherished, not required to risk your life again and again."

Verica shied. Here lay the source of the awkwardness between them. Ever since Morirex's death, indeed if not before, Ivomagus had made his interest in her clear. And though Verica found many things to admire in the shaman, she refused to place her heart in peril to any man. Never again.

She drew a breath. "Ivomagus, none of us might have chosen these roles we must now play. We will nevertheless stand strong in them."

"Yes, Mistress. May I speak plainly?"

She gave a grim smile. "You usually do."

"I would do aught I might to make your lot easier. You must know why."

"Master Ivomagus, now is not the time to consider matters of the heart."

"I disagree. It is the perfect time to consider the state of our hearts. Please, let me offer you mine."

He already had, if far more subtly. She shook her head, but before she could speak he went on in a fierce undertone.

"Morirex did not deserve you. He did not appreciate you."

"Mayhap not." She met his intense gaze. "Would you place yourself in the same terrible position I occupied?"

His gaze softened. "It would not be so."

"It well might," she told him, speaking now as truthfully as he. "I am no longer capable of love."

"Ah, Mistress Verica, do not be too certain of that. Love is a gift. Who can say where it may be bestowed?"

Chapter Five

The storm hit like a phalanx of Gaelic chariots and drove Wick to ground. He'd now grown accustomed to the cold. Heavy snow made travel difficult, but his body possessed the strength he believed his spirit lacked. The wind, however, threatened to defeat him, bewildering his senses and befouling his sense of direction.

When he could no longer feel his fingers or toes and feared he might walk straight into a Gaels' encampment, he dug himself a hollow beneath a pine tree and hunkered down.

He did not want to think. He'd found that while on the move he could shove the dark doubts and painful memories away. Now he lay prey to them with no escape.

Toward, or away? The question continued to dog him like an unwelcome hound. He might claim he went to locate his father's old allies and secure an alliance that would save his tribe. As he lay staring up into the branches of the pine, watching the snow blow through in wafts, he admitted the unsavory truth: he ran, pure and simple, because he could no longer endure his lot.

He, son of Radoc map Dumno—the bravest man he'd ever known or ever hoped to know—had proved a coward.

He'd run from his responsibilities, from the place

of tribeschief that he should have held with pride, from the folk upon whom his father had looked as children.

The goddess forgive him, for he could never forgive himself.

His younger sister Barta possessed more courage than he did. Heedless and ill-judged Barta might be, but valiant. And his little brother, Tally—he possessed a spirit that combined their father's hard-earned endurance with their mother's facility for magic.

Let either of them lead in his, Wick's, place.

But no, it would be Brude, without dispute the Epidii's finest warrior, who took over—Brude, Wick's one-time fast friend who'd taken to questioning Father's every decision even before Radoc's death, with a view to usurping him.

Let Brude have it, Wick thought again, just as he had back at their settlement when something snapped within his heart and he abdicated his place. Let Brude have the sleepless nights, the weight of responsibility, and the endless self-doubt.

Perhaps he, Wick, would die here, buried by the storm. He might slip away into sleep like a beleaguered wolf and never awake into the world any more.

Protest niggled at him. What of the promise he'd made to the goddess? He'd vowed to live for her, not die.

He could not give up, not just yet.

Yet the storm might well defeat him. Even huddled in as he was, the wind found him and bit deep in an effort to chill his blood. He felt the remaining warmth draining steadily from him.

And closed his eyes.

What followed must have been another dream—an

inexplicable mystic visitation such as had already beset him. For, slipped halfway into unconsciousness, he thought he heard something—someone—stir, out beyond the branches that sheltered him. The light changed and shifted. A wall of fur and warmth encircled him, blocking out the wind; Wick heard snorting and the restless movements of body and hoof.

His eyes moved wildly, and even in the dream his heart began to pound. Impossibly, sweat broke out on his brow.

Yet gradual warmth seeped into him. The herd of deer, if such it was, closed in more tightly, and his muscles eased.

Precisely when the wind died, he never knew. He slept soundly, the deep rest providing a measure of healing, and when he woke feeble light trickled into his hollow.

No bodies surrounded his shelter; no deer stood there. Instead, a wall of snow enclosed him, piled up against the lower boughs.

Had he indeed imagined the rest?

Either way, he lived still.

He dug his way out through the snow and fought to gain his feet. Squinting his eyes against the light, he gazed about like one reborn. He had no grasp of where he might be—how far west, how far north. The new dawn seeped through a wall of cloud to the east, and the world lay so silent he could hear his own heart thudding in his chest.

Where to go? The Gaels could be anywhere—west, north, south. In the storm, he might well have crossed into their territory. That meant he should get moving before they did, before they dug out from their encampment and, presumably, reset their patrols.

That would be difficult in so much snow. Wick, traveling alone, should be able to outdistance them, if only he had a direction.

Upon the thought, his eyes caught faint depressions in the snow. Not a trail but the suggestion of one. Like a trench, it encircled the tree which had provided him sanctuary, and led away northeastward. The same direction in which he'd followed the deer yesterday.

Ah, then, maybe he hadn't dreamed—or imagined—it. Possibly a wall of deer had surrounded him while he slept.

But why? Such a magical occurrence made little sense. He had no value and little worth in the world.

He did not deserve such favor.

What was it his mother always used to say? *We cannot divine the minds of the gods.* All at once Wick almost thought he felt his mother standing beside him, almost heard her whisper, "The goddess must have plans for you."

And who could fight such intentions? Who would dare? Wordless, his stomach growling, Wick shouldered his thin pack and followed the faint path away through the snow.

****

Day and night followed one another; darkness came and went. Wick, fighting through the snow and with no food in his belly, soon fell victim to a weariness deeper than mere exhaustion. Yet something within him—a heretofore undiscovered will—kept him moving. The half-buried deer trail he followed led on and on.

Once or twice he caught the faint impression of a

hoof print that let him know he did, indeed, follow a herd. Then unexpectedly, at midday, he came upon a gory scene.

Murder. That thought entered his mind even though it made no sense. He'd spent his whole life surviving on wild game and had hunted countless animals for food. If they did not die, he did not live—an ancient adage that for him incorporated both mercy and deep gratitude. He'd eaten more than his share of venison.

Why coming upon the site of just such a kill should disturb him now, he could not say. Yet both anger and protest arose and filled him.

Perhaps it was the wanton waste he now saw before him—the animal, a fine stag, had been felled and butchered on the spot. The head, boasting an impressive rack of antlers, remained lying in a vast pool of blood, as did the legs, hooves and a good portion of usable meat.

Surrounding it Wick could see the tracks of at least two and probably three men; the footprints led away through the trees and westward.

Gaels.

To be sure, he could almost smell them. He stood with his nostrils flaring like those of a wild beast. If seen, he would suffer a similar end to that of this hart.

Some of the Gaels' tracks lay outlined in red from the stag's blood, and he wondered if they meant to return to pack out the rest of their kill. If so, they would doubtless see his, Wick's, footprints.

And follow him?

Ah, what to do? No matter what direction he took away from this place, he might indeed be tracked.

Given the Gaels returned.

The rest of the herd had fled. He could see their divergent trails as clearly as those of the Gaels. They had abandoned their fellow to death and sacrifice.

So should he. But first…he felt his mother's spirit move beside him as he whispered a prayer, soft yet fervent with gratitude. A prayer closely followed by a request.

Starving, he might help himself to some of the found meat like the scavenger he'd obviously become.

Please, he requested the god. Then he fell to his knees in the snow and applied his knife. The flesh, already half frozen, tasted divine on his tongue.

As the flesh of a god should.

He took all he could fit in his pack and, hands stained red, stepped carefully into the tracks of the herd, hoping his footprints might be overlooked in the churned slush, should the Gaels return.

He never noticed that, as he passed, his tracks turned to hoof prints in the snow.

Chapter Six

"Mistress Verica, the storm has passed. Should we now prepare to fight?" Segovax stood before Verica, his dark eyes wide and his expression distracted. Behind him, snow lay deep across the settlement, roof-high in places.

As a girl, Verica had loved winter, a season of rest when the monsters from the west fell back and left off dealing death. She and her friends might have the chance to sit cozy by the fireside, gossiping and spinning dreams.

One such dream had been that of catching the eye of the finest man the tribe Caerena had to offer—its handsome and powerful war chief. Verica had snared his interest in the end but failed miserably to live up to his expectations.

These days, winter brought only hardship and no respite. The settlement would need to be dug out so folk could reach the wood stores and the midden. There were wounded who needed care and sadly, overnight, dead to tend. And the threat of attack never ceased.

But surely the Gaels would be buried as deeply as Verica's own tribe. They could not possibly attack so soon.

She regarded Segovax with unjust annoyance. Impetuous, he was quick enough to argue with her decisions yet still came to her for answers. She had few answers, and at the moment felt weary enough to crawl beneath the snow and stay there.

Before she could so much as snap at Segovax, a second warrior joined them—Motius, he with the missing ear. The sight of his wound, still not dressed since yesterday's battle, turned Verica's stomach.

"Mistress," he burst, "Sennin sent me to tell you we are almost out of food." Sennin, Motius's wife, tended the communal cook pots, another site that would need digging out.

Verica snapped at him, "Why have you not had that ear tended? What is the matter with Sennin that she has not bandaged it?"

He grinned uncertainly, revealing a chipped tooth. "She said it would do better if the cold got at it and stopped the bleeding. So it has."

"It is filthy. Go at once and have Callorix look at it." If, that was, the healer could spare the time.

"But Mistress," Motius protested, stuck at his wife's instructions, "what about the cook pots?"

"And," Segovax interposed, "should we not set a guard in case of attack?"

Verica sighed and tried to force her weary thoughts into motion. "Set a watch. We want to know as early as possible about any movement from the Gaels. I do not see how they can attack through so much snow." But they were tricky bastards. And Verica had learned how fatal inattention could prove.

"We already have two lads on the lookout for game. Everyone is cold and hungry."

"Dispense what food there is. Tell Sennin to feed the wounded first, at least those who are able to eat. And the children."

Both men sagged. Verica knew how hungry they were—so was she, and the cold only served to sharpen the appetite.

She rattled on, her brain, once jogged into motion, seeming to run more smoothly. "Set someone to clearing trails so the healer and his assistants can get about. We will organize a hunting party as soon as we can."

They nodded, looking miserable. Motius turned to leave, and Verica reiterated, "And get that ear tended."

He gave her an uncertain nod and left. Segovax stood on.

"Mistress?"

"Yes, what is it?"

"If the Gaels come now, do you think we can fight them off?"

No. But she did not want to say it. Fierce her young cousin might be, but he had seen things so terrible they fair burnt the eyes, and the heart. They all felt afraid on some level, all the time—she no less than anyone else. Each passing day seemed to deplete their stores faster— of food, warriors, and courage.

That thought softened her voice when she said, "I do not think the Gaels will be able to attack so soon. They will be buried, as are we."

Doubt filled Segovax's dark eyes. Verica clasped his shoulder. "Let us use this time to provide our people with what they need. Set a watch—men, not lads. And fit a party for hunting."

First things first; immediate needs must be met and bellies must be filled—beyond healing, all else could wait.

****

The raw flesh of the god—the first food to pass Wick's lips in days—lent him strength as he trudged on. The trail he followed climbed steeply through waist-high snow and bore so far westward he nearly abandoned it. He asked himself over and over again why he continued to follow. He'd seen the Gaels' tracks leading in this direction.

Yet the herd had broken trail for him—he did not know if he had the energy to break one on his own. And surely the herd would not venture too near those who hunted them, not when they'd already lost at least one of their number.

So he pressed on, never looking back at his own footprints, while the cold air seared his lungs. Once or twice he thought he caught a glimpse of russet brown up ahead of him, visible against the white snow—the herd. He ached to pause and rest but feared that, if he did, he might not be able to force his limbs back into motion.

And then, abruptly, the deer ahead of him froze; he caught his first good look at them through the bare trees. He froze also, precisely as if he numbered one among them. His limbs trembled with strain.

He widened his eyes at the sight—at least half a score roe deer, led by not a stag but a pale hind which now raised her head and scented the air to the west.

Following suit, Wick caught a hint of it—smoke from at least one cook fire drifting over the snow, twining through the trees.

Gaels, so close he could smell them roasting the venison from their kill.

The hind snorted. She turned to the east and, breasting through the unbroken blanket of white with unfathomable strength, bounded away. The other deer followed. As if catching the fire of their alarm, Wick forced his body back into motion and trailed them. His legs, weak only moments before, gained unexpected strength, and the cold air surged into his chest.

They skirted the curve of the hill, high above the floor of a deep glen, twining through trees unending. How far they went, Wick could never later say— seemingly far, yet no great distance. He was one of the deer, the herd his home. As they went, the heavy clouds cleared and a weak sun shone through, reflecting from the snow and dazzling his eyes.

Perhaps that explained why he saw nothing before the first arrow came arching in. It struck one of the does, taking her in the side, and the entire herd shied as if they all felt the pain.

Wick's mind rebelled at the impossibility of it— how could this happen here, when they had left the Gaels well behind?

Red bloomed on the doe's side and dripped into the snow. The hind at the head of the herd snorted and changed direction violently, the herd struggling to keep up. The wounded doe collapsed into the snow, and the deer between her and Wick leaped over and around her; abandoned, she flailed feebly.

Only Wick, bringing up the rear as he had for so long, paused. With a surge of pity, he looked into the doe's deep, dark eyes. He watched the life fade.

He heard a cry then—a human voice—issuing from the trees. Before he could turn, an arrow took him in the shoulder, biting deep with a blaze of pain so intense it stole all breath.

And took him to his knees.

He saw the men break from the cover of the trees and streak toward him and the doe, kicking up the snow and whooping in glee. Not Gaels—these were Caledonian tribesmen like him. Not his fellow Epidii, no, for he had fallen far from home.

Would he die here in this unknown place, bleed out into the snow just like the doe? He arched his body in agony and caught a glimpse of his own arms—nay, front limbs, for once more they ended in hooves rather than hands.

The men ran in brandishing knives, eager to dispatch him.

He bellowed like a stag in its death throes. In response he saw a flash of bright light—and nothing more.

Chapter Seven

"Who is he?"

"I know not, other than a Caledonian tribesman; you can see his tattoos. I do not recognize any of the markings."

"Mistress Verica! I must tell you—"

"Pray, Segovax, not now."

The words, exchanged above Wick, washed over him the way waves of water might shush over rocks, rushed and sibilant. He could tell that people—strangers—stood directly above him, but to save his life he could not open his eyes. Pain possessed him, along with a dire weakness that hinted of death.

One of the voices stood out among the others. It belonged to a woman, carried a sharp edge, and spoke to Wick on a level deeper than understanding.

"But mistress," insisted the first speaker, a male, "we took down two deer, a hart and a hind. The hind fell first, and when she did, the hart paused. Perhaps he was her mate. My shot took him in the shoulder—a fine shot it was. He went down in the snow. But when we got to the place..." The speaker abruptly faltered. "We found *him*—a man. A hind lying there, and a man, just as you see him."

Wick wished with all his might he could open his eyes. The ensuing silence made him ache to see, but his eyelids might well have been weighted by stones.

At last, the woman with the tense voice said, "You must have been mistaken."

"No, Mistress. How could I be mistaken at that distance?"

"As you can see, you have shot a man through the shoulder. Not a hart."

"Ask the others who were with me. Ask what they saw. It was a deer, a male deer. It must be magic."

Again the woman said nothing. The pause lasted longer this time before she breathed, "Bring Ivomagus."

Footsteps hurried away. Wick wondered where he was, into whose possession he had come, but all wondering abruptly ceased when a hand touched his brow. The touch held unexpected tenderness and struck through him even more deeply than the voice.

A thumb urged one of his eyelids open; the other eyelid followed obediently. A face swam into his view, hazily.

She hung above him, one of the most exquisite sights he'd ever beheld. A strong, angular face she had, stark at jaw and cheekbone, framed by black hair and marked by strong brows of the same hue. Her gaze narrowed when it met his—eyes of a deep, vibrant blue. Wick lost all his breath, and not from the pain in his shoulder.

"Well," she said, her lips twisting into a wry curl, "and do you intend to survive?"

It seemed so. Wick tried to speak the words, but they did not come. Though his lips moved, he emitted only a groan.

"Can you tell me your name? The name of your tribe? How you come to be on our land?"

Unable to so much as shake his head, Wick

groaned again. She seemed to glimpse the answer in his eyes; something in her hard gaze relented.

"No? Well I am not surprised; you are badly wounded. The arrowhead passed clean through your shoulder—clean being the important part. You will be happy to know I removed the shaft while you were still senseless."

Wick found no ability to be glad or otherwise. Her face so entranced him he could think of nothing else.

Her hand still rested on his brow as if she'd forgotten to remove it. The intimacy of her touch seemed to unite them, a feeling made still stronger when she leaned down and whispered, "My warrior thought you were a hart. To me, you look like a man. And then"—she seemed to muse, a new expression invading her eyes—"there is what Ivomagus said."

Before he could gather the strength to answer, a flurry erupted at the door to the hut—a structure similar to an Epidii hut back home—signaling the entrance of a tall man wearing a deerskin cloak. He had a severe face, hair nearly as dark as the woman's, and kind eyes.

"Mistress Verica?"

The woman glanced at the newcomer over her shoulder; in profile, her face looked still more beautiful.

"Ah, Ivomagus. The very man. Will you take my place? It seems we find ourselves faced with an incidence of magic."

"So I have heard." The man's brows quirked. "Talk outside is of little else. A deer turned into a man?"

The woman shrugged. "Or a man turned into a deer. He seems to be a man, at the moment."

They exchanged a look Wick could not interpret, and she rose, taking her hand from his brow. He felt the loss deep within. The man shed his heavy cloak and assumed her place.

A shaman. Wick, seeing him up close, recognized that at once. The Epidii had always kept at least one shaman; they now had Pith, well-advanced in years. Indeed, most of their holy men had been much older than this individual appeared.

Still, he possessed an aura of subtle power and the scent of herbs hung around him. Complex tattoos twined up both cheeks and across his forehead. The kind eyes looked bright with curiosity.

The woman—Mistress Verica, so the young tribesman had called her—said, "He does not seem able to speak."

"Have you examined his markings?" the shaman asked.

"Yes."

"Does he bear any brandings you recognize?"

"No. But you have been farther afield than I, Ivomagus, and have met members of many other tribes. You look."

The shaman hesitated. In a soft, patient voice he asked, "Do you hear me, master?"

Wick jerked a nod.

"Can you not try and speak?"

Wick made an effort so painful sweat broke out all over his body. As before, a groan made the only result.

Respectfully, the shaman asked, "Will you permit me to examine you?"

His touch, as he opened the front of Wick's tunic, remained deft and impersonal. He swiftly eyed the tattoos Wick bore, the first given soon after his birth and the others marking every significant occurrence of his life.

The eyebrows twitched again. "He is a warrior, the survivor of many battles. And possibly born to a noble house."

"What tribe, can you tell?"

"That I do not recognize." The shaman swiftly closed Wick's tunic. "We will discover nothing more, Mistress Verica, until he can speak for himself. I advise we let him rest and heal. He has lost much blood and needs to regain his strength." The shaman glanced at the woman. "For now, I would not leave him alone."

"Why not?"

"We do not know who he is—what he is—and we are not certain we can trust him."

Wick thought of his sister Barta's lover—the man she insisted on calling True—who had appeared among the Epidii in a manner not unlike his appearance here. For the first time, he understood how True must have felt, unable to explain his presence or the hint of magic that hung about him.

The woman bit her lip. "But you said—" She caught back whatever other words she'd been going to say and gave the shaman a hard stare. "Very well, I will be guided by you in this and will set a guard—at least until he can tell us who he might be."

Stay with me, sit beside me, Wick asked her silently. *No guard, just you and me together.*

But of course she didn't hear. Instead she told the man, "We will speak further of this, Ivomagus, and the strange coincidence of his arrival so soon after you—" Again she broke off.

The shaman rose and turned to face her. "So we shall, all in good time. Meanwhile, do not, I urge you,

Mistress Verica, linger alone with him. You are far too valuable to the tribe to risk your safety."

She looked surprised. "Surely I am at no risk. You see how weak he is, too weak to speak. Do you sense any darkness in him?"

"I am not sure what to make of his presence."

Verica frowned in consternation. Wick wanted to say he would not hurt her—never under any circumstances. But his tongue served him no better than that of a stag.

The shaman touched Verica's shoulder. "Have a care for my sake, if not your own."

The woman gave a bleak smile. "Worry not. What do you mean to tell the tribe? They will be all too ready with their questions."

"I will tell them the truth and that we know little as yet. I shall advise patience." The shaman, too, smiled. "Which does not always make for welcome advice."

"I fear few of us possess your patience, Ivomagus."

The shaman reassumed his cloak, shot the woman an intense, uninterpretable look, and went softly out.

Wick began to pray. He prayed that despite the shaman's advice this woman—*Verica*—would resume the seat she'd taken before. He prayed she'd remain close to him, so close he might gaze into her eyes—that she might once more touch him, providing that same sensation of deep comfort.

But she merely stood gazing at him. He looked back at her, willing her without words. After a moment she sighed. "I would that you could speak."

So did he.

"But deer—and perhaps half-beast men of whose arrival I've been forewarned—do not use human language, do they?"

Wick did not know what she meant. He began to lose track of his thoughts again, as if a mist rose between them. Nay, surrounded them together like a spell of magic.

"A curious thing." She came and sat in the place beside him, just as he wished, though she did not touch him. "Had you been a deer, you should have arrived here naked. Deer do not wear clothing. Yet you do—ragged and torn, yes, but clothing, all the same."

And his pack. Had he lost that? Everything he possessed had been in there, plus the flesh he'd taken from the stag the Gaels killed.

Gone.

"Though I suppose," she mused on, "a deer wears its hide, does it not? And most of what you now wear is made from deer hide."

Wick let his heavy eyes droop shut. He willed her to touch him, but she did not.

Instead, her soft voice went on, "A warrior, Ivomagus says you are—the survivor of many battles."

Wick opened his eyes and once more found himself gazing into hers, deep blue like an evening sky.

She whispered, "That means you must be valiant. And, my mysterious stranger, it is a quality my tribe much needs at this season."

Him, valiant? Ah, Wick thought sorrowfully, she had no idea how sorely she was mistaken.

Chapter Eight

"Has he spoken yet? The stranger, has he said anything?"

Wherever Verica went around the settlement, she heard the same questions. Folk who should have enough other things to occupy their minds seemed wholly taken with the arrival of the valiant warrior, as Verica had privately dubbed him.

Their curiosity and wonder had not been at all dampened by the stories Motius and Segovax had to tell. As far as Verica knew, they'd repeated their tale to anyone willing to listen. And most everyone proved willing.

Verica had to admit it made a grand story. And her folk, so badly beaten down, could certainly use some evidence of magic.

She answered the oft-repeated question with a shake of her head and the words, "He sleeps still."

So he did, caught in a deep sleep she could not help but think of as unnatural, but which the healer, Callorix, called restorative.

"Exactly what he needs," Callorix insisted. "His wound heals well and cleanly. He is strong."

Verica could tell that much. She'd seen enough of the body beneath the rough clothing to judge his physical condition. Precisely like a hart in its prime, he had a deep chest, well-muscled and generously covered by both scars and tattoos. His hands—broad in the palms—bore still more scars. A man who had indeed battled, and battled hard.

What she needed to do was corner Ivomagus and charge him with the veracity of the prediction he'd made, following his claimed Vision—that a man-beast came, and possibly for her sake. For the tribe's benefit—yes, that she could warrant. The Caerena needed such an ally, a hero. As for her, despite the tingling of awareness when she touched the stranger, she had no interest in men.

Might he prove to fill the role of savior for the tribe? Verica could not tell. Quite likely born of a noble house, Ivomagus declared, yet not above five-and-twenty in age. Not handsome in the accepted sense—not as her husband, Morirex had been—he nevertheless had a compelling face, broad in the brow, with bold cheekbones and a strong jaw.

And his eyes—now those Verica could not help but call beautiful. Those first moments, when he'd come awake and had gazed so intently at her, she'd felt their impact. Dark and fathomless, holding emotions she had no hope of naming, they might well be the knowing eyes of a hart.

When brought in covered in blood, he'd been carried to one of the storage sheds. Verica had since ordered him taken to her own hut, and that against Ivomagus's advice. She'd reasoned the healer's hut—already overcrowded—was no place for him, at least not until they discovered whether they could trust him. She would rather risk her own safety than that of the wounded, and besides, she rarely took to her own bed.

She'd spent time sitting beside him once or twice,

watching him sleep. Hoping he'd awaken and speak to her? She could not say.

Meanwhile the weather, that uncertain ally, decided to betray them, bringing a thaw which would eventually dissolve their protective walls of snow. Verica met with her advisors again and again, saw to the burial of the dead and the healing of the wounded. She set a strong guard. Eventually, on a chilly and windy evening, she cornered Ivomagus and refused to let him pass.

"You and I, Master Ivomagus, need to speak together."

He sighed, eyeing her with weary acceptance. "Mistress Verica, you desire answers I do not have. I have prayed about the arrival of the stranger. I have sued the goddess for answers; the only reply I receive is a request for patience."

Verica snorted. "You understand I am not the most patient of women, especially in this instance." She leaned closer to him. The wind seized her hair and swayed her where she stood, rattled the bare branches of the trees overhead. "You made a prediction, a particularly unbelievable one."

Ivomagus's pale brown eyes crinkled. "I believed it."

"So, tell to me—is he the man? The—the man-beast whose coming was foretold?"

"It would seem so, would it not? Could he in truth, Mistress, be anyone else? It is too steep a coincidence that I should foresee such a thing only to have him brought in, and Segovax claiming he shot a beast rather than a man."

Verica searched Ivomagus's eyes and shook her

head. "So what does it mean?"

"That is the question I cannot answer. Not until he awakens and we can speak with him, to find out the name of his tribe and ask why he has entered our territory."

"You said—you said he came for me."

"Yes."

"What does that mean?"

Ivomagus did not look happy. "Mistress, I cannot answer that either. I can only bid you wait until we determine the truth of it. The goddess has given me no answers; hence I have none for you. I would be happier if you would house him elsewhere—not in your hut."

"Where, then? Whom should I endanger, other than myself?"

"Anyone. No, I understand you do not like that answer. But, Mistress Verica, it comes from my heart. I do not know what this man may mean to you. There is one thing I hope he will not come to mean."

"Master Ivomagus…I have made it clear I have no time—no patience—for the kind of relationship you desire."

"You have made that clear, yes."

"Well, then, why should this be any different? Clearly, this man is a warrior. The most I hope is that he may prove of assistance to the tribe. We stand in dire need."

Ivomagus bowed his head in assent. "I pray you be careful, for the sake of the tribe if nothing else."

"I will. Meanwhile, if you wish to pray, pray for another storm." Or for the Gaels to move back westward. That they might withdraw even a small distance, and give the Caerena breathing space.

Not two days after that conversation, on a clear, bright morning, one of the young lads, called Penri, came running up to Verica with a companion in tow, a bedraggled object dangling from his hand. Excitement filled the youths' faces. "See what we found!"

"What is that?" A deer-hide pack, dark with wet and stained by what might be blood, she saw, answering her own question.

"I found it in the place where Master Motius and Segovax made their kill," Penri declared. "We went looking for dropped arrowheads. This might belong to the stranger."

So it might, yet anger nearly blotted out the possibility.

"You went there? So close to where the Gaels are encamped? Why would you take such a foolish risk?"

Penri's excitement deflated. "Every arrowhead is precious, so Master Motius always says. Besides, we wanted to see if the Gaels are still there."

"Did I tell you to go out scouting? Did anyone tell you?"

"No, Mistress."

"What if you had been captured, eh? What would your mother say?"

"We were careful and made sure not to be captured." Penri, who had all of twelve years, drew himself up. "We have our knives. And we are very nearly warriors."

Verica, trying not to choke on her outrage, held out her hand insistently. "Give that to me."

The lad passed it over without question. It stank. "Have you looked inside?"

"Yes. There is meat and a flask for water, not much

else."

"All right. I do not wish for you to go off on your own like that again."

"No, Mistress, but…" The boys exchanged excited glances before one continued, "We think the Gaels have withdrawn. We could no longer smell their cook fires or hear any sound of them. It is good news, no?"

"It is, indeed." Good and welcome news, if true. "But not worth you two risking your lives. Now go."

They pelted off. Verica thought hard about their news. The tribe desperately needed a respite—her warriors needed time to finish healing and decide whether they should abandon this place and move eastward.

The Gaels withdrawing from their doorstep seemed like a gift.

She carried the malodorous pack directly to Ivomagus's dwelling. He sat outside the door and arose with alacrity as soon as he saw her.

"What is that?" His fine nose wrinkled involuntarily.

"Penri and Margovax discovered it, back where the stranger was found."

"What were they doing out there?"

"I do not know. But they seem to think the Gaels have withdrawn."

"A blessing, if true."

"Indeed. They also think this pack belonged to the stranger. Penri found it amid the melting snow."

"It reeks."

"It does. Will you help me examine the contents?"

His nose twitched again, but he nodded. Verica untied the thongs with her own hands and dumped the contents out onto his doorstep.

Strips of meat, poorly or perhaps hastily wrapped in cloth, tumbled out along with the aforementioned water skin, a tunic—now stained with blood—and several other less readily identified objects.

"That is venison," Ivomagus observed.

"Yes."

The shaman met Verica's eyes in a hard stare. "It would be a strange deer indeed that devoured the flesh of its own kind."

Verica returned his look questioningly. "You think you were mistaken about him?"

"Mistaken, that someone of importance approached? No. That the someone is the man asleep in your hut? I cannot tell."

"You continue to ask for answers about him?"

"Constantly."

"Have you not received any?"

"Not yet. But can you not sense a hint of magic surrounding him?"

Verica hesitated. Magic was not and never had been her domain, even before she lost her faith. But yes, she'd noticed. Magic hung about the man like a whiff of fragrance. Ivomagus, as she knew, insisted magic turned the wheel of the world. Trees, rocks, sky, clouds, weather—all operated to a magical rhythm that affected the lives of men...and women. Then there was also the kind of magic that needed to be summoned by supplication or an act of will. Which was this?

"Do you believe him a danger to us?"

"To the tribe, you mean? No, although as I said before, I will need to speak with him. What is this?" From among the spilled objects, Ivomagus picked up a stone. Smoothed as if by water, and well speckled, it fit in the palm of his hand.

Ivomagus closed his eyes and clenched his fingers around the stone. "This comes from well south of the Moray," he declared.

"Are there any markings on it?"

"None."

"Why would the stranger carry a stone? A keepsake?"

"And there is this." The object Ivomagus next picked up dangled from his fingers—a necklace, its cord singed. Had it belonged to a lover? The delicacy of its design argued it had, at very least, once adorned a woman. Perhaps the stranger had a wife.

Again, Ivomagus closed his fingers around the trinket and closed his eyes. "There is loss connected with this, and deep sorrow."

Had he lost his wife even as Verica had lost her husband?

"Yes, well," she mused, "none of us is exempt from grief."

"That is so." Ivomagus looked thoughtful. "Mistress, if this pack did indeed belong to the stranger, and if you return it to him, these objects may well prove restorative."

"Do you think so?"

"Odder things have happened. Let us take the necklace and the stone to him."

"Very well. First, allow me to send a patrol to scout the area west of here, beyond the place where he was found. Then I will go alone and take the necklace to the stranger. He may find that less overwhelming."

"Very well—but pray go carefully. You do not

know how he may react."

****

Wick dreamed he ran with the deer. His heart boomed deep in his chest and his hooves pounded the ground in time with those of the others who surrounded him. He could feel the blood rushing through him in a fierce song. The song was life, the music shared among himself and his companions.

The herd crested a rise, moving as one; he looked ahead and saw her—the white hind that led them, heat steaming off her snowy hide into the cold air.

Did they run away, or toward? He needed the answer to that question.

As if she heard his thoughts, the hind turned her head and looked back at him.

Their eyes met.

Blue eyes she had, the color of a winter sky at midnight.

Someone opened his clenched fist, pried apart the fingers, and placed an object against his palm. His hand closed around it instinctively.

"There now," a voice said softly. The sound of that voice washed through him the way the song had while he ran. Only he did not run now. He lay flat on his back, immobile.

He squeezed the object tight and new images flooded upon him. His mother's face, lit by joy. Her smoke-gray eyes gazing into his, and her hand, warm with approval, patting his cheek.

It is beautiful. Thank you, my son.

Mother…

Her warmth suddenly faded, dying away like a snuffed flame. She lay upon the ground, her eyes closed, and the smell of burning filled Wick's nostrils.

No, no, no—he did not want to relive this. He hadn't wanted to live through it the first time; he couldn't endure doing so again.

He opened his eyes. Like a sun coming up, the room came into view.

He saw the same face he had before—not his mother Essa's face but that of the beautiful woman with the blue eyes. He tore his gaze from hers and focused on the object in his hand.

His mother's necklace, the one he'd given to her at winter solstice the year he turned thirteen. The same he'd taken back from her the night she died, just before he laid her in her grave.

The pain of that moment returned to him, a river flowing. He closed his eyes again.

And heard his mother's voice.

Come awake, son. Come alive. To this place you have been led by magic.

Magic? Him? But nay—of Essa's three children, he was the least likely to experience such grace. His sister, Barta, the defiant and rebellious one, had claimed a kind of fierce, heedless enchantment Wick could never attain. His little brother, Taloc—Tally—carried the spark of their mother's affinity for the magical, the ability perhaps to see beyond the ordinary and peer into the future.

He, Wick, was the practical one, the accomplisher of ordinary tasks—the work pony. He could expect no assistance from the gods.

Except—he had made a promise to the goddess. He ran with the deer. And if he could believe what he'd heard this woman say, he'd been felled as one.

Live, his mother bade him. *Live and fulfill your vow*.

What could he do but obey?

Chapter Nine

"He says his name is Wick map Radoc of the tribe Epidii. Son of a slain chief. His father was killed by the Gaels in a raid. You were right, Ivomagus. The necklace brought him back to himself and allowed him to speak."

Ivomagus gazed into Verica's eyes, a troubled look. They stood together outside the door of Verica's dwelling, where the wounded man—Wick map Radoc—still lay. Snow had once more begun to fall, the flakes spinning down like feathers tossed from on high.

"Was he able to tell you how he came here?" Ivomagus asked.

Verica shook her head. "Not yet, but at least he speaks. Surely, that is the important thing." She laid hold of Ivomagus's sleeve. "You come and speak with him. See can you determine whether he is the man from your Vision." The one who may have come for her, Verica. After speaking with the stranger—Wick map Radoc—and gazing once more into his eyes, she ached to know.

Ivomagus looked unhappy, but he said, "One thing is certain, Mistress—the gods have sent him, for good or for ill."

"Go speak with him," Verica urged again, her lips growing tight. "Determine which it is."

The shaman gave her a look she could not

interpret. "I will."

Verica preceded Ivomagus into the hut. Wick map Radoc sat propped up against the wall with a rug behind his head. Dark auburn hair lay tangled on his brow and, forehead creased by pain, he did not appear much of a warrior. Yet at the sight of him Verica's heart lifted unaccountably.

His dark eyes embraced her before moving to Ivomagus in question.

"This, Master Wick, is our tribe's shaman, called Ivomagus."

"I remember seeing him before—and you." His voice sounded rusty, a gravelly rumble. Caution filled his eyes.

"Please relate to Master Ivomagus what you told me."

Wick shifted uneasily in the bed. Ivomagus took the place Verica had occupied just moments ago; his eyes moved to the necklace Wick still clutched in his hand.

Wick map Radoc focused his dark eyes on the shaman, seeming to weigh and measure him. Some of his tension eased.

"How did I come here? Am I your captive?"

He had asked Verica the same questions but did not seem to grasp the answers she'd given.

Ivomagus shook his head. "No, you are not captive. You were picked up by our warriors after one of them shot you with his arrow while hunting."

"Shot me?"

"He thought he aimed at a deer," Ivomagus said carefully. "The arrowhead went through your shoulder, as you see. Our healer has tended your injury. Can you tell me why you were on our land?"

Wick seemed to struggle to find an answer. Once again he asked a question. "These are not lands held by the Carvorst? Or Chief Enestimus map Saccus?"

Ivomagus shot Verica a questioning look. "No. I have indeed heard of a tribe called the Carvorst, but they hold lands far east of here. We have no alliance with them."

Verica put in, "We heard, from tribesmen fleeing northward, the Carvorst have been routed. Were you traveling to their lands?"

Wick looked confused. "The Carvorst chief, Peldomus, was on good terms with my father. I had hoped to sue aid from him."

"Your father, Radoc?"

"Of tribe Epidii."

"You said he was killed," Verica inserted gently.

"Yes." Wick clenched his fingers still more tightly on the necklace in his hand. "My tribe is fair destroyed."

"A common tale among the Caledonii." Again Ivomagus cast a look at Verica before he asked, "So you come to our lands looking for assistance?"

"I lost my way. There was a storm, and a band of Gaels—their encampment cannot be far from here. I followed a herd of deer away—we were pursued." He frowned, as if puzzled by it, but Ivomagus visibly relaxed.

"Ah, that does explain it. If you fled amongst a herd of deer, our hunter must have mistaken you for one."

"Our apologies," Verica added softly.

Wick map Radoc nodded, though he didn't appear

satisfied. Verica could not blame him. It would be difficult to mistake a man for a deer, even in deep snow.

Gently, Ivomagus questioned, "Your tribe Epidii, how far south of here do they reside?"

"Far. I am no longer certain how far. As I say, the storm threw me off my course."

"And the Gaels, just as here, press your tribe hard?"

"Yes. They overrode our settlement and nearly destroyed it. Killed both my parents and badly wounded my young brother." He raised the necklace in his hand. "This belonged to my mother."

"Had you an older brother, as well?" Ivomagus asked.

A shake of the head made Wick's only reply.

Ivomagus frowned. "Forgive me, but I do not understand. Were you not, then, left as chief?"

Wick map Radoc said nothing.

"Why," Ivomagus pressed, "would you, in such case, leave your tribe?"

Wick lifted his gaze from his hands. What Verica saw in them made her leap to his defense. "He says he came in search of assistance for his tribe. That is, surely, also the role of a chief."

Ivomagus looked at her in surprise. Seldom did she speak for anyone; she could not imagine what made her do so now.

Wick map Radoc remained silent, but the pain in his eyes, stark and raw, conveyed much.

Verica told him, "Since one of our tribesmen has injured you, you are welcome to stay here while you heal. But we have little other aid to offer. Like your own tribe, we Caerena are hunted and hounded from the west, displaced, and woefully reduced in number."

"Throughout Caledonia, it is the same," he replied. "Traveling northward, I scarce recognized the country through which I passed. Tribe after tribe has relinquished its territory, either through necessity or defeat."

"A sad state," Ivomagus agreed. "But we are not defeated while yet one of us remains alive. The water that runs through these rivers and streams runs also through our veins. We are Caledonia."

Wick gave a tight smile. "Those sound like words my mother might have spoken. But the Gaels now hold much of our land. Are they also Caledonia?"

"They are Del Riada and far too greedy. We will not go down to defeat while yet one of us stands, while the memory of even one ancestor remains."

"My ancestors travel with me," Wick map Radoc agreed, "in blood and bone. But I am not sure I can agree with you any further than that."

Ivomagus touched Wick on the arm. "Enough for now. Rest while you can, Wick map Radoc. Our guards watch for any movement from the west. Hopefully we will have a small respite which will allow you to regain your strength."

Ivomagus rose; with a murmur for the man in the cot, Verica followed him out. They stood huddled together beside her door.

"Well?" Verica asked, hushed.

Ivomagus's kindly eyes looked thoughtful. "A curious circumstance, and no mistake. The fact that he followed a herd of deer might account for Segovax's error in felling him."

"Perhaps."

Ivomagus smiled wryly. "I, like you, Mistress Verica, do not feel entirely satisfied by that explanation."

"And the rest of it? Is he the man you saw in your Vision? The one you said…said came for me." Verica felt unaccountably anxious for it to be so. A part of her she did not trust, upon which she dared not rely, longed for her to mean something to the man lying inside her hut, and he to her. But she'd finished with such impulses, and such feelings. She would have no more of it. She refused to be seduced by a pair of fathomless dark eyes.

That being said, even she, her senses half blunted by battle and loss, could sense the magic in Wick map Radoc.

As if he followed her thoughts—and Verica hoped he did not—Ivomagus said, "There is strong magic connected to that necklace he cherishes. But it is a fair and gentle magic."

Verica blew out a breath. "You do not believe him to be a danger to us?"

"A threat, do you mean? I do not. I sense anguish in him, but it is personal."

"Anguish?"

"He carries a load of sorrow."

Ah, Verica thought again, and who did not?

She drew a breath. "As I told him, we cannot send him away while we stand responsible for his injury."

Ivomagus eyed her thoughtfully. "Mistress, please allow me to make arrangements for him to be lodged elsewhere while he recuperates."

"Where? There is no place."

"There must be. You need a private abode where you can withdraw when the responsibilities grow too heavy. Besides, I would be sure of your safety."

"You have just finished saying he is not a threat."

"Yes. But you are precious to—to the tribe. Should any harm befall you, I do not know how we would contrive to go on."

"The same way we have continued to fight on without Chief Ammin, without Morirex and countless others. I am not indispensable, Ivomagus."

"You are, Mistress; you just cannot see it."

Verica did not know how to reply to such a statement, or to the warmth in the shaman's eyes. Instead she looked away and said hastily, "I do not think it wise to move the Epidii chief just yet."

"Chief?"

"Is that not his rightful place in his tribe?"

"It sounds to me as if he has forsaken his place. Whatever the case, there is a story in it, far more than he has yet told to us."

Verica leaned closer to the shaman. "I will just have to deepen my acquaintance with him, Ivomagus, and see can I discover it."

Chapter Ten

Verica once more dreamed that she ran, her gait swift and sure over the broken ground, her body reaching, reaching, celebrating its strength. A cold wind rushed past her, stinging her eyes, filling her nostrils and streaming past her…

Fur.

She realized she possessed hooves rather than feet, and a coat—not of brown but of pure white. She led not a tribe of the Caerena but a herd of deer.

Slowing her pace, she turned and looked back at them. They had run far and breathed clouds of steam into the icy air. Behind them lay the churned tracks of many hooves. The members of the herd seethed together in a mass of brown, only one of them standing out to her eyes. A large stag, bursting with life; his hide held a reddish gleam. He lifted his head and looked at her; their gazes connected with a surety that sounded through her. She fell into his gaze—dark, deep, and wild—and his essence enfolded her like scent.

Verica awoke with a start, her heart pounding. So real had the dream seemed, for an instant she wondered how she came to be lying in a heap of blankets instead of standing out on the hillside.

What did it mean?

She lay drawing deep breaths until her heartbeat calmed, absorbing the stillness within the hut.

The stranger—she supposed she should think of him, now, by name, Wick map Radoc—slept quietly in her cot. Unwilling to move him, she'd made a separate bed for herself against the far wall. Listening, she wondered if he breathed.

Had he perished at some time during the night? Surely not, young and strong as he was. A warrior. She'd seen warriors endure far more terrible injuries than an arrow through the shoulder.

Yet fever—or renewed bleeding—might have taken him in his sleep. Most certainly, she needed to check.

She sat up; her head, still half stranded in the odd dream, spun slowly, and her hair swung across her back. She felt a sudden dread of finding the man on the other side of the hut dead, and remembered the night Morirex had died.

Like Wick map Radoc, Morirex had been strong— a fair bull of a man. He'd carried more than one wound at the time of his death. A tribal hero, he'd gone into battle time after time bearing injuries that made Verica marvel at his endurance.

He'd fought against the pain and weight of them defiantly—roared aloud and denied the terrible wound that at last overtook him. Hollered at her, his wife, and demanded she lend him her strength.

She had tried.

Why would she think of that now, when the hut— Morirex's hut—lay so peaceful, as did the night outside? No cry from the sentry, no apparent danger within or without.

Still fighting her feeling of disorientation, she arose and lit a rush light. Tiptoeing to the cot she'd once shared with her husband, she half feared she'd see Morirex's corpse lying there, bloodied and torn, a grimace distorting his features as it had in death.

No. The stranger—Wick—lay quietly with his good arm bent across his brow, like a child. The deep breaths raised and lowered his broad chest.

Her legs gave out and she sank down beside him. Why should she feel so much relief? This man meant nothing to her.

No man would ever again mean anything to her, save as an ally or tribesmate. She'd sooner thrust her seared hand back into the fire than care for another man.

As she had a hundred times before, she asked herself why Morirex had despised her so. Was it because she'd never conceived his child? It wasn't as if Morirex hadn't made the effort to impregnate her. He'd used her body in the manner of a breeding boar. Even after it became plain she'd never carry his child, it had not kept him from his pleasure.

His, not hers.

An unbroken maiden when she came to him, she'd been shocked by how unfeeling—how violent, even— the act had been. She'd heard otherwise from her friends, been told of drugging kisses and the touch of a calloused hand, the tenderness of lips at a breast.

Morirex had used her as he might one of his weapons—merely because he needed to. But that, she once more assured herself as she had a hundred times before, had taught her endurance. It had lent her a strength upon which the Caerena now relied.

It had taught her she did not want a man in her life.

Now she sat and studied the man who had, indeed,

been thrust just there—into her life—through no act of her own. There was magic in it, Ivomagus said. Gazing at Wick map Radoc, and despite her own lack of faith, she believed it.

Had he been sent for her? No, surely for the benefit of the tribe, who lay under her care and domain. A strong warrior, even sorely wounded, made a desperately needed addition.

Wick map Radoc might have been dropped from the sky by request. That did not mean he would choose to help them. They could not offer him much in return.

Verica propped an elbow on one knee, set her chin in her palm, and continued to regard him.

Not handsome, no—yet something about him fascinated her. Fascinated, not attracted. Like notions of love, she had put passion behind her. Perhaps it was those dark eyes, so like the eyes of the hart in her dream. Or the broad chest that somehow made him seem reliable—like an earthen bulwark. Or the tendrils of magic that enfolded him. She had put prayer behind her...but no one could dismiss magic.

Still and all, the weaving of magic had never been a skill she sought, any more than Morirex had sought her company. She respected it. One had to respect it, but she left its management to others.

Surely her dream, Ivomagus's warning, and the stranger's odd and unexpected appearance made her prey to fancy. Just as when the guards, pushed past ordinary weariness, began seeing shadows turn into enemy attackers, she began to see something in this man that did not exist.

Not that she doubted him for a hero. Valiant he must be, without a doubt.

****

Wick, at the age of eight, sat beside his mother's knee, watching her carefully. Morning sun flooded into the hut through the open door, lighting her hair with glints of red and catching the movement of her fingers while she wove a complicated pattern above the fire.

"Pay attention now, son."

Wick obeyed. He adored his mother and always listened to her requests. Well, nearly always. Sometimes he ran off and played with his friends when she'd asked him to gather kindling. Sometimes he followed after his father, eager to accompany him on the hunt.

But deep inside, his spirit responded to this—not the magic his mother espoused so much as the time spent alone with her, as the object of her attention.

Well, they were more or less alone. His sister, Barta, played in one corner. Wick wondered if Mother had placed a charm on her, to keep her quiet. Barta, rarely still, loved to run and chatter and draw notice to herself.

Now, though, she cuddled with one of Father's great hounds. Give Barta a hound to love, and she became as contented as she ever got.

Dismissing her from his mind, Wick focused once more on his mother. She'd belonged to him first, even before Barta came along, because he was firstborn. His father's pride and, he liked to think, the possessor of his mother's heart.

"There, Wick my darling. Did you see how I did that?"

He shook his head. His deep auburn hair, caught in a rough plait, skittered across his back like a snake.

Essa's smoky gray eyes examined his face with kindly exasperation. "It is important, son. Were you not paying heed?"

"I was, but it looked hard. Do it again, Mother."

"I shall, and more slowly." Her graceful hands moved like birds, and light entered her eyes. "Gather the power from the air around you. Channel it through you and into the stones. That will guard you from all harm, see? Weave together the water and the fire, for opposites must become one." Again her fingers moved in the complex pattern. "Breath love into it."

"Love?"

Her gaze turned still more kindly. "Love is the true power, Wick—at the center of everything. The heart that cannot love has lost all hope of protection. When we approach the gods, we do so through love. Only then will they hear us." She picked up one of the enchanted stones, warm and speckled, and handed it to him.

"I love you, Mama."

"And I love you, my strong and valiant son."

"What is *valiant*?"

"It means brave."

"Like Dada."

Essa smiled. "Your father is the bravest man I have ever known, and I do adore him for it."

Wick stowed away that nugget of information like the stone, inside his tunic: bravery brought the most dearly sought approval and love.

"But I do not speak of that kind of courage when I speak the word valiant. Courage comes easily to your father. I sometimes think it is second nature to him. No, Wick, valiance is a thing more hard won. It is of the spirit as well as the flesh. It means summoning courage even when one is afraid, and pushing on."

She reached out and cupped his cheek with one warm, graceful hand. "Remember, my darling, the best a man can be is valiant and wise."

Wick awoke to deep silence, his whole body protesting the loss of his mother's presence. How many times had he mourned her since her death? Too many to count.

But no—for he could feel her yet, the fragile and tenuous bonds of love.

Surely she remained close to him.

He opened his eyes. The soft radiance of a rushlight lit the hut—not his parents' hut back home but that of the woman who led the Caerena. That woman herself sat beside the cot where he lay, with her hands lightly entwined and her sleek, dark head bowed.

Asleep.

Ah, and why should she be sitting here beside him instead of in her nest of furs across the hut, where she'd retired before he fell asleep? Had he cried out or made some other sound in distress, during the dream?

And why should her presence echo for him his mother's? The two women shared little beyond being women, and being beautiful.

Mistress Verica of the Caerena must surely be the loveliest woman he'd ever seen, even when, like now, those glorious eyes of hers lay closed.

She looked a good deal younger in sleep, the hard edge she had still present but muted. Wick wondered again what had put her in the position she held—ironically, the same he'd abdicated back home.

Perhaps the goddess had directed him here—by

hoof and by magic—to shame him.
No more than he deserved.

Chapter Eleven

"I need to get up." Wick gritted his teeth against the pain in his shoulder—strong enough to kick any man back down—and cast a look at the woman who stood beside his cot with her hands on her hips. She appeared ready to try and keep him in the bed by force if necessary.

Could she?

A shocking thought barreled through Wick's mind. She could keep him there with one kiss, with one touch, if she chose. Bed him for days uncounted, if she would but remove her clothing and join him.

And by the goddess's holy light, from whence had that image come? He rarely focused on women. Or on coupling. Back home among his own tribesfolk, he'd always been considered a good catch. The future chief, so the young Epidii women supposed him. A few had displayed their interest. But, struggling to fill his father's place, he'd had little time for them.

None, for all their efforts, had done to him what this woman did with a single, casual glance.

Now she interposed her body between him and freedom. "You are not fit."

"Fit or not," he told her with a dour glare. "I cannot lie here like an infant."

"You are clearly still in pain."

"Pain is just pain and means nothing. Do you know

anyone who's not injured?"

The retort caused her to back off, though she continued to watch him through narrowed blue eyes. Wick wished she wouldn't. He felt weaker than he liked to admit, and did not welcome such an intense regard.

She bit her lip. "Perhaps I should call the healer."

"Go ahead." That would get her out of the hut and give him a chance to piss, a pressing need he certainly did not want to perform in her presence, even though last night the healer had left him a crock for just that purpose.

She seemed to measure him from the top of his head down to his toes. She scowled. "Here, let me help you."

Before he could draw breath to object, she stepped in and propped her shoulder beneath his.

The action brought her body up against him, her side pressed close, one of her arms wrapped around his body in a supportive gesture. He could feel the heat of her, could feel one small breast cleaved to his chest. Sensation slammed through him, stealing what breath he'd managed to hoard. *Softness. Warmth. Strength.*

How could all these things be present together, in one woman? She proved smaller, there beneath his arm, than she'd appeared, given her staunch stance—the top of her sleek black head barely reached his ear. And he could smell her—spice, old leather, and the intimate, arousing scent of woman.

Could she smell him, also? By the goddess, he must reek of filth and blood.

"All right?" she puffed. "Don't go down, or you will surely tear that wound open." Her fingers dug hard into his side, and he felt her body flex. He closed his eyes against a fierce wave of desire, and she looked at him doubtfully.

"Perhaps we should return you to the bed."

Perhaps they should.

Not looking at her, he said, "Better you should leave, so I might use the pot."

Surprisingly she laughed, a deep, dusky sound. "Is that all? Why did you not say?

"I just did."

"Very well. I will go find us some breakfast. Try not to fall down while I am gone."

She hurried out the door, and Wick struggled to master himself. His half-arousal had surged to full-blown while her hands remained on him. In such a condition, he did not know how long it would take him to accomplish his stated purpose.

A fine thing if she returned only to find he hadn't used the crock.

Plainly, he could not stay here—not with the Caerena and most definitely not near Mistress Verica. The tribe, as reduced as the Epidii back home, had nothing to offer him in the way of assistance, just as Verica, attractive as she might be, had nothing to offer him.

More correctly, he had nothing to offer her.

He ought to leave as soon as possible, head east, and continue searching for his father's old allies. That, or lose himself in the forest and die there like an aged hound.

He used the crock and carried it to the corner, his shoulder screaming at him with the movement. Then he walked to the door.

Heavy snow had fallen during the night, which

probably accounted for the silence. The settlement appeared little more than a series of white mounds. He could see Verica's tracks leading away from her door, the path from which sloped upward, and little else.

Like their huts back home, these had been dug into the ground with only their roofs showing, the vent holes in which now disgorged lazy puffs of smoke into the heavy air. Snow still fell, big flakes that spun and twisted much the way his mother's hands used to when she spoke a prayer.

Protection. But there was none, not anywhere. All his mother's prayers and charms had not kept the Gaels from their door.

They had not made Wick valiant.

Mistress Verica, he suspected, thought him something he was not—a brave chief, a hero. He must leave before being forced to disabuse her from that belief.

Two children ran by with a hound, breaking a trail. They might have been himself and Barta back in the days when the world held a ray of happiness. Both children stared at him, and the hound gave a deep woof, regarding him through suspicious yellow eyes. For some reason, it made him think of Barta's companion, the young stranger she called True.

Then he caught sight of Verica on her way back to him, following the children's trail. She came with her head down against the swirling snow, flakes like white feathers in her black hair.

"Brrr, it is cold," she greeted him. "Why do you stand here in the chilly air? The healer, Callorix, says he will come after he tends some of the others, to look how you are mending. Here."

She thrust a cloth-wrapped packet into his hands before squeezing past, her body brushing against his.

"It is not much," she warned. "There is not much to spare even given the doe Segovax brought in." Wick turned his head, and she wrinkled her nose at him. "Part of the catch proved to be a man."

"Better mayhap, had I been a deer."

She shrugged. "Better for the cookpots." Her deep blue gaze touched his. "As it is, I am not sure what to make of you."

"I am a complication, an unwelcome one," Wick acknowledged dryly.

"The very last thing I needed. But come, sit. Eat. Once the healer does his work with you, I doubt you'll want to."

Wick took a place beside the fire, which she quickly stirred to life. She accepted the packet of food back from him and laid the meager repast out on a hearthstone.

Eyeing it, Wick said, "You go ahead. I have little appetite."

That sharpened the expression in her eyes. "Just because we have little, do you suppose I will fail to extend my hospitality?"

"Give it to the sick and to the children." It was what his father would have said, and had on more than one occasion. Among the Epidii, the chief's house went hungry as often as anyone else's.

Mistress Verica retorted, "You *are* sick—or at least wounded and recovering." She snapped again, "Eat."

Wick's brows twitched. Clearly a woman to be obeyed. He took up a small portion of food.

"So," she asked then, one warrior to another, "how

bad is it?"

When Wick did not reply and merely stared at the scraps of roasted venison in his hand, she acknowledged, "A foolish question, eh? I can see you are hurting."

That stiffened Wick's spine. "I will be well, soon enough."

"No doubt. I saw your scars; you are no stranger to battle wounds. Tell me about the plight of your tribe."

Again, when he did not immediately speak, she prodded, "It must be dire, if you left them to search for assistance."

"It is dire."

Still he stared at the food, unwilling to elucidate. He could barely remember a time when the Gaels had not been a threat. They figured in the stories Caledonian women told their children at bedtime, monsters who came from the west. In the beginning, the threat had seemed a distant one. Greedy, the Gaels were, and merciless, unwilling to be satisfied with their own kingdom. They fought without quarter and used their battle chariots to cut the Caledonii down like ripe barley.

A fate suffered by Wick's own father.

Everything changed then, he acknowledged. His father had survived and continued to lead the Epidii, but he lived with constant pain. And the Gaels pushed in closer—so close the Epidii could feel their breath on the backs of their necks.

In answer to Mistress Verica's inquiring look, he said, "The Gaels press us hard in the south, and the tribes around us have fled eastward. Those we might have counted as allies are there no more."

Verica's gaze turned sympathetic. "So you have come farther afield, looking for them?"

Wick shrugged and immediately regretted it as his shoulder complained. "The country through which I passed has changed, become barely recognizable. I do not know where our allies have gone—moved or dead, who can tell? I found burned and abandoned settlements and the reek of the Gaels everywhere. I was very nearly captured by them." He remembered his promise to the goddess and his flight as a stag. Had it been mere imagining?

"And those back home?" she asked tentatively. "How will they fare in your absence?"

Dangerous ground, Wick thought. Did he want to admit he'd abdicated his place and handed over leadership of his tribe to another? He saw a measure of respect—perhaps even admiration—in this beautiful woman's eyes. Perhaps he did not deserve that, but he discovered he desired it.

He shifted uneasily in his seat and said, "Winter comes. I hoped that, as in past years, the attacks would ease up and felt it the best time for me to strike out." Swiftly he turned the conversation back on her. "And you? How did you wind up leading this tribe?"

Her lips curled in a rueful smile. "It is a strange thing, is it not? A woman acting as a warrior."

"Not strange at all. My sister, Barta, has long numbered one among our warriors, as fierce and twice as stubborn as any of them."

"My tribe has come apart at the seams. Our chief and his son, both killed. My husband was war chief. When he too fell, our chief's widow, Mistress Cunarda, appealed to me to step into his place. I am certain your sister would have done the same."

Wick imagined Barta would. "When did you lose your husband, Mistress?"

"Late in the summer." For an instant, Verica's eyes grew distant, filled with pain.

She must miss him and mourn him still. But Wick could tell she wished to display no sign of weakness.

"We have all lost someone," she observed. "Now eat. I would not want you also to perish."

Chapter Twelve

"Mistress Verica!"

Verica turned her head sharply when the leather door curtain flew aside. Hectia's head appeared, a mass of snow-dusted, red-gold plaits above troubled gray eyes.

The girl swept Verica with a keen glance before focusing on Wick map Radoc, who sat beside the fire.

"Hectia, what is it?"

"Mother sent me," Hectia admitted in a burst of honesty, "to see if you are all right."

"Our guest has not yet killed me, if that is what you mean—nor have I killed him. Come in, girl. You are letting the cold in."

Hectia slipped into the hut, her gaze all over Wick. "We grew concerned when we did not see you."

Verica bit her lip. Cunarda, no doubt urged by the erstwhile Ivomagus, had done her best to persuade Verica to find lodgings elsewhere for the incomer.

"Where else should I house him?" Verica had retorted. "Should I leave him at large to endanger others? As war chief, should I not absorb any threat?" Not that she believed Wick map Radoc to be a danger. Ivomagus merely acted from an overzealous sense of protectiveness.

Now Wick stirred and returned Hectia's piercing look. Did he resent being considered a threat?

With irony, she told Hectia, "You may return to your mother with word I yet do live."

"I will. But I have other news, from the guard. They have detected movement from the Gaels."

That got Verica to her feet, her heart sinking with dismay. "I'd hoped they had withdrawn. Are our men certain?"

"It seems so."

"Do the Gaels mobilize to attack us?"

"They could not tell."

Verica turned to Wick. "They would not organize a raid through such deep snowfall, would they?"

He frowned. "Who knows what they may do? They thrive on battle. If they do come, at least they will not be able to maneuver their accursed chariots. That is an advantage."

"I must go and see." Verica snatched up her cloak. "Master Wick, you remain here and await the arrival of the healer."

Disregarding the advice, he rose. "No, I will come also."

Verica might have argued it. She did not believe him fit to be on his feet. Besides, the affairs of her tribe fell to her alone. Yet she could not waste time arguing it with him.

They went in a little knot of three, following the narrow trail Hectia had made, and found the Caerena guard gathered at the edge of the trees that enclosed the settlement—three young men and one older.

The elder, Motius, greeted Verica with a hiss. "Sss—listen."

She did, stretching her ears like those of a hare, and caught a faint rumble on the clear, cold air. Voices? The movement of chariots? She swore under her breath—she'd been hoping the lads were right, and the Gaels had withdrawn. But Wick spoke truly; at least they would never move those vehicles through this deep snow.

"What do you make of it?" she asked Motius in a breathy whisper.

He shrugged unhappily. "Cursed if I can tell. It was the hound who first alerted us." He laid a hand on the head of the deerhound at his side. "At first I thought another herd of deer passed by. But that is something more."

"Yes." Verica thought furiously. "Send out scouts—no more than two men with a hound. Tell them to go carefully." They could afford to lose no one else.

Motius nodded. "Nactovus," he said to the lad standing by, "you and me. And Swift, here."

Hectia edged closer to Verica. "What shall I tell Mother?"

"I will go speak with your mother." Verica turned to Wick. "Will you return to my hut?"

He frowned, an expression all too frequent with him. His dark gaze rested still in the distance, and Verica wondered what thoughts filled his mind.

Troubling ones, without question. But he nodded and began to turn away before catching her by the arm and drawing her closer.

So close she could once more smell him. She'd spent the night, to be sure, in the same hut with him and become all too aware of his scent—musky, male, and not unpleasant. Now his gaze engaged hers with an intensity she felt pass through her like a spear.

"Mistress, I scent battle."

"Eh?" she responded, startled.

"I know it does not make sense, an attack in such weather. But I feel it. Don't you?"

****

Verica shook her head, looking alarmed, and Wick drew a breath, wondering how to impress his certainty on her. "It comes upon me this way sometimes," he confessed. Not all the time, curse it—he'd had no warning the night his parents died. Having no hint of danger, he'd failed to be on guard—he did not mean to make that mistake again.

So why should he receive warning now? He could not tell, but by the goddess, he refused to fail this woman.

"Very well," she said, not removing her gaze from his. "Segovax, go alert our warriors to the danger of attack. Have everyone collect his or her weapons. Motius, you take Swift and go see what you can discover—but go carefully."

Motius did not immediately move. "But," he protested in surprise, also staring at Wick, "you mean to listen to him?"

Verica rounded on him. "Would you rather stand unprepared?"

The man, lads, and hound all left without further protest.

To Wick, Verica said, "I must go speak with Mistress Cunarda. You return to my hut."

He nodded, though he had no intention of staying there. He too would collect his weapons and prepare to fight. Something he understood.

Curse his shoulder, though, he thought as he watched Verica jog away in the company of the girl,

Hectia. Uneasiness stirred again in his heart. He'd never liked the idea of his sister entering battle, although he couldn't deny she made a strong showing, especially with her war hound, Loyal, at her side. But Loyal lay dead, slain as a result of Barta's own rash actions. And Wick could not imagine Mistress Verica, for all her obvious strength, leading her tribe against a band of murderous Gaels.

Death, as he'd learned, came all too swiftly and easily. He did not want it to find this beautiful, courageous woman.

If she expected him to sit meekly in her hut while she faced battle without him, she made a serious miscalculation.

****

As all too often when Verica arrived at the chief's house, Mistress Cunarda looked frantic. The events of the past year had not dealt easily with this woman, whom Verica both respected and called friend.

Cunarda had adored her husband, Ammin. Unlike Verica's husband, Morirex, Ammin had loved his wife in return. Now her courage, if not her will, seemed to have shattered. She lived in a near-constant state of anxiety and sometimes worried to the point of making herself ill.

She turned a pale face toward Verica when she entered the dwelling. "So—he did not rape you during the night, then?"

Verica snorted. "I should like to see the man who would succeed in raping me."

"You will, if the Gaels have their way and overrun us. They will force us all." Cunarda glanced at her daughter, Smerta, present in the room as well as Hectia, who'd entered in Verica's wake. "Lest the goddess prevent it."

Verica fought the impulse to snort again. She'd learned to hold her tongue on the subject of the goddess's mercy. "Wick map Radoc has neither forced nor killed me, as you see."

Cunarda blew out a breath. "What of the Gaels? Smerta says they may be on the move. Impossible, surely!"

"Our guards have heard…something. Master Wick has warned me of attack."

"Master Wick has?" Cunarda stared.

"You know very well a good warrior often has an instinct for such things. We need to prepare. Smerta, gather your weapons."

Cunarda halted in her pacing. "You are mad. They may be on the move, but surely only to withdraw. They cannot attack through deep snow."

"I would be prepared, whatever happens."

Piteously, Cunarda returned, "But surely we are safe a few days longer?"

"It will cost us nothing to stand ready."

"What if he is a spy for the Gaels, this Wick map Radoc? Have you thought of that?"

"A Gaelic spy? With the marks of a Caledonian warrior all over him? Oh, Cunarda. I got a good look at him whilst I sponged all that blood away. The marks are old, and genuine."

"He may have been bought. You know what the Gaels are. They may hold someone dear to him—his wife or child—and so force him to their will."

"So they may, but I do not believe so. He has spoken to me, some, of his past." He'd not mentioned a wife. That did not mean he lacked one, or children. "There is a story in it." And magic, could Ivomagus be believed. "But I do trust him."

"Why?" Cunarda challenged. "How can you trust anyone, given what we have suffered?"

"I don't know," Verica admitted. "But I do." She could not explain it, but her heart insisted there was goodness inside Wick map Radoc, and courage.

A cry came from outside, shattering the quiet of the morning. She swung toward the door, her long knife already in her hand.

"What was that?" Cunarda gasped.

The call to battle. And proof that Wick map Radoc had spoken truly.

Chapter Thirteen

Wick had not yet reached Mistress Verica's hut when the shout sounded across the settlement. He whirled, every instinct leaping to attention, his nostrils quivering like those of a war hound.

During the last year, when danger in the south had grown so constant, he'd found a facility for slipping into the role of warrior, pushing all else aside, including his innate feelings. To be sure, on some level he remained concerned for those he loved. But it did not do to fret while facing a ruthless enemy, and besides, since the deaths of his parents any softer feelings felt blunted.

Now, without conscious thought, the knife came into his hand. He started back through the snow toward the center of the settlement. Other folk joined him, streaming out from their huts, most looking apprehensive. Verica appeared with both of the chief's daughters as well as the chief's widow on her heels.

"Who was it hollered?" she demanded.

"I!" one of the lads replied—the warrior called Segovax ran, his face white, with a hound at his side. "They come. By the goddess, they do come!"

Wick had time to exchange one look with Verica, no more. He wanted to bid her round up the other women and flee with them away through the trees to what safety they could find. But like his, her knife was in her hand, and her eyes burned with what could only be battle light.

"Positions, positions!" she called. "Mistress Cunarda, gather the mothers and children. Move them away into the forest."

Wick grunted. His role here did not include giving orders. In truth, he had no role here. Verica might well command him to stand down.

Instead, her gaze sought his; briefly she measured him. "Are you fit to fight?"

"I am."

"With me, then."

They ran through the trees, leaping like the deer of which he'd dreamed, forming along with others a ragged line. This would not do; Wick knew it for a poor defense. But why would the Gaels choose to attack at such a time? What had they to gain by coming hampered by deep snow, and without their chariots?

"This makes no sense," he gasped to Verica even as he took up a place on her left hand.

She shook her head. "They have never before attacked in such weather. Seeking to destroy us, you think? Deliver the finishing blow? Take our settlement for their winter camp?"

Wick's only answer came in the form of another grunt. Other Caerena warriors pushed in beside him, including Motius, still with the war hound at his side.

Without looking at Motius, Verica asked, "You saw them? How many?"

"Two score. No chariots. But they break a trail and come swiftly."

"Hoping to take us by surprise, no doubt—fall upon us in our beds." Verica bit her lip savagely. "Wipe us away like harvested barley."

"Yes." Another warrior, an older man Wick had heard called Ramoc, pushed into the line beside him. On the far side of Motius stood a boy of no more than fourteen, who looked terrified. Beside Verica, one of the chief's daughters—Smerta?—took her position. She appeared frightened also, if determined.

As he did before every battle, Wick wondered if he would die—here among strangers where he did not belong. If he meant to spend his life resisting the Gaels, should it not be in defense of those he loved?

He caught it then, the sound of the Gaels' approach, a barely perceptible vibration comprised from the rattle of weapons, the crunch of snow, and the shush of guarded voices.

Verica turned to him; her blue eyes blazed in her face. "May you fight well, valiant one!"

****

"Wick! Wick map Radoc!"

From afar off someone called his name. He knew the voice but could not immediately place it. Then fingers touched his shoulder and reality snapped into place with the abruptness of sudden awakening.

Mistress Verica. *She survived the battle.* He experienced a fierce rush of gladness at the knowledge, followed by an equally strong wave of disappointment. *So did he.*

"We drove them off." Verica's voice sounded muffled, and Wick realized the shouts of battle and the clash of weapons still echoed in his ears. He blinked furiously and managed to focus on her face.

He would not have known her, with all her color flown and lines of exhaustion visible beneath a liberal splashing of blood. In stark contrast to her pallor, it ran down her cheeks in crimson streaks. Examining her farther, Wick saw the leather of her tunic had been rent and more blood seeped through from beneath.

But she still stood firm. Her fingers clutched at him, curled like claws into his good shoulder.

"Are you badly hurt?"

He shook his head. In truth, he did not know whether he'd been touched. He must have taken wounds in so sharp an encounter.

They stood together in a wide swath of red snow. Looking around, he saw that Gaelic dead lay everywhere. The aged warrior, Ramoc, sprawled dead beside him. Smerta sat in the red snow clutching her arm and weeping.

Verica's hands—including the one clamped to Wick's shoulder—were red to the wrists.

She said, her gaze fierce on Wick's, "We drove them off. It was because of you."

"No." Not possible.

He gazed away in the direction the Gaels had fled. He barely remembered the encounter, or their flight. "We must follow and finish them."

"What?" Verica stared as she might at a madman. "I did not hear you right."

"Follow them." The wide trail appeared like a pathway of blood. "Rout them. Burn their settlement." Wick did not know from whence the words came. Certainly not from his conscious mind.

"But…" Verica looked stunned. "We are too few."

"They are too few. It will not take many of us. A small force." They sounded like words his sister, Barta, might say—rash, dangerous words—and that halted him.

But Verica's gaze took light. "I will go. You and me. Who else?" She looked around. "How many do we need?"

"But two more," Wick heard himself say.

"I will come." The chief's other daughter, Hectia, swayed on her feet, but her eyes held steady.

"And I." The youth, Nactovus.

Again Verica asked Wick, "How badly are you wounded?"

He shook his head; he still did not know. His eyes moved to her rent tunic. "You?"

She shook her head also and cried to their companions, "Bring fire."

What followed seemed like a wild dream, even to Wick, who proposed it. They followed the bloody tracks, stepping into the Gaels footprints and trying to move as swiftly as possible. Wick became aware of his injuries then—the wound on his shoulder that had been half-closed now gaped open, by the feel of it, and other cuts stung in a number of places. No one, after such a bloodbath, could possibly go untouched.

They came upon the Gaels' settlement—a rough, hastily erected group of skin huts—without warning. No guard had been set, and no warriors were in sight. As one, they hunkered down and everyone, including Verica, looked to Wick.

"There still may be a lot of them," Nactovus whispered.

"Not expecting us to follow. They are in disarray. Easily routed."

Approximately two score Gaels had attacked. Wick tried to remember how many lay back there on the ground. Not as many as the boy feared could remain. He counted the skin tents silently. Eight of them, easily fired even in the snow.

"Give me the flint." He held out a hand to the lad. "I will circle round to the left and fire the first of the shelters. See that trail? It is where they must have dragged their wounded."

"No," Verica said quickly. "It is my place. I will go."

"They will not see me." Hectia snatched the flint and darted off before Wick could halt her.

"What of us?" Nactovus asked nervously.

"As soon as the first tent fires, we run in. Kill everyone you can see."

The lad swallowed convulsively. "Am I going to die?"

"If you do," Wick said, just as his father had, before almost every battle, "the goddess will receive you."

Nactovus nodded. Time for no more—the last tent on the left fired; a cry went up from within, and smoke billowed from the damp hide.

"She's done it," Verica breathed. "Bless her."

"Courage," Wick told Nactovus, and darted forward.

Later, he thought as how he should have let Verica lead the way. Later, he thought many things. At the time, he had but one aim in his head: kill. His mind turned red. He never looked into the eyes of those he encountered, many of whom came running from the burning shelter, all wounded.

It felt like slaughter. Back home, Wick seldom took part in the slaughter of stock; he had no heart for it, although, to be sure, he'd gutted his share of game.

Game already felled during the hunt.

He half saw Nactovus go down beside him, victim of a lucky slash from one of the wounded Gaels. He didn't know where Hectia might be—she had not returned from firing the shelters.

Then suddenly he saw no more opponents. In the sudden, unnatural stillness Verica fell to her knees beside the lad.

"Dead." The word broke from her in a sob. "Poor lad, poor brave lad."

"Come. Where's the girl?"

"She went ahead of us."

Wick lifted Verica bodily and stood her on her feet; he couldn't imagine from whence he got the strength. "Come," he said again.

"But—"

"We need to go." And he would not leave without Verica. He'd sooner die than leave without her.

Verica swayed where she stood. Her face appeared to be painted with blood, to match her hands. Her gaze met Wick's. "Wait."

She turned from him and moved off through the churned and reddened snow, bending over the fallen Gaels one by one. At first her movements looked solicitous. Then Wick caught the swift, small motion of the knife in her hand.

Slitting throats. Making certain they were all dead.

He watched in fascination while she completed the grim task and returned to him. Then he hefted up the body of the lad and slung it over his shoulder.

"Come," he told Verica for a third time.

They did not run; they had no need. Behind them

everyone lay still, the settlement burned, only a breath of smoke rising. He guessed they lacked the strength to run, in any case.

He turned his head and looked at Verica. "Were you wounded?"

She failed to answer him.

Chapter Fourteen

Hectia ran ahead of Wick and Verica with news of their victory. As a consequence, Verica found herself greeted as a hero when the two of them—the three of them, she amended hastily—came limping in.

The smoke from the Gaels' burned settlement seemed to accompany them, carried on the wind. A great roar went up when she and Wick emerged from it and cleared the trees.

Verica looked at her companion, whose expression remained tight and grim. She could not begin to guess how he'd managed to carry Nactovus's corpse so far, but neither did he reveal any physical strain. At the center of the waiting crowd, he laid the boy's body down with tender care.

Ivomagus stepped forward and acknowledged the gesture with a nod before turning to Verica with concern in his eyes.

"Mistress, are you badly hurt?"

An interesting question, one Wick had already posed to her several times. She'd been sore injured even before they launched the raid and now kept her feet mainly through will power alone. The sting of many wounds had resolved into one massive throb, but the wound that worried her, located on her hip, bled steadily.

She knew very well that he—or she—who led

could not afford to display weakness. Morirex had taught her that. So she refused to answer Ivomagus even as she had Wick and instead declared, "We are victorious. The Gaels' camp lies destroyed."

A howl went up all around. It drowned out the wailing of Nactovus's mother, who had fallen to her knees at his side, in the snow.

Victories had been so few and fear so bright this year past, Verica's people needed this, despite the high price.

"A miracle," Ivomagus pronounced. "We owe this victory to the mercy of the god and goddess."

Verica lifted her chin and added loudly, "And to the valiance of this man here beside me, Wick map Radoc."

Wick turned his head sharply and stared at her in what looked like horror. "No," he began.

But Ivomagus interrupted, beginning a speech about courage and divine guidance. Verica, struggling to retain her feet and only half listening, wondered about what she'd just seen in Wick's eyes.

Then they were ushered toward the chief's house. Cunarda embraced Verica and thanked her for bringing both her daughters back alive. She too looked into Verica's face and asked, "How badly are you wounded?"

Still Verica did not answer.

There in front of the chief's door they were toasted with heather ale and praised once more. Beside Verica, Wick stood silent as a rock. Hurt? He must be. How, with a badly wounded shoulder, had he fought so hard and carried Nactovus so far?

At last Verica stepped forward and lifted her hand.

Most of the tribe had gathered around them, and she raised her voice so all might hear. "It is a great victory, this, one that will allow us time to recover and make plans for the future. But it has come at a price. We have dead to grieve and wounded to tend. Everyone who took part should report to the healer at once."

The onlookers, eager for a greater show of triumph, scattered reluctantly. Those who had participated in the battle moved obediently toward Callorix's hut. Verica swayed; someone seized her arm and steadied her.

Wick? No; instead she found herself staring into Ivomagus's eyes. "And you?" he queried. "Will you also report for care?"

"Of course." Eventually. First she wanted to return to her own hut—alone—for a chance to see how badly her body had fared.

Ivomagus swept her with an appraising look, up and down, almost as if he could see every one of her injuries. "I will accompany you, to make certain you reach there safely."

"No, wait. I must speak with Nactovus's mother." She cast a look back toward the grieving woman, who still knelt above her young son.

"He will be carried to her hut, and I will follow there to counsel her—after I escort you to see Callorix."

Verica glanced around surreptitiously. "Where is Wick map Radoc?"

"He has gone."

"Where?"

"I saw him head toward your dwelling."

Ah, and had Wick the same idea as Verica, a desire to get alone to lick his wounds?

"I must check on him. Ivomagus, I've never seen

anyone fight as he did this day, with no thought for himself. Not even Morirex could have matched his courage."

An unnamed emotion flooded Ivomagus's eyes. "We will both go there, then—to your hut—and assure ourselves he is well."

"No. You should stay and assist Apulla to take Nactovus's body home. Comfort her and speak the prayers she will wish said. She needs you far more than I do."

Ivomagus nodded reluctantly. Verica turned, staggered as her leg tried to go out from under her, and forced her body on.

A body, as she'd learned full well beneath Morirex's tutelage, was just flesh and bone; the power of will could force it to accomplish nearly anything. Endure a cruel touch that should have been tender, push through illness or exhaustion. Ignore wounds.

She reached her own hut and shoved aside the door curtain. Wick had, indeed, arrived ahead of her. Already he had slipped off his blood-soaked tunic; the sight of his body made the breath seize in Verica's throat.

The arrow wound at his shoulder oozed blood. Several new cuts marked his skin, adding to the extent of his gore—a deep slash to the right side of his chest and another to his forearm, both still bleeding heavily— and those were but the ones she could see.

Her heart fell violently and she fought for words. Nothing more than a choked sound came from her. Stepping in, she closed the leather curtain carefully and moved to his side.

For one long moment they stood so, gazing into

one another's eyes. Verica saw no pain in Wick's eyes and soundlessly acknowledged his courage once again.

Promptly forgetting her own hurts, she hissed through her teeth. "Sit."

When he failed to move, she planted her palm against his chest and gave him a shove. He went down with a grunt, possibly one of protest. Verica, who had dealt with stubborn males in the past, chose a matter-of-fact tone when she forced her voice through her throat again. "You are a mess."

A second grunt made his only reply.

"These wounds are deep and have bled heavily. Why did you say nothing?"

"What warrior worries for himself?"

Now she grunted, an agreement. "How did you manage to carry Nactovus so far?"

His eyes once more met hers. This time she thought she identified some of the deep emotion teeming there. Grief? "My father taught me not to mind pain. He—he lived with a terrible, heavy amount of it."

"So you have said. It never got any easier for him?"

"No." The word came out hard-bitten. Wick did not wish to speak more of this; Verica sensed that much. She gave him a fierce stare. "Have you any other wounds?"

"A slash to one leg."

Verica wondered if it matched the one she carried. "You should go to Callorix."

"The healer will have all he can handle with his own tribesfolk. Why trouble him with an incomer?"

"An incomer who carried us to victory, back there."

"Do not exaggerate."

Verica knew she didn't, but hesitated to argue it with him. This man possessed modesty unlike any she'd ever encountered. So different from Morirex, who would have had Verica on her knees, pulling off his boots and tending him like a servant. On that thought she turned away, filled a basin with water, and searched out some cloth for bandaging. Like all else, such supplies had become scarce.

With her back turned to Wick, she said, "I suppose I shall need to tend the worst of your hurts myself, then. Best take off your leggings."

"Eh?" The shock in his tone might have made her smile, had she the strength. As it was, her weariness allowed her only a sigh.

She stole a look at him over her shoulder. "Unless you would rather await Callorix after all."

"I will wait, yes."

"I doubt many men so brave as you have suffered for the sake of modesty. Most I've known have been all too eager to remove their clothing in the company of a woman."

When Wick made no immediate answer, Verica turned to face him, a cloth in her hands.

Of all the things he might have said, he chose but five words in reply.

"Do not call me brave."

That made her eyes widen. She walked back to the fire with the basin.

"Why ever not? Do you forget I was there and fought at your side? You fought like three men."

His dark eyes fell, and an odd expression came to his face.

At one time, after she first handfasted with Morirex, Verica would have dropped the matter. She knew when a man wished to keep his own counsel and when he believed a woman should hold her place—and her tongue. Since then, she'd done a thousand impossible things. Buried half the people she knew, her husband included. Clawed the tribe back from the brink of destruction, led them to fight. Survived.

One man's wishes no longer intimidated her.

She sank down beside Wick, next to the hearth.

"Why don't I tend what I can see, before you bleed to death? Then we will take up the matter of your leggings."

The corners of his mouth quirked up. "Determined to get me out of them, are you?"

She shrugged and dropped her gaze in turn, so he would not see what lay in her eyes. She felt impossibly eager. Surprisingly, she would not mind lying down with this man whose strength came wrapped in magic and mystery. The thought shocked her; she hadn't wanted anyone since the very beginning with Morirex, and she'd had little enough actual pleasure with him.

Wick watched carefully as she wrung out the cloth and moved to sponge his shoulder.

"This will sting," she warned.

Yet he sat like a stone while she wiped away the blood and packed the torn shoulder wound. So much blood. How much could one man shed? Lost in her task, she concentrated on causing him as little pain as possible, and started when he spoke suddenly.

"What of you, Mistress Verica?"

"Me?" She jerked up her gaze and once more met his. Barely a whisper separated them, and Verica lost her breath at what she saw in his eyes.

Another smile quirked his lips and warmed his gaze. "Do you not need your wounds tended? Will you take off your clothing, also, for me?"

Quite an improper suggestion, even under the circumstances. But the soft mischief in his voice lent no offense; instead Verica felt a stir of titillation.

With the native honesty that marked most of her utterances, she said, "I might."

His fingers rose and cupped the back of her head. Gently—so very gently—he drew her to him. Their lips met.

A caress. A whisper. Verica had never been kissed this way, by lips so warm they wooed, coaxed, and persuaded. Tentatively he tasted her, decided he liked the flavor, and dove deeper.

Verica had a sudden flashback to one of Morirex's kisses—swift and brutal, teeth clashing on teeth, the taste of blood. The pain of invasion accompanied by the overwhelming subjugation of her body. Hard-learned experience told her a man took what he wanted without asking.

But Wick map Radoc's lips asked. They sought, thrilled, and comforted. His fingers slid lower and caressed her cheek, the calloused thumb stroking lightly like the touch of a butterfly, and Verica's entire body melted.

She opened for him. Possibly for the first time in her life, she invited, as opposed to endured invasion. Their mouths molded together on a wave of lazy heat.

Oh, by all that was holy, what was this? Verica felt her mind, her spirit, expand on a blaze of white light. How could she hope to resist?

She did not try; instead she surrendered to sensation and suspended even her breath until Wick broke the kiss and rested his forehead against hers.

"It is not often a beautiful woman makes me such an offer." Humor filled his voice and went straight to her head.

But she faltered, "Beautiful?"

Again his thumb caressed her cheek. She went weak in every limb. "You are the most beautiful woman I have ever seen."

Shaken, she tried to match his humorous tone. "If you think so, you must have taken a blow to the head during that battle." Once she'd been considered lovely. She'd fancied that made Morirex look her way.

Now her body bore scars, her hair—a former source of pride and perhaps even conceit—hung tangled and dirty, caked with blood.

But he said, "So beautiful," and whispered his lips over hers again.

She wanted to offer herself to him then, to pull him down on top of her, run her hands all over his body and join with him. But he bore heavy wounds. So did she. Anyway, it would be madness, would it not? This thing that had sprung up so unexpectedly between them must be a reaction to the danger of battle and the exhilaration of their victory. Just like when Morirex had returned from fighting and forced her.

Ah, but what to do with the desire that beset her? For she couldn't deny she wanted this man, even though she'd been a stranger to desire so long she barely recognized the impulse.

She withdrew from Wick just far enough to look into his eyes. Before she could see what lay there, he dropped his lashes.

She caught his face between her hands. "Look at me. Please, look at me."

He did. Once more their gazes connected, and Verica's world trembled; the very colors of it changed.

She drew a breath that hurt. "We—"

An interruption occurred in the form of Smerta, bursting through the door of the hut without warning. "Mistress, Master Ivomagus asks if you—"

The girl stopped speaking, and her eyes went wide. "Oh!"

Verica drew away from Wick hastily and sprang to her feet. "Yes, Smerta, what is it?"

"Ivomagus calls for you, Mistress."

"I am tending Master Wick's wounds."

"Is that—?" The girl caught back what she meant to say.

"Tell Master Ivomagus I will come as soon as I can."

"And you, Mistress?" Smerta's gaze touched Wick's naked torso before examining Verica in turn. "Have you also been tended?"

"Not yet but I will be," Verica assured her.

Without another word, Smerta left.

Wick raised his eyes. "Go. I am well enough."

Verica did not want to leave. She had accepted Wick map Radoc into her hut only to keep an eye on him, but now everything had changed. Whatever she felt developing between them went far beyond the instinct to protect, and could prove dangerous in the extreme.

She said, "I will finish binding up your wounds before I go."

"As you will, Mistress. You are in charge."
Was she? In her heart, she no longer felt sure.

Chapter Fifteen

After Verica left, Wick sat alone in the quiet hut, his thoughts skittering away from him like dry leaves before a rising wind.

He did not know what to make of Verica, did not know what to make of himself when he got near her. The young women of the Epidii, back home, behaved in predicable ways; they flirted and followed the young men of the tribe with their eyes, sought them out if they wanted to make their interest known. Such things had always seemed to rush by him like a river. He'd never yet been in love and tended to dismiss the emotion as nothing more than a byproduct of desire.

Indeed, he would have disbelieved the state entirely, had he lacked the example of his parents' union, which while enduring so much grief and difficulty had never wavered.

It would be the height of foolishness to lose his heart now. To Verica, who believed him something he was not.

A courageous man. A hero.

He closed his eyes, remembering the words she'd said to him just before they engaged the Gaels. "May you fight well, valiant one."

Just because she'd stood beside him during one battle, watched him face off against a handful of Gaels... Battle, as he knew, was the easy part. In the face of immediate danger the blood came up; a man had no choice but to fight.

Kill or be killed.

Facing the unbearable made a far more difficult prospect—a trial Wick had failed.

He gritted his teeth and peeled off his blood-soaked leggings, recalling the long slash he'd taken to his left thigh—filthy and still bleeding. That, he would tend himself with the supplies Verica had left to hand. It could not hurt any more than his heart.

What had he seen in Verica's eyes when she looked at him? What had he tasted in her kiss? He could not tell, but he'd be willing to bet his life on the fact that she desired him.

Yet such desire could get a man in trouble and had, more than once, when it came to his friends and companions.

If anything, what he felt toward Mistress Verica should serve as a warning. He needed to leave this place as soon as possible, move on before he became any more deeply involved.

Because he did not want Mistress Verica to find out what kind of man he truly was—one who'd turned his back on his tribe and all those who needed him.

He dealt with the cut on his thigh without mercy, sparing himself nothing in pain. When it came to mercy, he deserved none.

****

"What was that? What did you say?" Verica could not concentrate; it might be due to her weariness, but she'd already found it necessary to make people repeat their words more than once, and the malady showed no signs of improving.

Her latest victim, Ivomagus, gave her an odd look and patiently repeated his previous statement. Ivomagus was nothing if not patient.

"I asked what you wish to do about the burial rites. With the snow so deep and the ground frozen, it will prove a challenge to lay Nactovus and the others to rest. Yet we must so honor them."

"Yes. Yes, we must." Verica felt again the brush of Wick's lips over hers and the caress of his thumb at her cheek. So gentle. Who would have believed a woman could be undone by mere gentleness?

Was she undone? Oh, she feared so.

"Mistress, are you sure you are well? Have you had your wounds tended?"

"Not yet."

"Perhaps we should discuss this after you have seen Callorix."

As if on cue, Smerta appeared at Verica's side with both Cunarda and the healer in tow.

"Mistress," Callorix said, "I have time to see you now."

Verica drew breath to protest.

Cunarda spoke before she could. "Go with him, Verica, or I will have you carried bodily."

Verica looked into Cunarda's face, saw the depth of her concern, and relented. "Very well."

Ivomagus bowed. "We will speak of this later, Mistress."

Cunarda took Verica's arm. "I will come with you, to see you right."

An unpleasant interval followed in a curtained area of the healer's hut. Usually, fortitude allowed Verica to endure the binding of her battle wounds. This time she went lightheaded and nearly blacked out, there on the stained pallet.

When she fought her way back to full consciousness, Cunarda held both her hands and spoke softly, tears in her eyes.

"There, that is the worst of it done. You must stay strong, Verica. We cannot stand to lose you. I do not know what I—or the tribe—would do then."

"Struggle on," Verica answered weakly, "as we have been doing."

"No." Cunarda shook her head decidedly. "You are the heart of this tribe—you cannot see that, but I can. Callorix," she appealed to the healer, who carried out his duties with a closed expression, "is that not so?"

He nodded and permitted himself a tight smile. "I do not suppose, Mistress Verica, there is any use asking you to rest?"

"To be sure, Master Callorix, I will try." Although scores of duties awaited her, not least the postponed meeting with Ivomagus. "We should have some respite now that the Gaels' camp has been destroyed. We may lick our wounds and settle in to endure the winter."

"Not an easy prospect, that," Cunarda murmured. "Yet no one surpasses us at hard endurance."

"Ivomagus calls it our greatest strength. I must go and speak with him about the burials."

"I will do that," Cunarda said quickly. "You return to your hut and rest until your strength returns. What of the stranger—does he also need the attentions of Master Callorix?"

"I have tied up the worst of his wounds, but, Master Callorix, I will send him to you if I see the need. That arrow wound on his shoulder tore open during the fight, and he lost a lot of blood."

"There is also the risk of fever. Hold a moment, and I will give you a mixture for him."

Callorix hurried into the other part of the hut, and Cunarda leaned close to Verica. "I ask you again to let me find other accommodations for the incomer. You will rest more easily on your own in that hut."

Would she? Verica doubted it. Even now, in a strange way, she craved Wick's company.

"Other accommodations where?"

"Here, perhaps."

"Callorix is already overflowing with wounded. Mistress Cunarda, I do not mind housing Master Wick with me."

"I am still not easy in my mind about him."

"I am. Did he not just stand to defend us? I tell you, were it not for his presence in this last fight, I do not know that we would have won out against the Gaels."

"Yes, Hectia said how bravely he fought. Still, you are a woman alone."

"Do you truly suppose him so eager to tumble into my bed?" Verica might only wish.

"He could make unwelcome advances."

Verica bared her teeth. "I have told you, no man will take advantage of me."

"Morirex did."

Verica's smile died. "Morirex was my husband."

"And he used you shamelessly. From what little you have told me…"

"I should have told you nothing."

"Still." Cunarda lowered her voice and laid a hand on Verica's arm. "Have a care."

"I always do." The reminder, she acknowledged, was a valid one. Hastily she went on, "I will stop by the cookhouse and fetch something for us to eat. Master Wick must be famished." She hesitated. "Is there sufficient food?"

"We have not much, but take what you need. Both of you have earned it."

Callorix returned with a small bag of herbs. "Mix these in water and give Master Wick a draught tonight as well as in the morning. Send him to me if he becomes feverish."

Verica nodded and left, feeling restless. She passed Smerta, who looked at her curiously, and hurriedly changed course to avoid Ivomagus, who did not see her. Let Cunarda decide on the burial rituals, as she'd offered. Verica could not face it now.

At the cookhouse, she accepted two small portions of food before turning for her own hut.

Perhaps, she thought, even as she ducked in, it proved fortunate she and Wick were both hampered by wounds. It might well provide a rein on the desire.

Wick looked up sharply from his place beside the fire when she came in. He'd changed his clothing to the less stained garments from his pack and made an effort to tame his hair. He must have tended his other wounds also, for he'd put away the basin.

"Here." Verica went to him, bent, and placed the larger portion of food in his hands. "You must be famished."

"Thank you." His dark gaze moved over her slowly. "Have you had your wounds tended?"

"Yes."

"How bad are they?"

An innocent question, yet the look that accompanied the words heated her blood. "The healer says I will live. Here, he sent me a draught for you, to fight fever and ease your pain."

Laying her own portion of food aside, she mixed the herbs with water and passed the cup to him. He did not immediately drink. "Should you not have this rather than me?"

"I have a better cure." Verica snagged a jug of heather ale from the hearthstone and unstoppered it for a long drink.

Wick grunted, looking at his draught without favor.

"Drink," she urged him, and lifted her brows. "Then I will share."

He drained the portion with a grimace. They ate in silence, Verica wondering why she suddenly felt so comfortable. With a close look, she passed him the jug. "Here."

He drank before handing it back to her. She put her lips where his had been and took another swig, but found it disappointing. Not half so pleasurable as touching her mouth to his.

"That is good ale."

"Our brewers, both of whom have been miraculously spared to us, declare it the best in Caledonia. It is said they—or their forbears—made a deal with the goddess." She snorted. "If you believe in such things."

Wick crooked an eyebrow at her. "I take it you do not?"

"I used to," Verica replied. "But the goddess does not keep her promises."

Did he look shocked by her blasphemy? Verica

couldn't tell, and she took another drink to stave off any discomfort. He had not walked her path or learned her lessons. He did not know what she felt.

"I think," she mused on, perhaps allowing the ale to speak for her, "it is one of the worst aspects of being overrun by the Gaels—losing the skills, the arts and talents that make us Caledonii. Things like brewing heather ale and the songs sung at handfastings. I fear if our trials continue, a day will come when no one remembers the names of our ancestors."

"You sound like my brother, Taloc."

"Ah yes, you mentioned a sister and a brother who still survive. How old is he?"

"Fourteen. We call him Tally." Wick gazed away at nothing.

"You miss him."

"More than I can say. There were but the three of us, you see. Tally took most after Mother. Barta"—he smiled—"is most like Father, though she would not thank me for saying so. She is a warrior." His gaze found Verica's face. "Like you."

"Ah, yes. And where do you fit, Master Wick?"

"I am not so certain I do fit."

"You are firstborn, no? The adored son. Future chief."

He froze with a morsel of venison halfway to his mouth. "Some bring grace into the world; some bring strength. Some few just endure."

A curious thing for him to say. Something in his manner, though, kept Verica from asking further personal questions. Instead she challenged, "We were just speaking of this at Callorix's hut. Is there not strength in endurance?"

"Perhaps."

"And may not those who endure also hope to find grace?"

That made him look at her again. She caught a glimpse of some intense emotion in his eyes. Yearning?

"Mistress Verica, I have no answer to that."

"You told me your mother was a wise woman. Would she not insist there are kinds, and kinds, of strength? Possessing valiance the like of yours, Master Wick, I should think you could accomplish anything."

He surged without warning to his feet and laid the rest of his food aside. Without looking at Verica, he turned to the door.

"Where are you going?" she asked, all her comfort flown.

"Midden."

"It is cold out. Why not use the—"

"I need air."

He went out, closing the leather curtain behind him carefully.

Though Verica waited long, he did not return.

Chapter Sixteen

"Have you seen Wick map Radoc?" Verica, huddled in her cloak, asked the question over and over again. Dark had now fallen over the settlement; once again snow and sleet pounded down, thick and fast. The cold bit at her fingers and toes, but she did not want to go home.

Not without finding him.

She carried but one thought in her mind: he could have collapsed somewhere, prey to loss of blood—the same thing that had killed Morirex. He might lie beneath this chilly blanket of snow.

She'd traced the path, well-enough defined, from the main part of the settlement to the midden. After that she'd searched the rest of the settlement, inquiring of everyone she encountered.

Most people just shook their heads and hurried away, heads tucked well down. A few of the men looked curious.

One suggested, "Perhaps, Mistress, he has decided to move on."

"Why would he do that?" she returned, the fear in her gut growing sharper.

The fellow shrugged. "He may just go as mysteriously as he arrived."

Mayhap so. Maybe the magic that wrapped around him had whisked him away or turned him back into a wild hart.

If only Verica could turn into a hind in order to follow him.

She would not let herself contemplate that thought too long; she dared not. Eventually she encountered Ivomagus, who caught her shoulders between his hands. "Mistress, you should not be out in this weather. Callorix says you are far too badly injured."

"We all carry wounds, Master Ivomagus." Including Wick map Radoc. "I must continue searching for Master Wick. I am afraid he has collapsed somewhere."

Ivomagus's pale brown eyes grew kind. "Go you home, Mistress. I will carry on searching, and call upon others to help if need be. When I find him, I will take him to Callorix and send you word."

Not at all what Verica wanted, but how could she object? It did not seem reasonable to express so much concern about a near-stranger.

"Thank you." She nodded.

They parted, and Verica headed home. Part way there, she paused as a chill breeze struck her cheek, turning her head. It caressed her much as Wick's calloused thumb had. She stared into the trees, her eyes searching. There—beneath tree boughs heavy with snow, she saw the faint impression of footprints leading away.

Breath caught, she traced them, her whole body hurting and her fingers stinging with cold. She came at last to the place where the trees thinned at the northeast edge of the settlement. She blinked in surprise.

There, she thought she saw a deer. No, it was the figure of a man.

The breath left her lungs in a rush of relief. Silently, she moved forward and took the place at Wick's side.

He did not stir or so much as glance at her. Instead he gazed away into the dark, face far too shadowed for her to read. But she felt the impulse streaming off him, that to leave. She would lose him even before she'd had him.

That thought made her seize his forearm, her fingers closing tight. Still he did not look at her.

"I'd best be off," he told her at last.

Her heart thudded in protest. "Where?"

He formed a gesture that said he did not know. "Away to look for my father's allies."

"You can leave in the morning. Not now, so sorely injured as you are. Not through the dark and cold." She tried to catch her next words back, and failed. "Give me at least one night with you."

That made him turn to her. "Verica, what are you saying? I am scarcely fit."

"I did not mean—" She broke off; she had meant it. She wanted him, like a fire burning. "Just stay with me for the night. If your wounds prevent you from doing more than keep me company, that is fine. We need not...not couple."

She wished she could see what lay in his eyes then, longed for it the way she used to long for a glance from Morirex. The thought should have given her pause; matters with Morirex had not ended well. But at times in life, the heart would not be held; it leaped of its own will. The reasoning mind could but follow, helpless.

"Do not leave me," she begged in a whisper. She slid her fingers down his arm and closed them on his hand. She tugged him into motion—back beneath the low-hanging boughs of the trees and through the settlement to her door. She tugged him in through that portal, turned, and pressed her body against his.

Not a tall woman, she needed to stretch up far in order to place her mouth on his. Hunger blossomed between them, immediate and all out of proportion with their exhaustion. Verica's vision turned white and her whole body tingled. She'd never imagined such desire.

The sense of connection followed swiftly, almost as fierce. Her heart trembled, terrified by her overwhelming desire to lose herself in this man.

Ever since wedding with Morirex, Verica had been holding on hard to her courage and sense of identity. She'd learned that a man could destroy a woman if she allowed it. Now suddenly she cared far less about protecting herself than having Wick near her at any price.

But his hands came up and caught her shoulders in a gesture that argued caution. He broke the sweet contact of lips on lips and said, "No."

Mutinous, Verica stared into his eyes. She wanted to beg but instead chose persuasion.

"Ah, come. Where is the harm in us lying together for one night, if you are bound to leave in the morning?"

Wick looked torn. His throat worked before he said, "Much can happen before dawn. I could well leave you with my child."

Or your heart. Verica did not speak those words, but quite possibly he saw them in her eyes. As before, he caressed her cheek gently, the contrast of rough fingers against soft skin striking her deep.

"It will not happen," she assured him. "In all the years I was with my husband, I never conceived."

"Years?" he repeated hoarsely.

"Three years we were together." A long period of suffering. Not woman enough for it, Morirex had tossed at her often enough, with that sneer that served to lacerate her soul.

"I see," Wick said.

Did he? Could he see the lonely nights spent lying beside a man who used her body the way he might a mere tool, only with less care? Who caused her pain for his own pleasure?

She needed to know, needed Wick map Radoc to show her if it must always be thus, if no kindness might be found for even a single night. Yet she no more wished to compel him to couple with her than she'd wanted Morirex to force her.

She said, "Lie with me in my bed this night, Wick map Radoc. We will keep one another warm. I ask nothing more."

He gave a gusty, incredulous laugh. "Stay near you? And keep from touching? I am not strong enough."

"Did I say we would keep from touching? Come."

She towed him to the bed, where she paused and kissed him again softly. Her sleeping bench was wide—Morirex had insisted on that—and piled with furs. The madness that now possessed Verica's mind insisted she would wipe out all the bad memories by lying here with this man. One night to remember when she was old, when she lay dying.

But he said, "Wait."

She did, hanging upon his gaze and the words that

might fall from his mouth. At that moment she knew she would willingly wait forever for this man.

"Even if I disregard my own hurts, Verica, I cannot dismiss yours. You are sore injured."

"What harm is there in us lying in one another's arms, to sleep?" She began working the laces on the front of his tunic, but he caught her hands and clasped them hard. Again, his breath gusted. "Lie with you, naked as born, and not take you? You must be mad."

"I offer you whatever you would have of me this night. Your choice; your desire."

He kissed her then, kissed her as he had before, with that deep-reaching combination of heat and tenderness. Together, wrapped tight in one another's arms, they tumbled onto the bed.

Chapter Seventeen

Wick never later knew at what point he abandoned all hope of good sense or when his mind flew away. It might have been at the moment his body, with Verica's cleaved to it, hit the sleeping bench. But he thought he still hung onto a few shreds of sanity then.

It might well have been when she once more pressed her mouth to his and, in a wild and glorious movement, touched his tongue with hers. Or when her fingers, soft and insistent, succeeded in opening the front of his tunic and then, in an act that stole all his breath, the leggings beneath.

To be sure, that must have been it, when he felt her take him between her hands and wrap tight, because he remembered very little clearly after that.

Flashes of what followed remained with him, yes—pictures and feelings, like dreams. The sheer heat of it and the way their bodies fit together without effort, as if they'd done this a hundred times or more.

Had anyone asked him, he'd have declared himself incapable of what happened next. Shoulder torn, weak from loss of blood, leg barely able to support his weight. Yet all that fell away, lost in the pure beauty of their joining. Verica's warmth enfolded him; her spirit steadied and uplifted him. Her body became an extension of his own, wound for wound, movement for movement, desire for desire. At the height of it all, he would sooner have died than have broken the connection.

Spent and tightly entwined, they slept only to awake and mate again. Another dream, Wick told himself, as wild as those others wherein he ran like a deer. None of it real, none of it truly happening.

He loved her gently so as not to hurt her, and she gave back to him unsparingly, matching kiss for kiss and touch for touch. When he slid again into sleep she accompanied him; they ran together, a hart and a white hind.

Wick awoke much later and wondered where he was. Not back home and not out in the forest. Warm, warm. The heat passed right through him, providing comfort to places that had been cold a long while. His heart, his spirit.

He moved, and his body protested; the new wounds had stiffened while he slept and screamed at him in complaint. But someone lay cuddled into his chest, the source of all that delicious warmth. His hand rested on her bare back, skin so smooth it made his fingertips tingle.

Verica.

He didn't realize he'd said her name aloud until she stirred, interesting parts of her sliding against particularly sensitized parts of him. Her dark head rested on his good shoulder just beneath his ear; a wealth of black hair flowed over both of them. She looked so beautiful in the soft light that filled the hut, all the breath seized in Wick's throat.

"Has morning come?" she whispered.

Wick did not know. Dim, filtered light seeped in around the edges of the door curtain; he guessed it must have.

He needed to leave this day. Rise from the bed and walk away from this woman forever. Whatever it cost him.

She opened her eyes with a sweep of black lashes. The smile started there—in her eyes—before it reached her lips.

He began to vocalize the words in his head. "I need to…"

"No. Lie quietly for just a moment more. Please."

A woman like this should not ask. She should not beg. She should command all she encountered with a mere wave of her hand, including a man's heart.

He stayed where he was.

Her eyes found his. "How do you feel?"

Like he'd been dragged over rough ground studded by boulders and populated with gorse bushes, behind a fast-moving pony. Quite possibly, he wouldn't be able to get out of the bed if he tried.

He surprised himself, though, by saying, "Wonderful." Or perhaps it wasn't so surprising.

Verica shifted, raised herself up on one elbow and looked into his face. "Your wounds?"

He grimaced involuntarily. He'd never before followed a battle with a night of lovemaking, though he knew men who did. Never had he acted so irresponsibly.

The black lashes dropped half way. "I hope I did you no harm."

"Or I you." Had she truly climbed on top of him and rocked them together in a rhythm that spoke to his very spirit?

"There are times in battle one does not pause to

consider one's wounds. It seems to be the same in bed, with you."

Wick ran his fingers through her hair. "I would never want to harm you." Which meant he needed to leave. Today. But by the goddess, it would go hard with him.

She traced one of the tattoos on his chest with a careful finger. "You did not. Everything I gave to you last night, I gave willingly."

And generously. Wick remembered that. He slid his palm down the smooth curve of her back and encountered a bandage at her hip. His gaze flew to hers. "You took this wound yesterday? You should have said—"

"And if I had, what would you have done?"

"Kept from touching you."

Her eyes gleamed. "You truly think so?"

He smiled and corrected. "*Tried* to keep from touching you."

"But I wanted what we shared last night." Softly, she kissed him. "Even more, I suspect I needed it."

She climbed from the bed, giving him the first real chance he'd had to see her body. Battered and with bandages at hip, leg, and shoulder blade, she nevertheless remained lithe and beautiful. Her breasts, small, high, and pointed, peeked at him through the black hair that flowed wild over her shoulders. Lower down, the patch of dark hair between her legs shielded the secret place where he'd spent himself last night.

Wounded he might be, but the very memory had him rising for her, high and hard, the desire so intense his throat went dry.

"You will be hungry," she said. "Wait here; I will

dress and go fetch us some breakfast."

"What will your people say?"

"About what?" Swiftly she began donning her clothes. Wick watched helplessly.

"About you having lain with the stranger?"

She tossed her head. "How will they know? I will not tell them."

"They will guess."

"How?"

By the look of her, but he did not say so.

"Besides"—she drew on her boots—"why should they object?"

"They will think you deserve better." And she did.

She shot him a look. "Better than the hero who drove the Gaels from our doors? Is there any better man?"

Before Wick could reply, she snatched up her cloak and dashed out, admitting a rush of cold air that swept clear across the floor to the place where he lay.

With a groan he stirred himself in the bed. The groan came not so much from physical pain, however biting, as from mental agony. He hadn't lied when he told Verica he'd learned to ignore physical discomfort. What had happened last night proved another matter again.

He did not know what to do about his desire for her. Such a woman as Verica deserved a hero in truth, a man as strong as she, who would stand beside her, staunch as stone, and never let her down.

Not one such as Wick map Radoc.

He dressed hastily and built up the fire before drawing on his own cloak and heading for the midden.

Folk were up and about early—or perhaps he and

Verica had slept longer than he'd thought. Each one he passed greeted him warmly; some smiled. But he tucked his head down and made his way back to the hut as swiftly as possible, engaging no one. He returned to find Verica back before him. She stood in the center of the floor glancing around in a distracted manner. When Wick came in, she whirled and relief flooded her eyes.

"I thought you had gone."

"Just to the midden."

"I thought you'd left for good. As you meant to do last night."

"No. But, Verica—"

Once more she interrupted him. "I brought our breakfast. Sit and eat. On the way back here, I ran into Ivomagus; he wants to hold a service later this afternoon for those who died in the raid. They cannot be buried yet, I fear. That will need to wait. Come," she reiterated, "sit."

Wick joined her beside the fire, put his elbows on his knees, and forced his fingers through his hair. "Verica, listen to me."

"No. I—"

"Please listen."

She sprang back to her feet. "I will not. Not if you will speak of leaving."

They stared at one another, Wick flooded by consternation.

"I need to move on."

She drew a breath. "I understand, but I have been thinking about it. You should not go yet, not before your wounds heal and, perhaps, the weather eases. It is unusual to have so much snow this early in the winter. Travel will be easier for you if you wait."

Perhaps so, Wick acknowledged, but waiting would make leaving her far more difficult.

Before he could speak, Verica rushed on. "I know you are eager to procure help for your tribe and how you must worry for them. But there is no sense setting out before you are ready, only to founder on some snowy hillside where you cannot find shelter. Better to stay here until you can safely travel. A few days…"

A few nights. The words remained unspoken, but Wick saw them in her eyes. He did not dare spend a few nights; if he did, he might never leave.

"I will see how I feel later today," he suggested gently. "And see what the weather does."

She did not look satisfied but dropped the matter. "I must go meet with Ivomagus after breakfast. Will you come?"

"He does not want me there. Caerena business is none of mine."

Her gaze challenged him. "And if I want you there?"

"I bid you to reconsider."

An uncomfortable silence fell. What if he told her the truth about himself? What if he dragged out all the ugliness, disabused her of any wrong-headed admiration she might hold?

She'd kick him from the warmth of her bed then, right enough.

He should do it, he told himself. He should tell her just how lacking in courage he'd proved after his father died, when the impossibly heavy responsibility of leadership had landed squarely in his hands.

How would she look at him then? With disparagement, just as he deserved.

Could he bear to see the expression in her eyes change, given all they'd shared last night, the gentle kisses simmering to passion, intimate enough to chase every other thought away?

No, not that.

Better, better she never knew. Better to slip away through the trees as he'd intended last night. Just keep walking, never look back.

Never see this woman again.

Ah, and what did he need with a woman? Apart from the warmth, the mind-numbing pleasure of coupling, and the soul-deep sense of belonging. He'd never taken time for women before, and he'd survived well enough, hadn't he?

Hadn't he?

Except his life had felt hollow, striving day after day to live up to his father, leading men via orders that were never his own. Struggling always to be something he was not.

But if he was not Wick, son of Radoc, chief of tribe Epidii, then who was he? He could not say, other than unworthy of this woman who sat opposite him.

"You had best go on your own to meet with your shaman," he told her at last.

"And"—she hesitated, her gaze searching his face—"will I find you here when I return?"

"You will."

"Do you promise it?"

"I will not leave this day."

"Or tonight," she insisted.

Wick merely returned her gaze somberly. Face grown tight and eyes shadowed, she arose and left him there.

Chapter Eighteen

"Mistress Verica," Ivomagus demanded gently, "are you listening to me?"

Recalled from the depths of her thoughts, Verica lifted her gaze to the shaman's face. He sounded as if he struggled to keep his voice patient and hide any irritation; still, it showed.

"I apologize," she said swiftly. "What you and Mistress Cunarda have planned sounds like a fitting rite to honor our dead."

"And the additional component?" he pressed.

Caught, Verica narrowed her eyes. Lost in thoughts of Wick, she had in fact failed to listen.

She should feel ashamed, but she seemed able to focus on nothing except what had taken place last night, how it felt when Wick ran his roughened palm up her leg so slowly and tenderly. She'd never been touched that way, as if she mattered; every part of her longed to experience it again.

There had been no pain in Wick's arms. A first for her.

Ivomagus's gaze softened with compassion. "You must be tired, Mistress, and sore from your wounds. Perhaps you are not yet fit for tribal matters."

Before Verica could answer, he went on, "I saw you and Master Wick returning to your hut last night. It is as well, as I was able to call off the hunt for him."

Verica flushed. She should have sent word that would have allowed this kind man to return to his fireside.

"I am glad. It was inconsiderate of me not to let you know."

Ivomagus shrugged. "I doubt you were thinking straight."

That was truer than he knew.

He went on, "You ask much of yourself. Each of us needs rest from time to time. And relief can be as crushing as a blow."

"Relief?"

"The defeat of the Gaels on our doorstep, the removal of a threat that has dogged us so long, must prove a staggering relief."

"I had not thought of that." Verica smiled wryly. "I am afraid I view this victory as temporary. One thing we have learned of our enemies—they always return."

"Yet we are safe for the time, perhaps until spring. It is a gift that will give us a chance to recover and grow strong."

"I do not doubt you are right."

"If you wish to absent yourself from the ritual this afternoon—"

"No, I need to be there. It will be expected of me."

"Well, at least go home and rest until we are ready to begin. I will send a lad to summon you at the proper time."

Verica shook her head. "I must go to visit the wounded."

"I have already done that. All are holding their own. You know, Mistress Verica, I have spoken of this before…"

"Yes?" She tried desperately to focus on him.

"Your duties are many and heavy. You could use someone at your side."

"There is Cunarda. And you."

A smile crossed Ivomagus's face. "I did, in fact, speak of me."

"Yes?" she repeated, stupid with lack of sleep and with desire for Wick map Radoc.

"As I mentioned before, winter is a good time to wed."

Wed? Herself and Wick? An impossibility. She began to shake her head. "I do not think—"

"Mistress, please do not refuse too swiftly. I know you have not been a widow for long, and you have likely not recovered from the loss of Morirex. He was a singular man."

That was one way of putting it. "So he was."

"But if our tribe is to recover from its losses and grow strong again, we need to build."

Verica could only agree with that; she nodded.

"That said, I wish you would consider handfasting with me."

"You?"

"It cannot be a surprise. I understand I am not a warrior, or worthy of your regard, but you must know how much I admire you."

"You are more than worthy of my regard."

"I cannot help but believe we would make a good pairing, you with your strength and me looking after the tribe's spiritual needs."

"I…" Verica sought desperately for something to say, something that would not hurt this good man's pride.

She faltered. "I am honored beyond what I can express. But I do not believe I am ready to handfast again." Liar, she sneered at herself. If it were Wick holding out his hand to her, how might she answer then?

Ivomagus bowed his head. "Mistress, I ask you only to think on it, give the matter your fair consideration. The winter is long. We have time."

"Yes, so we do." Verica floundered helplessly. "And I—I will consider on it."

Again he bowed his head. Like an untried maiden without more than a score of battles behind her, Verica fled.

She arrived at the chief's house disheveled and with her mind truly scattered. She found Cunarda sitting alone at her hearth, working at mending.

Cunarda looked up, when Verica burst in, and lifted a brow. "Verica, what is amiss?"

"Nothing." Everything. "Where are your daughters? How do they fare this morning?"

"They are well enough. Smerta has gone to assist the healer, and Hectia is with Nactovus's poor mother, seeking to lend her some comfort. Hectia's wound kept her up most of the night, but she will heal. Forgive me saying it, but you look far from well. And far from rested. What has happened?"

Verica wondered how much to say. As a rule she kept her affairs and her feelings to herself. Some details of her relationship with Morirex had crept out and been confided to this woman after they became close. But certainly not the worst of it.

She'd confided that to no one.

Cunarda knew Morirex had not been an easy man

to live with and that his hard nature had often caused Verica pain—little more.

Now Verica sat down opposite the chief's widow. Cunarda—formerly as youthful looking as her daughters—had aged these past months. Well, so had Verica. But kindness regarded Verica from Cunarda's hazel eyes.

"What is it, my dear?" She laid her work aside.

"I have just been speaking with Ivomagus about the ceremony later today."

"Ah, yes. It will not be easy to face. We have lost so many, and Nactovus was so young."

"Ivomagus excused me from attending and then asked me if I would handfast with him."

"Eh?" That caught all Cunarda's attention.

"He said we would do well together and our joining would help heal the tribe."

"Well! I have heard of more flattering approaches, but he is not wrong. And is it so surprising? He has had his eyes on you ever since Morirex was killed, possibly before."

"Not surprising, no. He's certainly hinted at it before, but never come out and spoken so baldly. It has shaken me."

Cunarda pressed her lips together. "Ivomagus is a good man, but perhaps you are not ready. The winter is long, and the Gaels have been pushed back. There is time."

"Exactly what he said."

Cunarda swept Verica with a perceptive look. "You know, many a widow of this tribe, and we are generously endowed with widows, would welcome his interest." When Verica did not respond, she pressed,

"What did you tell him?"

"That I am not ready to take another husband. I did not wish to injure his feelings so did not speak the truth, that I could not imagine myself and Ivomagus... together. I do value him beyond measure, both as a shaman and a friend."

"Ah. You cannot imagine taking him to your bed."

Verica shook her head violently.

"Perhaps that will change now that he has declared himself. Mayhap it is just that you have had no one in your bed since Morirex."

Verica dropped her eyes, and Cunarda, like a war hound on the scent of a battle, leaped. "Have you?"

Again, Verica failed to reply; Cunarda pondered it.

"One of our warriors? Not one who's since been felled, I hope."

"No."

"Then..." Not a stupid woman by any measure, Cunarda contemplated the matter. Leaning closer to Verica, she lowered her voice. "Not—the newcomer?"

In answer, Verica lifted her eyes.

"By the goddess! When?"

"Last night. We came together even though both of us are sore wounded. I am not even certain how it happened, Cunarda, save I persuaded him to lie with me, just for comfort and so we might keep one another warm..."

"You persuaded him?"

"It was I who asked him to share my bed. All my doing."

Cunarda spoke a soft curse word, no doubt learned from her late husband. "That is not at all like you, Verica."

"I know. I've sworn off men, vowed never again to risk my heart."

"Well, and was it just about comfort? Nothing more? No, don't bother to answer. I can tell just by looking your feelings are involved. What will you do now?"

"Nothing. Whatever last night means to me, it meant little to him. He intends to leave as soon as he can, journey on and continue searching out assistance for his tribe."

"He would not stay, if you asked?"

Verica shook her head miserably. "I have no right to ask such a thing. A man like that—strong and valiant—will always put the needs of his people first. And we, reduced to bare bones, cannot offer him the help he needs." If only the Caerena had the men and might to form an alliance with the Epidii…it might well make an answer.

Cunarda clicked her tongue.

Verica looked at her imploringly. "How could I let such a thing happen? And how, appearing from nowhere, could he so swiftly become this important to me?"

"It does happen that way sometimes. It was like that for me and Ammin, you understand. Oh, things were different in that I already knew him, but I wanted nothing to do with him whilst we grew up. I thought him haughty and arrogant. But our fathers negotiated the match. Before the day we handfasted, I'd never even been kissed."

A faraway look came to Cunarda's eyes. "Then there was our wedding night. Me, so embarrassed I did not know where to look. Ammin—nothing like I expected, but kind and full of gentle teasing as he tried to reassure me. I fell in love with him then, that first time we coupled."

"Not before?"

Cunarda shook her head. "Not before. But oh, it came powerful when it came, that love. And it never wavered between us, not even through all the sorrow that followed."

"You were fortunate," Verica said, thinking again of Morirex.

"I was blessed. My point is attachment may well follow a mating. Was it a good mating?"

Heat promptly flooded Verica. Arousal provoked by tenderness and a sense of belonging so deep it terrified her. "Yes."

Cunarda thought about that before she said, "Then I pity Ivomagus."

Verica shook her head. "I tell you, Wick map Radoc has no intention of staying. I will not be able to hold him."

"Are you certain?"

"I am."

"But," Cunarda concluded sadly, "that does not truly matter, does it? I suspect Ivomagus has already lost you and any chance at winning your heart."

Chapter Nineteen

Verica returned from the burial ceremony wearing a grief Wick could easily feel. She came with her eyes downcast and her shoulders drooping. Even so, her presence changed the very air of the hut.

He'd been sitting and contemplating his departure tomorrow morning, fully intending to advise her of his plans as soon as she arrived. Cold or no cold, snow and winds aside, he dared not spend more than one more night in her company.

In her bed.

To be sure, he'd argued with himself over it, speaking his protestations aloud like a mad man, sounding them to his own ears. The day, already advanced, would soon fall into night. Good sense dictated he should wait and depart in the morning.

Yet perhaps better to spend the night out in the frozen forest than risk touching Verica, falling into another of her deep kisses, and landing in that place they'd shared last night.

Trees and snow, and even predatory Gaels, he understood. The way this woman made him feel confounded him.

But the sight of her entering the hut bowed by grief kept him from speaking his intentions. Instead he rose and gently led her to the fire.

"Come and sit. You are chilled to the bone."

Her fingers, stiff and icy, contracted on his. He urged her down and stirred up the fire, which had died down in her absence.

Just like the one in his blood, Wick thought ruefully. That too now leaped up again.

"How went the ritual?" he asked. He knew how it felt, struggling to keep one's composure during these events. How many good friends and tribe members had he seen go beneath the soil? After a time the tears stopped coming and there were no more words to express the pain.

He rarely spoke of his feelings. He'd learned it did little good. Yet now he sought to draw Verica out and, perhaps, provide her a measure of comfort.

She'd lost so much already, including her husband—a hard man, from what she'd said, but one of unquestioned valor.

What would she say if she knew the sort of man she'd taken to her bed in his place?

"It was…" She seemed to search for words. "It was difficult. The women wept." She lifted her eyes to Wick's face. "Women always weep."

"Still, it is good to honor the fallen. Our old shaman back home, called Pith, always says it brings comfort envisioning their spirits flying free into the keeping of the god and goddess."

Verica said nothing but clenched her hands together in her lap.

Wick, in an effort to distract her from her grief, said, "Your shaman seems a good man."

"Ivomagus? He is a very good man indeed. Not aged, as you say your shaman is, as our old priest was. Like the rest of us, Ivomagus accepted the duties thrust upon him and has stood strong. No one could ask more of him."

And, as Wick knew, people asked much. Gently he told Verica, "Your tribe will have time now to rest and heal before you must again face the Gaels."

"I hope so. I confess I no longer know what it means to rest."

"I hope, Mistress Verica, you find a measure of respite and peace. You deserve it."

That made her eyes fly to his, just as if she could see what lay in his heart. She breathed a single word. "No."

"Mistress?"

"You still mean to leave."

"I promised I'd stay this night, and I will. But it is best that I leave come morning."

"No," she said once more.

When he rose, she came to her feet also and stood foursquare, facing him. "I insist you should stay here until you heal. There is plenty of time to find help for your tribe before the winter ends."

"There is." He let his gaze touch her face before he shook his head. "But I fear if I stay with you, I will want you in my arms. And if I have you again in my arms, I will not be able to leave. And leave I must."

She lifted her chin. "What of tonight? Will you refuse to share yourself with me tonight?"

Wick swallowed hard. "I am not sure I dare." How to lie with her again, indulge in the intoxication of her kisses, and then force himself away?

"That is honest."

Ah, honesty. Were he truly honest, he would lay before her all his faults and weaknesses. But then she'd cease looking at him the way she did right now, as if she admired as well as desired him, as if he deserved her admiration.

No, he could not lie with her again, unless he corrected what she believed of him. And once he did that, she wouldn't want him in her bed or in her settlement.

"Yet," she went on, pain bright in her eyes, "if you leave, we two may never see one another again. Is it so much to ask for one last night, in the face of a lifetime?"

When Wick did not answer, she rushed on, "I don't think I mistook your enjoyment of what we shared last night."

"You did not mistake. It was…" Once more words failed Wick.

"Magical," she breathed.

He could only agree. "So it was."

"Do you suppose two people find that more than once in a lifetime? Wick, I know you carry the interests of your tribe always at your heart and care only for saving them. I know you can afford few distractions. But I ask you for one more night."

"Verica—"

"If you dare not couple with me, I understand. Let us but spend the night together. We can talk, if you like, talk all night. You can tell me about the man you are so I will have the memory to hold once you have gone."

"The man I am." Wick closed his eyes on a wave of dismay.

"Is it too much to ask?"

He opened his eyes and gazed at her. "If I stay here with you, what happened last night will happen again. I cannot hope to resist."

She stepped closer to him, her gaze capturing his like a promise of seduction. "Whatever you want, I want also. I will need something to hold, something for after you are gone."

Honesty, indeed. He felt it in equal measure then, the pain that would result from losing her, balanced against that of telling her the truth about himself. Ah, but could he set his mind to leave her in the morning, following the warmth and blinding pleasure? If he went without telling her the truth, he might live forever in her mind as a hero.

Dishonest, and beguilingly tempting.

Another step closer, and she raised a hand to his face. He should step away, just as he should have refused her bed last night. But he stayed where he was, for the same reason.

Verica kissed him, and he felt her need reach for him, raw hunger that matched his own. Her lips parted beneath his, inviting him in. He felt the impact of it clear to his toes.

He wanted to draw back, break the contact, pick up his pack, and go out into the snow. To lose himself, but not in her.

Her hand slid from his cheek to his shoulder, lightly touching the bandages there, before she caressed the muscles of his chest. Not pausing, her fingers slid still farther down and captured his hardness through the fabric of his leggings. She groaned.

Desperate as a man denied air beneath deep water, Wick broke the kiss. Verica gazed into his eyes, seeking to hide nothing from him.

"One night," she urged him, "to last us forever."

Could the memory of one night last forever? Yet there was magic in this. And Wick knew if he stayed each moment would be burned upon him—each kiss, touch, and taste.

She stepped away from him, and his heart thudded just as if he'd once more transformed into a hart. A forthright woman, her gaze held his even as she unfastened the ties at the front of her tunic, as she shed her clothes with more haste than seduction. When she stood before him naked save for her bandages, he knew himself lost.

Lost.

"Wick map Radoc," she whispered, "I give you whatever you would have this night. If you would love me, love me. If you would but lie with me, that I also welcome. But stay."

Wick gathered her reverently into his arms and carried her to the bed.

Chapter Twenty

Wick map Radoc dreamed. The depths of sleep held him like a cradle, rocked him in a place beyond mere slumber where he ran. Once more he leaped with the shadowy forms of other deer all around him, through a forest that glowed with its own light.

And once again he followed the herd rather than led. Ahead of him, throwing up clouds of mist from her hooves, raced the white hind. Wick strove hard to catch her.

He knew her now, and knew he would follow her anywhere, all his life long.

The deer running beside him abruptly vanished. Only the hind remained. He lengthened his stride in an effort to reach her, muscles bunching and straining impossibly.

Verica, he thought, calling to her with his mind, but she did not pause.

Before them, the mist billowed outward and the trees opened into a clearing. The white hind turned to face him and abruptly transformed...not into Verica after all, though he'd been certain of her identity. Instead, shining bright as moonlight on snow, she took on the form of a woman with flowing silver hair.

Wick skidded to a halt, the breath puffing from his nostrils in clouds, still a hart with a weight of antlers on his head.

"Kneel, Wick map Radoc," the woman ordered. "You will bow before your goddess."

Wick fell to his knees, entirely without intention, and so discovered he'd once more become a man. It felt precisely as if a powerful hand pushed him down. He sensed, rather than saw, the silver woman approach him.

"Look at me."

He strained his gaze up and studied her. Beautiful, she glowed like the moonlight, and magic swirled around her in visible folds.

Her voice sounded cool and imperious. "What have you to say to me?"

"Goddess." What more could he say? At this place, words meant far less than emotions. "How came I here?"

Disregarding the question, she took another step closer. He saw that her feet, positioned lightly in the snow, were bare.

"Wick map Radoc, you made me a promise."

He must have made her thousands, seeding his prayers with them—when he asked her to preserve him in battle, to hold the Gaels back. To awaken his mother's lifeless body that lay in his arms. But he knew she spoke now of but one—that he'd made in exchange for his life.

"Yes, goddess?" he agreed humbly.

"Not long ago we made a bargain. Your enemies pursued you through my lord's forest. You—who claim to value your life so little—nevertheless called upon me to help you retain it. You said, as I do remind you, *Goddess, please lend me the strength I lack. Lend it to me and I will devote what remains of my life to you.* I transformed you into one of my most beloved creatures—a deer. You ran faster than any man may run and made good your escape. Did you not?"

Wick's heart began to pound thunderously. "I did."

"And do you so devote your life to me?"

What could he say? That he would not keep his part of their bargain? That he lacked honor as well as courage?

The goddess did not await his reply. Instead she told him haughtily, "I call upon you now to repay your debt."

"What would you ask of me?"

"Act as bidden; go where sent."

"This is but a dream," Wick protested, his denial born of panic.

"And how does a dream differ from what you call life? Do not both arise from the spirit, guided by perception and given credence by the heart? What you call life, Wick map Radoc, is but a dream you experience through open eyes."

"No." Again he strove to refute it. "The things I have seen are real. Were this dreaming, I could call myself awake from it, find my father whole and my mother living."

A hint of compassion showed in the goddess's eyes. "One day you will awaken and find that to be so."

"When?"

"On the day of your death."

That stole what remained of Wick's breath. He contemplated it, fought for understanding, and said, "Then I fear death no more."

She smiled, and magic shone from her like the moonlight. "First must come the keeping of promises.

What did your father tell you of that?"

"To keep them, always."

"He was a man who did just that. And your mother? What would she say of such a promise as you gave to me?"

Wick did not need to ask himself; his heart already knew. His mother had walked the path of magic every day, whispered prayers with each breath, and conjured enchantment with song. She had seen beyond appearance and judged those around her purely by spirit rather than how they appeared—even taking the side of Barta's strange companion, True.

He groaned and got to his feet. "Lady, what would you have me do?"

"Act as I bid you, Wick map Radoc. Live for those other than yourself."

A prick of annoyance touched him. Was that not what he'd done always? Was it not how he'd spent most of his life?

Always for the tribe and never a selfish choice permitted. How had that served him? Badly, for his world had come apart, and the one time he'd rebelled against duty, it had taken him from his home.

And caused him to doubt himself.

But if his mother, who believed so deeply in the unseen world, had indeed taught him anything, it lay in the wisdom of the god and goddess.

He raised his eyes to the being who stood before him. "Yes, lady. How will you direct me?"

"Do you affirm you will keep your promise and place yourself in my hands?"

Wick grimaced, but he nodded. And what would she ask? What terrible feat? That he turn himself over to the Gaels? Die in a welter of blood?

"Have faith, Wick map Radoc."

Was that the command? To have faith? But no; she had not finished.

"There is a woman you have encountered among the Caerena."

"Verica."

The goddess smiled. "Wondrous how her name springs so swiftly to your lips. Or is it in your heart?"

"What of Verica?"

"Henceforth, it is her welfare must concern you, even more than your own."

"Yes, goddess." That was a vow easily enough kept. "But—"

"That means if she asks you to stay with her, you will stay. You will remain with her until she is healed of her wounds."

"Lady, please do not request this. I will not deny I might want to stay with Verica, but I must consider the welfare of my tribe."

"Did you not leave your tribe in the hands of another?"

Wick squirmed mentally. "I always meant to find them help and go back."

"Do not lie to me. You fled. You surrendered the place your father made for you and took a new path. Now, on that path, you offer me defiance. Is it your choice to behave like the sister you condemned?"

"I never condemned Barta." Envied her, perhaps. She seemed so easily to throw off the demands he, Wick, could not escape. "And," he said more softly, "I do not mean to offer you defiance."

"It seems I must teach you not only your own value

but the meaning of faith. You must find your way, as must your sister and your young brother."

"Tally? What has he to do with it?"

"Upon their births, your mother did bless each of her children and sue for my protection. And I, Wick map Radoc, do keep my promises."

"Very well, Lady." Wick sucked in a breath. "I will remain with Verica until she is healed. What more?"

"Is that not enough? Devote yourself to her as you would to me. She stands in my place."

Wick thought of the hind transforming into a woman, and into a goddess. He nodded. "And after?"

"Devote yourself to her and let the future unfold as it must."

The goddess gathered herself the way moonlight might, across the forest floor. As moonlight did when the moon slipped behind a cloud, she began to fade.

"Wait," Wick said.

"Merely love her. And so heal her." The words floated to him on the air, or perhaps only through Wick's mind.

He awoke to darkness and the warmth of Verica's arms wrapped around him. His whole body trembled and stung.

A dream, just another mad dream such as had plagued him since he left home. Yet his heart refused to believe it. He wished he could speak with his mother, wanted it so desperately he ached. He would trade much for one moment's leave to ask her what all this meant.

Instead he found himself without her wisdom, far from home, with this woman who should be a stranger yet did not feel like one.

He drew Verica closer in the dark. Not hard penance, being told to remain with her. Or was it? If he stayed, if she grew to know him full well, she would discover what lay at his heart.

Discover that he was not after all what she believed him to be.

Chapter Twenty-One

Verica opened her eyes to the dusky first light of morning and lay exploring the deep feeling of dread that weighted her heart. She prodded at it gingerly, as she might one of her wounds, and promptly turned sick inside.

On this day, Wick meant to leave her. He would gather his belongings, bid her farewell, and walk out of her life.

Panic struck, drenching her with cold and then heat. She wondered how she would bear it, she who had borne so much. Had she any hope of dissuading him? How could she even try? He had a destiny to fulfill, one with which she had no right to interfere.

He still slept beside her, quietly. She could feel the heat from his body and hear his soft breaths, one following another. Her mind raced as she thought about begging him to stay. But she'd sworn off begging from any man. Besides, if Morirex had taught her anything, it was that begging won nothing more than heartache.

And life, so it seemed, brought little except loss. She'd not thought it could get more difficult than what they'd endured this last year. But now fate had gone her one better, had presented her with something she desired while promising to snatch it away.

Not it, *him*. This man who lay even now in her bed. One unlike any she'd ever known, with magic in his eyes and a strength that manifested as kindness.

They'd made love so gently last night, with respect for one another's wounds. Once again, Wick's tenderness melted Verica's resistance and rendered her helpless. She'd never understood what joining with a man could be, until she touched Wick.

She remembered the last time she and Morirex had coupled. The exchange—like all those between them— had been born of need. His need. Following a battle, they'd come back here to their hut so she might tie up his wounds.

Instead, he'd shoved her down onto her knees and commanded her to pleasure him with her mouth before pushing her back onto the floor and pounding her without mercy, while her wounds bled and he found violent release.

The next morning they'd arisen and gone out to the fight during which he'd taken his final wound.

Verica contrasted that scene with the way Wick touched her, and cursed beneath her breath. What a fool she was—all she'd done, by compelling him to stay last night, was deepen the need, and put the pain off one short night.

Her heart beat fit to strangle her; all at once she could not breathe. She fought her way up in the bed, and Wick came awake from whatever dream held him. His arms tightened around her, a bulwark against the cold.

For many long moments they lay so, just staring into the dim air of the hut while Verica's pulse quieted and she fought to compose herself.

At length Wick stirred again. "Verica? What is it? Are you in pain?"

"No. But morning has come." That, to her mind, said it all.

She slewed around in the bed, gently so as not to hurt his shoulder. To her surprise, her own wounds stung less than they had the night before.

He did not acknowledge her words, yet she could feel the thoughts move in his mind.

Impulsively she told him, "Make love to me." If she could hold him here, she might delay if not put off the inevitable.

And had she learned nothing? That would only make her need him more. But she did not care, she did not care!

He made a soft sound that might have been a protest, and she added hastily, "I am sorry. If you do not wish to—"

"Not wish to?" he echoed ruefully. "Can you even suggest it, after last night?"

"What of your wounds?"

"My what?"

"Your battle injuries."

"When I am with you, Verica, I forget them." He kissed her, and emotion flooded through her, a tangle of relief, delight, and desire so strong it frightened her. Bonded with him mouth to mouth, Verica opened herself completely, spread her legs, and slid beneath him even as he eased his body over hers.

He interrupted the kiss to say, "I have no wish to hurt you."

"I know." She gazed into the depths of his dark eyes, suddenly serious.

Resting on his elbows, he caught her face between his hands. "Beautiful. You are so beautiful. Here." He kissed both eyelids. "And here." He slid down and kissed her breast before drawing the nipple into his mouth with arousing deliberation.

"Please," Verica implored, begging after all.

Maddeningly, he ignored the plea. Or perhaps not, for he unerringly followed the path of the desire that curled through her—tongue caressing one breast and then the other, the soft skin beneath them, and her navel. Lower still, he probed the hair that guarded her innermost heat.

Verica stiffened; though she'd often provided Morirex pleasure with her mouth, no man other than Wick had ever touched her here with anything more than rough fingers or brutal thrusts.

Did she want this? She'd earned the right to say, since Morirex's death. No more being pushed onto the floor to act as bidden. No striving impossibly to please someone who refused to be pleased.

Could she allow herself to accept such pleasure?

Then Wick's mouth found her heated, most intimate place; his tongue entered her, and she lost all ability to choose or to think. Sensation poured through her, pure and powerful: tenderness and strength; humility and command. A roaring chasm of pleasure. Dared she surrender to it? Had she the ability to resist?

No, for when the storm broke over her, it took every thought of refusal.

Verica knew much of the intimacies that might pass between a man and woman, or had thought she did. Now she lay wracked by slowly fading tremors while Wick once more stretched himself beside her and wrapped her in his arms, tight. A haven. The one place she wanted to be.

Her thoughts returned slowly as the tremors died away. She sought for words, failed, and sought again.

"What…?"

He gave a murmur and drew her still closer; his lips brushed her cheek.

She wished she could see him better in the dim light of the hut.

"Was that a gift?" she tried again.

"Eh?" He seemed to consider the question. "One for me, mayhap. You taste so good."

A residual thrill arced through Verica, a hope that more might come. Her mind flailed wildly. "But you took no pleasure."

"That was my pleasure, beautiful Verica." Did she hear a smile in his voice?

"Yet you had no release." Coupling, as she knew full well, was all about a man's needs, and his release. After her first time, she'd learned to hope Morirex's release might come swiftly.

Now she caught Wick—still hard—between her hands and cradled him tenderly, as she never had her husband.

He stiffened in turn. "Verica—"

"You must have your satisfaction."

"I am content."

What kind of man was this? How had he come into her life?

"Although," he conceded with a smile she could definitely hear, "I will not argue with your present activity."

Just as the first time he touched her, his gentleness undid her. She felt the tension and desire begin to build inside her again and fastened her mouth to his. Swiftly, she guided him into her, a knife coming home to its sheath.

Nothing had ever felt more perfect.

But now, in contrast to her previous absence of thought, the questions came pounding in.

If she meant to ask them, she'd better do it now before Wick rose and put on his clothing. Before he followed his intention and walked out of her life.

"Where did you learn to do such a thing as—as what you did to me?"

"Eh?" He sounded drowsy, steeped in peace. "Thing?"

"The way you pleasured me."

That caused him to lift his face from the crook of her neck, where it had come to rest. His eyes met hers in the dim light. "Have you never…before?"

She shook her head.

Wick seemed confounded. "But you are a widow. Surely your husband…"

Ah, it must be something a man and wife commonly did together. Or perhaps something only done by a husband who cared most deeply for his mate. Did that mean Wick had, in the past, loved some woman? Did he love her yet?

The thought started her heart to aching. But she pulled together the shreds of her dignity and said, "My husband, Morirex, did not deal out pleasure. He expected only to receive it."

Wick ran his fingers through her hair. "How could he resist tasting you everywhere?"

Verica swallowed hard. She'd never confided the harsh details of her marriage to anyone but Cunarda. If she did so now, would it make Wick think less of her?

159

What matter, if he meant to leave?

"My husband did not value me very highly. Not even here, in our bed."

"He must have been a fool."

Doggedly, she forced herself to go on. "Morirex was considered a discerning and intelligent man, among the finest this tribe had to offer."

Wick snorted. "Not so discerning, if he had you in his bed and failed to take full advantage of it. Me, I fear I could never get enough."

The bolt of desire evoked by his words reached all the way to Verica's toes.

"What of you?" she asked huskily.

"Me?" He reiterated, "I am still content."

"No, I meant have you ever been handfasted? Do you have a wife back home among the Epidii?"

"No."

Relief poured through her in the wake of the desire, leaving her weak. "Why not?" Such a man as this—strong, kind, a canny warrior, and hale enough to please any woman's eye...

"Never had the time—or the opportunity. After my father suffered his injury, there seemed to be a demand every moment of the day and night."

"Then how did you learn this wonderful means of pleasuring a woman?"

He laughed. "That is not something a man learns, Verica; it is something he desires with every part of his being. Especially when near a woman such as you."

"I do not understand."

"I ask you this, Verica: does a man learn to be hungry?"

"Well, no."

"I will tell you a secret." He lowered his mouth to her ear, making her shiver. "I am always hungry for you."

If anyone had told Verica she could surrender her will and lower her rigid guard to a man so many times in succession, she would have scoffed.

But what good would dissolving in Wick's arms do, if he meant to leave her?

Chapter Twenty-Two

Wick sat beside the fire in Verica's hut and watched her speak calmly and decisively to the group of people who'd turned up at her door only moments ago. They looked like a delegation, but listening with half an ear he ascertained each had his or her own concern. The worsening condition of an ailing child, not expected to survive. A shortage of men for patrol. The ever-present shortage of food.

And they all came to Verica.

What a wonder she was, he marveled, watching her while striving to appear as if he minded his breakfast, a bit of barley cake left over from last night. She was a combination of strength and forthright honesty. Was he the only one who sensed the terrible, tentative uncertainty lurking beneath her surface? She certainly fought hard not to display it.

His mother, Essa, had also possessed strength, but she faced her battles armed with magic and belief, not a long knife. Barta, near as doughty a fighter as any man, revealed little softness, ever. The few women he'd admired among the Epidii had been strong in their opinions but utterly focused on hearth and home, children and survival.

Verica wore her strength like a cloak, a shield, hiding that vast vulnerability. Did others behold only the strong competence when they looked at her?

He also wondered, given all she'd said of him, about that husband of hers—Morirex. When Wick contemplated the man, his fingers clenched around the barley cake and crumbled it. If Morirex hadn't already been dead, Wick would be tempted to do the job.

The hurt Wick sensed within Verica stemmed from her treatment at Morirex's hands; that he did not doubt. He tried to imagine having such a woman in one's bed and failing to provide her any possible pleasure. Since the first time they tumbled beneath the skins together, Wick had been able to think of little else.

And now the goddess bade him stay, a fact of which he'd had no opportunity to inform Verica. He'd begun to broach the subject when her tribesfolk came pushing in, causing both of them to scramble up hastily from the warm bed and don their clothing.

If the first of the arrivals, the mother of the dying child, felt shocked by the glimpse she'd had of them rising naked from a shared bed, she gave no sign, being far too wrapped up in her own concerns, just like the others who followed her in. Wick half recognized one of them as the lad who worked with the healer. He did glance at Wick once or twice.

Verica dealt with the questions and complaints calmly and patiently. The healer's lad stood silent until the others left, one by one, at which time he shot Wick another look.

"My master, Callorix, asks if you would like him to see to your wounds before you leave. And will you go to him, or should he come here to you?"

"I will stop by and see him," Wick answered, "in a short while."

The boy left. Verica tied the curtain shut with

careful hands before turning to face Wick.

He held out the remaining portion of barley cake. "Come and eat."

But she stayed where she stood, regarding him with those deep blue eyes.

Slowly, and employing visible discipline, she asked, "Is there aught I might say that will keep you from leaving here today? I understand your need. You are on a quest to help your people, and that is a powerful impetus. But I still say you need more time to recover, and travel will be hard."

"Please sit down," Wick repeated.

She took the place opposite him, caught up the poker, and stirred the fire.

Not until she returned her gaze to Wick's did he say, "I have decided not to leave today after all—that is, if you are certain I am still welcome."

She froze, the poker caught in her hand, before cautious joy took hold in her eyes. It flushed her face to a rosy hue.

"Welcome?" she echoed, as if she did not recognize the word. "Indeed, Wick map Radoc, you are welcome both among the Caerena and here with me. But may I ask why you have changed your mind?"

Wick wondered how to explain. His mother would have understood a debt owed the goddess. Would Verica? Never thinking how she might interpret the words, he said, "My heart bids me stay."

The light in her eyes flared; she nodded. Color ebbed and flowed in her face once again, and she seared him with one burning look before her gaze dropped. "I am glad. And I am pleased, Wick map Radoc, for you to stay as long as you will."

****

Who would have thought, Verica marveled a short time later as she walked toward the healer's hut, Wick might so swiftly change his mind? It almost made a woman believe, once more, in prayer.

He'd said his heart bade him remain with her. What was she to make of that? Had her kisses and the passion they shared in bed caused him to reconsider? Dared she hope she might win the love of such a man?

Ah, but she'd given up on love, had she not? Sworn off so much as thinking of it again. She'd lost faith in it, right along with her faith in a goddess who seemed to grant favors only to snatch them away again, or to cloak them in cruel deception. No, she dared not care too deeply for Wick despite the seductive softness of his touch, his deep kisses, and that fathomless look in his dark eyes. That path led to disaster.

Oh, and did it matter? He'd agreed to stay—for how long, she did not know, yet she could not keep her treacherous heart from rejoicing.

Might he stay till spring? There would be many, many nights just like those they'd already shared, a dizzying, intoxicating number of them.

Yet she could not dismiss a hint of uneasiness that he should change his mind so suddenly. She doubted her kisses were sweet enough to detain a man of such strong convictions.

She shouldered the thoughts, and the desire, when she saw Hectia waiting for her outside the healer's hut. The girl, arms wrapped tight around herself, appeared miserable, her eyes red and swollen.

She greeted Verica with the words, "He has died, wee Dreen. Only moments ago, he did."

"Lita's babe?" Grief touched Verica's heart. Indeed, Lita had come to her hut expressing her fear the child must lose his fight against the fever. Yet another loss, especially in one so young, felt crippling. Poor girl—no older than the chief's daughters, and one of Smerta's closest friends.

How could they hope to survive such blows, one after the other? This overshadowed even the victory against the Gaels.

"Oh, my dear," she murmured, and moved to take Hectia into her arms.

The girl wept. "First Nactovus, and now this! I loved Nactovus, Verica, truly I did. I thought he and I would be together one day, when all this sadness and grief was over. I will never love again!"

So she thought, Verica acknowledged ruefully, even as she patted the weeping girl's back. So Verica had thought. But now, when her mind—her spirit—touched the man she'd left behind at her hut, she feared for what she felt. Ah, it had been easier when she dismissed all softness from her life. Better when she'd refused any hope of happiness.

"I hate the Gaels," Hectia wept. "Oh, how I do hate them."

"They did not bring the fever, my dear."

"But they are responsible for Nactovus's death, and my father's, and so many others that, to my shame, I have lost count! And Callorix says this contagion might well have stemmed from some of their dead, or things we picked up in battle."

Grave news, indeed.

"Why could they not be content with their lands to the west and what they've already stolen? Why can they not leave us be?"

"I do not know, child."

"Nactovus had his whole life to live. *We* had his whole life." Hectia drew away from Verica and bared her teeth. "He was fighting within arm's reach of me when he went down. I stabbed the monster who felled him. Through the eye."

Good girl. Verica did not say the words aloud but squeezed Hectia's hands.

"When did wee Dreen pass?"

"Moments ago." Hectia jerked her head toward the hut. "Lita still weeps. She will not surrender his body. I could not bear watching it and had to come outside."

Verica, not sure she could bear it either, knew she nevertheless had to enter the hut, dredge up words of comfort from somewhere, and speak them to the grieving woman. It would call for both strength and softness. She didn't know if she possessed a sufficient store of either.

Resisting the impulse to flee back to her own dwelling, she set herself and entered the healer's hut.

Immediately, she heard Lita lamenting, a high, keening wail of pure grief. The stench of the place hit her an instant later—blood, overheated bodies, vomit, and the sheer, undefinable scent of sickness.

Ivomagus, on the far side of the hut, looked up and saw her. He stepped to her side quickly, his face tense and strained.

"Ah, Mistress, I thought I heard your voice. Has Mistress Hectia given you the sad news?"

"Yes."

"It is a hard loss. Indeed, they are all hard losses, but following on the others, to lose a babe..." Ivomagus seemed to catch himself. "But we must keep in mind, wee Dreen's spirit has now been released from all pain, all fear. Freed, it soars. He will visit for a time in the Everlands before returning to us again. So I have just been telling his mother."

And much good the supposed comfort had done, from the sound of Lita's continued weeping. Verica wanted to dismiss Ivomagus's concept of eternity out of hand. She might once have believed in such things—life had taught her differently. But the shaman had a true heart, and she would not dishonor him by allowing her own feelings to show.

Ivomagus, searching her eyes, seemed to perceive what she kept from saying. He grimaced. "I have told Lita I will hold a special rite for her child. See if you can persuade her to relinquish the babe's body to Callorix. I have not succeeded in doing so; nor has he."

Verica swallowed back a sudden rush of sickness. Suddenly she wanted nothing more than to run from this place, leave behind the death and grief, distance herself from the unbearable pain. But a leader—even one who had never requested the place—did not run.

She set her shoulders and nodded. With a passing brush of his hand on her arm, Ivomagus stepped aside for her to pass.

Scores of eyes watched her as she made her way through the crowded hut—those of the sick and dying, the fevered, and those who came to help care for them. In the near silence, Lita's wails penetrated straight to the heart. Verica had no notion how to approach this devastated woman. She sent Callorix a despairing look and turned her eyes on the young mother, who cradled her babe in her arms.

Instinct took over then, the same that brought words of encouragement to a frightened youth entering battle or to Cunarda's daughters when they despaired. She reached out and enfolded Lita, dead child and all, in her arms.

Broken, the girl sobbed against Verica's shoulder. For many moments, no other sound disturbed the silence of the hut. Lita's sobs gradually died to a soft moan. At last she raised her head enough to see who held her and murmured, "Mistress."

"My dear, I am so sorry."

"He was too small to fight the fever. Why has the goddess visited this upon us? Have we not enough, with fighting against the monsters from the west? Why this also?"

"I do not know," Verica admitted.

Lita hiccoughed. "Ivomagus says the goddess is merciful." She laughed harshly. "He says this to me, who holds a dead child in her arms."

"The goddess is not merciful," Verica said, unable to deny it.

"Then why spread such lies?"

"We give comfort as we can. And Master Ivomagus believes his own words." Verica wished she could give this girl some solace, just as she wished she had some to offer Hectia in the loss of Nactovus. And to herself, when Wick eventually, inevitably, turned his back and walked away from her.

It would not be today. That lent her the strength to draw breath.

"Ivomagus also says Dreen is now safe and at peace, beyond the reach of all harm," Lita spoke before Verica could.

"One day, so we are taught, we will all go to such blessed rest." Would she, Verica, stop longing for Wick map Radoc before then? "Come, give the child to Master Callorix. Dreen must be washed and readied for burial."

"I will do that!" Anguish twisted Lita's face. "I want for no one else to touch him."

Verica looked to Callorix, who nodded at her soberly.

"Mistress Lita," he said, "you and I will care for him together. Perhaps Mistress Verica will be kind enough to fetch your mother here to us. She can take you home with her once our task is done."

Grateful for an excuse to duck out of the hut, Verica went outside, where she stood drawing in great gasps of air. Hectia had gone, and no one else passed by; for an instant she stood alone.

She put her head back against the skin of the shelter and closed her eyes, wondering if she could go on. No, she corrected herself swiftly—not if, but how. She had no choice but to endure whatever might come.

She had never borne a child and never hoped to. At the beginning of her marriage, she'd desired Morirex's child in the worst way, thinking it would make a difference in how he saw her. She could only imagine the depth of loss Lita now endured—flesh of her flesh and love far-reaching.

The hut door behind her opened; Callorix stepped out, looking concerned. "Mistress, I saw the look on your face back there. Are you all right?"

Verica bared her teeth in what could not be called a smile. "Should you not be with Lita?"

"My assistant prepares the wash so we can bathe

the infant. But you, Mistress—surely your wounds need redressing. That deep cut at your hip—"

"Do not worry for me, Master Callorix."

"You do not want for poisoning to set in. Better to let me put on a clean bandage."

Verica assessed herself with some surprise. After a night of gentle lovemaking, the pain in her wounds seemed to have eased. Even the one at her hip pulled less, and the stubborn cut beside her shoulder blade felt as if it had at last closed over.

"I assure you, I am well enough. Do not waste time you might better spend on those inside, who truly need you. Does the fever still spread?"

Callorix grimaced. "We are holding our own. I only hope more of us do not fall ill with the same symptoms, in the days to come."

"We have few enough resources," Verica conceded, "and our strength is very nearly spent. I will dispatch everyone we can spare to hunt for game and gather fuel. If you need aught else, come to me—I will do my best to supply it. Oh, and"—in the act of turning away, Verica looked back at the healer—"you need not worry about tending Wick map Radoc before he leaves. He has decided to stay for a time."

Callorix looked surprised. "Has he? How long?"

"That I cannot say." However long he stayed, Verica feared his departure would come too soon, at least for her heart.

Chapter Twenty-Three

Verica slogged through deep snow after escorting Lita's mother to the healer's hut, trying to untangle the thoughts in her mind. Lita's grief had touched her deeply; it warred with the fierce gladness she felt at Wick's decision to stay. Uneasiness still gnawed at her, along with unanswered questions: did Wick have feelings for her? And if he did, what would that mean for her future?

Everything.

She faced that unwelcome fact with deep foreboding. The vulnerability of it fair stole her breath away. She'd struggled so hard to guard her heart. Yet Wick had walked in and claimed it as easily as if she had no defenses.

And what of Ivomagus's prediction? That must have some meaning. Wick had not arrived by chance. There was magic in it. Would that be enough to create a forever?

Had she still possessed faith, she might have prayed about it. Small, simple prayers were such a vital part of Caledonii life—a woman spoke a prayer of thanks when preparing a loaf of bread or drawing water. A man prayed while hunting, and sued the spirit of the beast he tracked for generosity and forgiveness. People spoke prayers for guidance and wisdom at the beginning of each new day.

If she thought it would win her forever with Wick, Verica might just whisper a genuine prayer of her own.

She shoved aside the door curtain of her hut, and her emotions spiked. Wick sat beside her fire; he turned his head when she came in, and their gazes met. Her poor, battered heart bounded unpreventably.

Concern flooded the depths of his eyes; he leaped up and guided her to the place where he'd been sitting. "Verica? Ah, that can't have been easy. Here, warm yourself. I kept the fire bright for you, but we are low on fuel. If you tell me where to find the stockpile, I will fetch more."

For you. How long had it been since anyone had done anything for her? How long since she'd allowed anyone to?

She sighed, relaxing into the seductive comfort of his presence. "There is no stockpile. All used up—it has been impossible to gather wood."

"Then that is something with which I can help."

She searched his face, suddenly desperate to ask him for the truth. Desperate, and yet afraid—she, who permitted herself to fear so little. She wanted him to love her. She wanted to be the reason his heart had changed. Could she bear it, if she was not? Ah, she'd fallen into the same old trap again.

She drew a breath. "The firewood can wait. I told Master Callorix he need not worry about tending your wounds this morning. He has his hands full, you see, and since you are not leaving…"

She waited for him to correct her, to speak the words that proved life had decided to deliver another of its hard kicks to her gut. He did not, but gazed at her steadily, the thoughts in his eyes indecipherable.

She stumbled on, her voice so uncertain it no longer sounded like her own. "That got me to wondering how long you thought you might stay. Not that I need to know; I told you, you are welcome, and that is so. But the tribesfolk will ask." Cunarda would. Oh, what would Cunarda make of this? And Ivomagus. He had foretold this man's coming but did not seem at all pleased his prediction had proved true.

Wick continued to gaze at her; still she could not identify what lay in his eyes. "I cannot say." He shrugged. "I will know when it's time to leave."

Verica choked down her disappointment. Not forever, then—there was no forever.

"I hope," he said awkwardly, "that does not make a difference in my welcome. I would give you a better answer if I could."

To be sure. Desire—if that was what he felt toward her—must war with the deep sense of duty he owed his people. From a man of his ilk, could she expect more? Did it make a difference how long he might give her?

With the honesty native to her, she said, "I have told you that you are welcome, and you are. All that I have is yours." *All that I am is yours*. But she did not add that. Her heart might well be lost, yet she needed to protect herself, to hold something back. Best to try and hide the depth of her need for him. Best to accept what he offered and express none of the longing teeming in her mind.

Softly he said, "Thank you, Verica. There is much I can do to make your load easier. I will organize a party to gather firewood. I can also help stand watch. I hope you will use me as you need."

Verica closed her eyes for one blessed moment.

"You may depend on it."

****

"I cannot say why he has decided to stay. I am but glad." Verica made the confession to Cunarda in a low voice so Hectia, working not far away, wouldn't overhear. The women busied themselves clearing snow from the meager wood supplies, uncovering the scraps so they could be distributed to needy households. Overhead, the clouds had flown away before a brisk wind; the branches of the trees clattered together like the antlers of fighting stags.

Cunarda gave Verica a sharp look. "You did not ask him?"

Verica shook her head.

"That is not like you."

"I know." Verica gazed across the clearing to where a hunting party mustered. Wick map Radoc organized that group; she could see him speaking with others of her men. Just the sight of him from a distance prompted a prick of longing. She wanted to lie again in his arms, taste his deep kisses. Yield herself to him as she'd never done in the past, not to anyone.

Feeling helpless, she murmured to her companion, "He told me he'd experienced a change of heart, whatever that means."

Cunarda lifted her brows. "It could mean any number of things."

Verica gave a hard nod.

"Curious. I thought he was on a quest to find support for his tribe. Has he abandoned that, then?"

"No, he would not do that." A man of honor to the heart. "I believe he has merely postponed it."

Cunarda mused, "There are many things that might

175

change a man's mind." Again she looked at Verica, her eyes kind. "I can think of one in particular."

So could Verica. Was that why she'd kept from asking? She wanted to hold on to that possibility for a while—believe Wick stayed for her, for the sake of love. She tried to snort, to deride herself for holding such a fancy, and found she couldn't.

"He gave no hint how long he means to stay?"

"He said he will know when it is time to leave."

"Ah, well." Cunarda paused with a load of soggy kindling in her arms. "You cannot deny we need the help."

"I cannot deny it." Best to be thankful she had him for another day, another night. But she could not help but feel greedy.

Hastily, she changed the subject. "Have you seen Lita? How is she doing?"

Grief flooded Cunarda's eyes. "She does not fare well. I don't see her getting over this loss quickly, if at all." Cunarda's expression changed suddenly, and she hissed, "Hsst, here he comes."

Verica, her mind still on Lita, spun about. Wick approached them at an easy, determined lope, betraying no sign that his wounds hampered him. The sun glanced off his hair, finding deep, warm strands of red, and highlighted the planes of his rugged face. Verica's heart jerked in response.

"Mistress." He nodded at Cunarda courteously before requesting of Verica, "A word, if you can spare a moment."

"Of course."

They stepped away together, Verica fighting the temptation to touch him—on the arm, on the shoulder, anywhere. Later tonight, she promised herself, she would be able to reach for him, twine her body with his, and feel his calloused hands caress her skin. Fall into the deep well of comfort that seemed to lie at his heart.

"What is it?" Uneasiness fluttered in her stomach, warring sickeningly with the desire. Had he changed his mind again, so soon? Had he come to tell her he must leave? She could not bear it. Ah, but neither could she allow herself to fall subject to this uncertainty.

Apparently oblivious to her inner turmoil, Wick said, "I merely wished to ask which you would rather put forward, gathering wood or the pursuit of game. With so many sick and injured, I would not spread your people too thin. The hunting band is ready to leave, yet it occurs to me game will do little good if you cannot cook it. And the sick need to be kept warm."

"Yes, so they do." Ah, he meant to defer to her, did he? To respect the status she'd won? Something Morirex would never have done. In fact, she felt surprised Morirex had not roused from his grave to protest her leadership.

"If the hunting band stands ready, go ahead and send them. I will organize the younger folk to gather wood."

Wick looked uneasy. "You mean to join them? But your wounds—"

"Are no worse than yours, or anyone else's. Anyway, I seem to be healing very swiftly and have little pain."

He nodded but said, "Allow me to lead the firewood detail. The young man, Segovax, stands ready to lead the hunting band. You tend to other matters here."

"Are you certain you are fit?"

"I am."

Verica thought about it. She had to trust—make herself believe he would not, having given his word, go from her and fail to return.

She nodded but knew her heart would be in turmoil till she saw him again.

Chapter Twenty-Four

Wick eased himself out of his tunic and squinted with some misgiving at the wound at his shoulder. He'd labored hard this day, hauling wood from beneath deep snow, toting and stacking it, which had done his injuries little good. And while he was good at disregarding discomfort and pain, he'd begun to wonder just how much abuse a man's body could withstand.

Now, finding himself alone in Verica's hut, he stripped down to take stock of himself. At some point during the afternoon, the scab at his shoulder had once more broken open. The slash to his thigh fared little better, and all the small hacks, nicks, and bruises between throbbed like a smacked thumb.

But he and his crew had managed to gather a decent amount of firewood, not nearly enough but sufficient for the time being. Even better, the hunting band had returned with a fair amount of game for the cooking pot.

Most of the fuel and food would go to benefit the wounded and, as Verica insisted, the children of the tribe. Verica had taken little for her own hearth.

Which meant Wick would need to keep her warm this night.

Now from whence had that thought come? Battered as he was, he shouldn't even be able to think about activities between the blankets.

But the desire came on its own, despite his aching weariness. All he needed to do was be near the woman or catch her scent for the heat to rise.

Unprecedented in his life, this kind of desire. Men commonly pursued women; it made up a large of part of existence. But the longing Wick felt for Verica outstripped anything he'd ever experienced.

He groaned as he peeled the blood-stiffened bandage from his shoulder. He'd had no chance to see the healer this day—what was the man's name? Callorix—and he hoped he'd have an opportunity to apply a clean dressing before Verica returned.

No such luck. He turned his head sharply when the door curtain rustled and she came in, her dark head bent over the bowl she carried in her hands.

"I have brought us some—"

She stopped speaking abruptly when she saw him standing naked beside the fire. Her gaze moved from the wound at his shoulder to the hair tumbling down his back, and still lower. The color ebbed and flowed in her face.

"By all that is holy, Wick! Why did you not say your wound had reopened?"

Wick grimaced. "The work needed to be done."

"Not at such a cost to you, it did not. Do you know what could happen if your shoulder takes poisoning?"

"I am strong; rarely do my wounds take poisoning."

"You should go at once to the healer."

"He is fully occupied, and his hut is full of fever."

Verica made a face. "Do not seek to distract me from the matter at hand. Here, let me look at you."

Carefully, she set the bowl on one of the

hearthstones and came to him. He stood quietly, vitally aware of his nakedness, while she probed the ragged wound at his shoulder with her fingers and her gaze.

"This needs to be cleaned."

"Do what you will." He meant it as an acknowledgment that he needed care. His body interpreted it differently, and his voice came out low and rough. Unpreventably, he rose for her, as a hart to the hind.

Again her gaze dropped and caressed him. She half reached out before catching herself.

"Nay," she breathed. "Sit. I will bring Callorix."

"Only fetch some water and a basin. I will cleanse it myself."

"You will not." She frowned prodigiously before adding, "I shall."

The following moments proved painful to both of them. Wick's erection subsided under the onslaught of pain, and, teeth gritted, he instead fought a sudden bout of wooziness.

Verica sweated right along with him. "I am trying not to hurt you," she said more than once.

He did not repeat the invitation for her to do as she would. Barely holding onto consciousness, he knew but dimly when she finished bandaging his shoulder and moved on to tend the rest of his wounds.

"There now," she murmured at last. "That is the best I can do. I am no healer. You will need to see Callorix in the morning."

"I will." He produced the words somehow, still fighting the blackness that threatened to overtake him.

"Wick. Wick?" Did Verica attempt to recall him from that dark place? Determinedly she engaged his eyes. "I brought some food. You sup while I fetch us more fuel."

"Do not go."

"But you need to stay warm this night. And I took little enough wood for my hearth."

"We will keep each other warm." Did he, in truth, speak the thought aloud?

Her gaze softened; she leaned up and gave him a gentle kiss, more comfort than passion. Yet her voice sounded husky when she replied. "All right. You lie down; I will come."

He watched her undress through hazy, half-slitted eyes, saw her slim flanks revealed as her clothing fell away. He saw her breasts peak in the cool air. She unbraided her hair so it came loose, swirling around her like a blanket.

She crawled in beneath the furs, and he made room for her in the bed. He wondered if she'd slept in this same bed with her husband. He wanted to ask but lacked the strength.

Instead he heard himself say, "You are so beautiful."

She stiffened for an instant before relaxing against him. "And you are quite plainly not in your right senses."

Mayhap not. For he began thinking it would be a fine thing to fall in love with this woman. The goddess protect him.

Doggedly he told her, "I mean it truly. I am not clever with words, and rarely do I compliment women. But what I say, I do mean."

"Hush your foolish talk and go to sleep. That is what you need."

"Sleep? With you lying naked here beside me?"

"I am here only to keep you warm—the nakedness merely helps with that."

"Do you say so?"

"I do. Here." She gathered him into her arms, his head finding the crook between her shoulder and jaw, and comfort flowed into him. His muscles eased.

"I wanted to say…" he began. He should tell her. Tell her that though he'd been bidden to stay in order to heal her, he suspected he could love her instead. That she should not make the mistake of loving him in return, for he was not what she believed him to be—not a hero—and unworthy of her admiration.

But the comfort reached so deep he lost the will. And then sleep enfolded him and all thought flew far away.

He dreamed. At first it felt familiar, a dream he'd experienced already many times. He ran with the deer in among the herd. He was a deer—one that had run too far and too long. The breath strained in his deep lungs, steam rose from his body, and his legs trembled beneath him.

He ran not toward, but away.

Suddenly the herd scattered around him. He turned at bay in the snow and stared into his enemy's eyes.

A hunter. A single man, a Gael with a head of rough hair made stiff by lime, standing like the crest of a bird and a savage expression on his face. The hunter's presence—strong, determined—and the gaudy garments he wore, as well as the bow and arrow in his hands, hit Wick with the impact of a hurled stone.

Did a man or, indeed, a hart recognize the moment of his death? Wick did now; he could see it shining in the hunter's eyes, knew that when the man loosed his arrow, Wick's life would end.

The eternal balance, his mother used to call it, that between man and nature, between man and his enemies, between light and darkness. Thin as a knife's blade, this place upon which they all stood.

Wick thrashed the snow with his hooves and snorted. He sought strength for a leap. He failed to find it before the arrow was loosed.

He seemed to see the missile flowing toward him—slowly, slowly—the very fabric of time bending ahead of and behind it. He could feel the pain of the wound even before the bolt struck, reaching deep, tearing flesh, sundering body and spirit.

But the arrow did not find its mark in *his* flesh.

The herd had fled—all but one. The white hind now appeared from nowhere like a thought, like an impulse. Hide gleaming pale as moonlight, she leaped between the hunter and the hunted, between Wick and his death.

The arrow struck her and penetrated deep. Red blossomed on her snowy hide, and her body bucked and shuddered before she fell.

She fell.

In his dream, Wick bellowed.

The bellow came with him, out from his sleep. He fought the arms that held him, trying desperately to escape the horror he'd experienced, half mad until he heard Verica's voice.

"Hush. Wick, hush! What is it? What happened?"

He left off thrashing then, unwilling to hurt her. Her arms came around him still more closely and held him tight.

"A dream," he gasped.

"Is that all?"

She did not understand. These dreams that had been visited upon him were more than dreams.

He corrected himself, "A Vision."

"A Vision? Of what?"

He dared not tell her. Not if she were the white hind—leading her tribe, leading him. Coming back to give her life to save his.

When he failed to reply, she spoke soothingly, "Who does not have evil dreams, given all we have endured, what we have seen? Dreams of blood and loss, and death. I myself have had them. The very children wake, weeping."

"I know." Perhaps, rather, it had been a warning. He must keep watch—just as the goddess had said. He could not let this woman, with her true and courageous heart, sacrifice herself.

Yes, that must be why the goddess had bade him stay, all for Verica's sake. And none of his own.

Chapter Twenty-Five

Wick awoke and lay quietly, watching his breath turn to steam in the cold air of the hut. His awareness returned to him in pieces, drifting in from what seemed like another world equally as real as this one.

The fire had gone out for lack of fuel, and pale light, accompanied by a trickle of cold, filtered in beneath the leather door curtain. Morning must have come some time since, though he heard as yet no sounds of anyone stirring, outside.

Verica lay in his arms, fast asleep—one small point of warmth in the chill. At some time during the night she must have ceased clutching him so protectively and instead burrowed in tight. Now her dark head lay on his chest and her breath skittered across his skin.

He felt…better. The pain of his wounds had eased, and his strength seemed to have returned—despite his troubling dream.

Vision.

The immediacy of it flooded back on him as he recalled that terrible moment the hind took the arrow meant for him, and he turned sick inside. A warning, without question, and one most likely sent directly from the goddess. What did it mean?

He needed to protect Verica.

He narrowed his eyes on the clouds his breath made, puffing beyond the warmth of the furs. And why, out of a world of men, should the goddess choose him, Wick map Radoc, for such a task? He who had failed to protect the ones he loved most in the world. Failed, and then abdicated the very place where he should have stood strong... What made him think it would be any different now?

Yet the goddess had spared his life, worthless as he might believe it to be. And now she exacted her price. There must be some significance in it.

He tightened his arms around Verica, and she stirred in her sleep, lifted her face groggily, and caressed his cheek with soft lips.

Tenderness flooded through him, swiftly followed by that heat which seemed to come alive so easily between them. No, he told himself hastily—whatever the goddess's aim, it lay not in the seeking of his own pleasure.

"Is it morning?" Verica whispered.

"Yes, but it must be very early. How do you feel?"

She stretched her body against his, skin on skin, and smiled. "Fine, I feel fine." Her eyes sought and engaged his, an instant connection. "I think sleeping with you does me a powerful good."

"Is that so?" He ran his hand down her back, fingertips brushing the bandage at her shoulder blade, and gently cupped her buttocks. "I am glad."

"And you?" she returned the question. "How do you feel this morn?"

Hard and ready for her. She must be able to tell that much, since they lay twined so closely together. He said only, "Better. Perhaps sleeping with you is good for me, also."

"We need to keep on doing it, then. And mayhap

something more than sleeping?"

He kissed her; he would defy any man to resist. She opened her mouth beneath his and invited him in. He pulled her body on top of his, where she molded to him, her soft flesh cradling his hardness. Kiss interrupted, she gazed down at him, her eyes bright.

"I fear I am a poor nurse."

"You are a very good nurse indeed," he corrected. "You kept me warm all night."

"And now I want very much to do things that might prove harmful to those wounds of yours."

"Oh?"

"In fact, I want to do these things over and over again."

Wick smiled. "Perhaps, if we go very gently, it will do me no harm."

The expression in her eyes changed, grew suddenly serious. "You are always gentle. I love that you are gentle with me."

"How else should I be?"

"Demanding."

"I am in no position to make demands of you, Verica."

Her gaze brightened again. "Perhaps it is I who should make the demands. You have a beautiful body, Wick."

His eyebrows twitched. "I fear the best that can be said about it is that it serves me well. These years past I have acquired far too many scars."

"We both have too many scars." She ran both her palms down his chest. "But I can see what lies beneath."

He hoped not, though her touch prevented him

from saying so, the way her hands caressed the muscles of his abdomen and slid lower still.

Huskily, he told her, "It is you who are beautiful, Verica." He cupped one small breast and felt her melt into him. She arched her body up in the bed and offered her breast to his mouth. He accepted it in a staggering flash of heat.

Verica cradled his head in her hands while he suckled her, drawing him in more closely. The heat expanded and consumed him, turning him heady with desire. Ah, if only he could spend eternity thus, with her body fused to his, bliss and need possessing him in equal measures. If only the world might fly away and allow them this.

She murmured, a wordless sound deep in her throat as he pulled more of her breast into his mouth, abrading the nipple with his tongue. She spread her legs and trapped the long ridge of his hardness between her thighs, an invitation. When he abandoned one breast for the other she gave a great sigh, shifted and, moving with astonishing lightness, took him inside her.

She seated him to the hilt slowly, slowly, and it felt exquisite. Wick gasped with pleasure so intense it felt like pain and lay looking up at her. Once more their gazes locked while she began to move.

"You lie quietly. Do not think to harm yourself." A smile of pure mischief touched her lips as she moved above him, her lithe body flexing like that of a woman riding a pony.

Wick, helpless, gave himself up to the demand her body made of his, to the searing heat of it, offering up all he had, and all he was. As if he had no control of his own flesh, and wanted none, he surrendered to the insistence of her strength and passion. It felt as if she reached into his body, caught hold of his spirit, and drew it to her right along with the rest of him.

Like a dancer she moved. Like a shaman, she enchanted. They came together in a rush of fire so bright he forgot he'd ever had wounds.

Ah, and no one told him coupling could be like this. Young men talked about it endlessly but mostly in terms of what they could get, not give. This, with Verica, felt like equal parts giving and taking, exquisitely balanced. His past couplings had been quick, awkward, and often rushed, all too often fueled by heather ale. They had meant nothing.

And none of them ever approached the tenderness that washed over him in the wake of this passion. Keeping him inside her, Verica lowered her body onto his chest, and he wrapped his arms around her, tight.

He wanted to make her part of him, wanted his tattoos to expand and flow over her skin. He had no idea what to do with such emotions, so he lay with his eyes squeezed shut, barely breathing.

Did she feel what he felt? Could she, possibly? Or for her, had what passed between them been mere release? An effort to stay warm?

He did not know, and life had taught him that what he wanted—even passionately—rarely if ever materialized. Unable to contemplate it, he allowed his mind to blank on the bliss of sheer feeling and floated.

"Have you fallen back to sleep?"

"Hmm?"

"Never before have I gone to sleep with a man still inside me."

That got Wick's eyes open. Did she mind? But

surely that was satisfaction he heard in her voice.

"If you would like me to move—"

"Do not dare." She stirred just enough to test the strength of their joining. "I like the way this feels."

He groaned, a sound of pleasure, of possession; he dared not let his thoughts go there even though the impulse shot through him with staggering power. He wanted to stay like this forever, bidden by the goddess or otherwise, wanted to offer his life for this woman.

Hearing him groan, she asked, "Have I hurt you?"

"No."

"Good, because coupling should not hurt. I know it often does, although never with you."

"Your husband—he hurt you." Here in this bed. Wick saw the truth of it as if she'd drawn him pictures. "Tell me about him."

Verica moved abruptly; their bodies parted at last, and Wick feared he'd ruined the moment. Why had he let himself break the spell?

But she snuggled in beside him again before she said, "I do not like speaking of him. He was…he was nothing like you."

Not a coward, Wick assumed, nor a man who fled his responsibilities.

But Verica said, "Oh, he was courageous as you are, but he had little patience, especially with me."

"Why?" Wick couldn't help but ask. "One should be most patient with those one loves."

"You are right. But Morirex did not love me. I should never have wed with him."

Wick huffed a breath. "Why did you?"

"I'm not sure I have the answer to that, even now. I was young and foolish. I thought I could make him care for me. I tried, in every way I knew, to make him care. I supposed if I were pleasing enough in bed, always serving his pleasure rather than my own, it would make him value me. I thought if I took up a place beside him in battle, it would chase his disdain away. That never happened; he just seemed to despise me more."

Wick's hand hovered above her hair. "I'm sure he did not despise you."

"Oh, he did. Perhaps if I'd been able to give him a child...but that never happened either." She lifted her face and looked at Wick. "It is as I told you at the outset—you need not worry about leaving your seed inside me. I am most certainly barren."

"Oh."

She gave a painfully tight smile. "Men do not like that. They like to think they will leave their mark where they have gone. You will not be so eager to couple with me again."

He knew she was wrong; he wanted her already. But he found he wanted still more to comprehend this pain she carried.

"Do not judge all men by this one who treated you so cruelly."

"No, I've never met another man like him. I chose with flawlessly bad aim." She sighed. "In the end, Morirex used me exactly as he might his own fist—with the intent of relieving the stress of battle. And with as little regard."

"I am sorry you had to endure that."

"You? Sorry? You did not treat me so—you never would."

"No. I hope he lived to regret it."

"I saw no signs of regret, not till his last breath."

"You deserve better." True, that. She deserved better than him. If he cared for her at all he should tell her so—tell her the truth about himself as she had just confessed the truth of her own painful past—rise from the bed and do her the favor of leaving her.

Yet the goddess bade him stay. That fact bent and twisted his own sense of decency; it made a mockery of the tenderness they shared. Heal her, the goddess had said. Could he?

"I deserve nothing, Wick. And I do not know why I am confiding all this to you except that you make me feel safe, more than I can ever remember. It is as if I've been searching a long while for the shelter of your arms."

With regret he said, "I cannot keep you safe, Verica. But you are welcome to say whatever you will to me."

Once more she raised her head and looked him in the eyes. "You are far too good to be true, Wick map Radoc. A dream."

"A true dream? That is what my mother used to call Visions." He recalled, with horror, the hind leaping in front of him and falling in a welter of blood.

Very gently he cupped Verica's breast with his hand, the place where, in his dream, the arrow had entered.

"Ah." Heat kindled in her eyes. "If you do that, I shall want you all over again."

"Yes?" He brushed her nipple with his thumb, and she shivered.

"We should get up and face the day," she breathed. "But, I am thinking, not just yet."

Chapter Twenty-Six

Verica, moving through a day that contained no end of demands, hard tasks, and problems to be solved, could not imagine why she felt so good. Energized and not as if she suffered half a score of wounds both big and small, and existed on a mere half bowl of cold broth shared with Wick, taken after they'd managed to persuade themselves out of her bed. Full of life and enthusiasm.

Her wounds seemed to have healed in half the usual time. A while ago they'd stopped pulling, and even the deep cut at her hip no longer caused significant pain. She needed to see Callorix about it but so far hadn't had a chance. And anyway, Callorix still had his hands full with the wounded and the fever victims.

As she worked gathering firewood, she wondered if lying with Wick had served to heal her. A mad prospect, yet she could not chase the idea from her mind.

One thing she knew for certain, she disliked being out of his sight, or beyond his reach. Even now they worked within eyeshot of each other, and she glanced at him often, touching on his presence.

Tribe members approached her in a steady stream with reports from the guards, with requests and questions. She had a lengthy conversation with Ivomagus about holding another burial ritual and perhaps one of purification against the fever, and another with Motius about the severe lack of supplies. During this last discussion, Wick came and stood at her side.

He listened quietly to all Motius had to say and held his tongue until the tribesman departed. Then he slanted a look at Verica.

"Your man says you need supplies to mend the huts, weapons, and clothing. I can think of a place we may obtain all that."

"Where?"

"The Gaels' encampment."

"Eh?" Startled, Verica stared.

He gave a wry smile. "Not everything there burned up."

Her eyes lit. "You suggest we steal from them even as they have stolen from us, all this while? I would like that."

"Yes."

Verica contemplated it carefully. "We would need to be very sure they are all gone."

Wick shrugged. "If you wish to raise a band and go discover what is left there, I am willing."

Her heart froze momentarily. Did she want to endanger Wick? Could she bear to?

"It is a fine idea," she hedged, "but if you go, I will go also."

He too hesitated before he shrugged. "You are the leader, Mistress, and the decision is yours."

****

Perhaps, Verica thought some time later as she peered from the cover of dense trees into the Gaels' ruined encampment, they should not have made this attempt in broad daylight. For broad it was—the sun shone down, blinding on the white snow, making her narrow her eyes against the painful glare. When she looked carefully, though, she saw not all the snow remained white; great swaths of dark ground, speckled with ash, bordered the ruins of the burned structures. The stained snow had refrozen, leaving ugly scars. Even uglier appeared the splashes of dark brown, which she recognized as blood.

Still worse, bodies—also now frozen—lay scattered where they had fallen. Proof, Verica thought, that no one here remained alive. The Gaels might be despicable murderers and thieves, but they did tend their dead whenever possible.

Regarding the scene, the hair rose on the back of Verica's neck. She turned and eyed her men, who included Wick, Motius, Segovax, and the young warrior Derux, who had volunteered with great zeal and yet now appeared less than enthusiastic.

Derux expressed his uneasiness in a low mutter. "I do not like this. It is too quiet."

"Yes." Motius grunted the word, and Verica could only agree. The place lay silent as an open grave.

"As it should be," she said softly, "given everyone lies dead. And look, Master Wick is right. Much has escaped the burning." Including the chariots. They sat in a neat row, all covered by snow.

Sourly, Motius commented, "Good thing it's so cold. These bastards already stink bad enough. Let's split up, Mistress, and do what we came to do swiftly, so we can get away out of here again."

Everyone nodded in assent.

"Locate anything of value," Verica instructed. "We

will gather it all and haul away what we can, then return for the rest."

Derux shivered. "Are we certain no one remains alive?"

Wick rested his hand on the hilt of his knife. "It appears so, but best to go carefully."

****

If there were chariots, Wick knew there must also be ponies. They would likely be in poor condition, left without feed in such weather; nevertheless, they might prove valuable. Circling away from the others, he went through the charred snow, passing body after contorted body, and slipped behind one of the half-burned structures, where he found the ponies—six of them— lying dead. A lad who had probably been their attendant sprawled near them, frozen eyes gazing at the bright blue sky.

Sickness rose into the back of Wick's throat at the sight. The ponies would be good for nothing but food. The idea sickened him, yet the Caerena's need was great, and it went against his ingrained belief to waste anything. Anyway, the animals' spirits had long since flown.

Would the starving Caerena care what went into their cookpots?

That idea spurred another. If they could uncover one or two chariots, they might transport a larger amount of meat and supplies.

He estimated some three-quarters of the camp had burned. Several structures, including the one directly in front of him, stood partially damaged but erect. Pulled apart, these would yield materials that might be used to repair the Caerena's own huts.

He stood quietly, listening for the others of his party, but could not hear them. He felt utterly alone—and as if he were being watched.

He swung around in the churned snow. And saw a man.

The fellow stood hunched over, bare knees nearly in the snow, clad in the gaudy if now ragged garb favored by the Gaels. A lurid wound marked one side of his face, and his bleached hair hung down his neck like a dirty pelt. His eyes burned feral as those of a beast.

It took Wick a moment to react; when he did, he wasted no breath hollering. Silently he leaped; the Gael, turning, attempted to flee.

He never stood a chance. Wick pounced on him in three strides, alarm lending him strength. A brief flurry ended with the Gael on his back in the snow and Wick's knife at his throat.

Wick's thoughts moved more slowly than his body had reacted; he possessed only a few words of the Gaels' tongue. The Gaels, as he knew, having taken countless Caledonii slaves, understood far more of his language.

He chose to speak in his own tongue when he said, "How many of you are here? How many left alive?"

The man spat at him, the only answer.

On a sudden surge of hate, Wick let the blade puncture the skin, just enough to start a thin line of blood flowing. He thought of his mother, lying limp in his arms when he carried her from the hut where she'd been murdered by these foul savages. Thought of his father who, despite his crippled body, had striven to rise and defend her.

"Die," he said.

"Wick. Wick!"

Someone seized his arm. The others, all four of them, stood beside him, staring. Verica hauled back on his arm, preventing him from slitting the Gael's throat from ear to ear.

"Not yet," she said. "He may know something of value."

Striving mightily to overcome his rage and hate, Wick nodded. He rose from the downed man, who made no attempt to stir.

"He's badly wounded," Verica observed. "Probably dying."

Good. Wick did not speak the word aloud, but Segovax glanced at him as if he'd heard it.

"Are there any others?" Motius asked.

"Look inside the building." Wick jerked his head at the hut. "He must have come from there."

Motius and Derux went.

Verica nudged the fallen man with her toe. "How many of you are there?" And, when the fellow glared at her. "Can you understand me?"

Segovax said, "He is no use to us if he cannot speak. I agree with Master Wick. Slaughter him."

Before Verica could reply, the two other tribesmen returned. Motius said, "There is another one in there—a lad. This one's son, maybe. He's in a bad way. Nearly dead."

"The only two survivors of the raid, perhaps?" Verica guessed. "Motius, stand guard here; I will go and see."

Verica moved off, and Wick followed. The interior of the skin hut—once a keeping place for gear and perhaps the ponies themselves—stank. Broken chariot wheels, some with their deadly spikes still in place, lay about, along with what might have been tattered harness. In one corner they found the lad, lying senseless on a pile of blankets, barely breathing.

Wick's nose wrinkled involuntarily. "Smells like death," he grunted.

Verica glanced at him. "We will need to take the man back with us. The boy also?"

"Your decision." The hind led the herd.

"If we drag him out of here, he may well die."

Wick suggested, "Leave him for now. Search the rest of the camp and make sure there are no others."

"Yes."

Wick followed Verica back out into the clean air, where she returned to stand over the injured Gael.

"Is that boy in there your son?"

The man's eyes, a curious gray-blue, spat hate the way his lips had. But Wick thought he caught an underlying thread of concern.

Verica must have sensed it too; she turned aside and gave orders.

"Segovax, you, Wick, and I will search the encampment for more Gaels. Motius and Derux, watch this one."

"What about the one inside?" Derux asked.

"He's not getting up on his own."

A thorough search of the camp revealed no other survivors, but the party did find a wealth of tools and weapons in addition to the slain ponies.

Wick suggested digging out two chariots and loading them with as much plunder as they could hold, in addition to the captives. That accomplished, they set out for home with Wick and Motius dragging the rattling carts with difficulty through the snow.

The younger of their two captives died before they reached their own settlement.

Chapter Twenty-Seven

"I have a bad feeling about this." Verica stared, troubled, into Wick's eyes and sought a way to put her uneasiness into words. "Perhaps we should not have brought that captive home with us. It might invite bad luck, having him here."

Wick shrugged, looking unhappy. Did he disagree with the decision she'd made back at the Gaels' camp? She went on, in more complaint than statement, "He says nothing of worth, nothing at all. And I have seldom beheld such raw hate."

"His hate I can understand," Wick admitted. "It but reflects what I feel toward him."

"Do you think that lad was his son? There was a"—Verica waved her hand—"a sameness about them."

"Son or not, he'd been keeping the boy alive, likely waiting for better weather that would allow them to get away, back west. He must have cared about him."

"Whatever their relationship, they were living on the meat from those slain ponies." The beast closest to the hut had been roughly butchered.

"A man does as he must."

"Yes, as does a woman."

Verica stirred restlessly. The two of them sat outside her hut, in the pale sunshine. The weather had warmed, and snow melted to slush underfoot. Trees dripped moisture on every hand.

One of the huts, not far off, had been converted to a prison for the captive, though Callorix said the man would not live long. His injuries, once uncovered, proved extreme; a wound to the gut that had already poisoned. Callorix, shaking his head, had declared, "I do not know what has kept him alive this long."

The intensity of his hate, would be Verica's guess. Whatever the man's physical condition, his hate alone lent him strength which he poured into resistance.

He refused to so much as speak his name or the name of his tribe. *Clan*, Verica silently corrected herself; the Gaels called their family groups clans. But the ties seemed similar to what bound the Caerena, and likely just as enduring.

Wick mused, "He may prove a valuable hostage, should we need to bargain with others of his kind."

"Do you think we will?" Dread—that familiar and sickening emotion—touched Verica once again. "I must admit, I've welcomed our freedom from threat of attack, however brief."

"One thing we've learned of the Gaels, they are persistent. I still do not understand why they cannot be content with their kingdom in the west. Instead, like greedy children, they push and push."

"They are like greedy children. I begin to fear they will never be sated. Wick"—she turned her gaze on him—"what will happen to us, the Caledonii?"

"Ah, Verica, I am not wise enough to give you an answer. If love could save us—love for this land and all who shelter in it—the Gaels would disappear forever over the horizon."

Longing stirred in Verica's heart; she regarded him with new attention. "If only." Then she might have hope of an ordinary life, with a man just like this one. "Do you think we will be conquered, in the end?"

He shook his head. "I do not know. The Gaels may be greedy, but we are equally tenacious. It will not be an easy contest."

Verica rested her chin on her hand. "Sometimes I long to just stop fighting."

"You are merely tired."

"Perhaps." Verica ached for him to take her into his arms, enfold her so she might lose herself in the sensation of warmth and safety he lent. An illusion, surely—none of them was safe.

As if his mind ran along the same course as hers, Wick said, "We need to find a way to make a stand."

"Here?"

"Here, in the south—anywhere. We need to gather strength, join with other tribes. Verica, what do you know of your former chief's allies?"

"Ammin's allies, you mean? Not much. I was not privy to such meetings before I took over from Morirex."

"He must have had ties with other chiefs, as did my father. Many of those ties are now sundered, but we need to find some who still stand. Now, when the battles have ebbed, is the time."

"Cunarda may know. Or Ivomagus, though even that seems doubtful. He was but an apprentice, before Ammin fell, and no more privy to important meetings than I. All of Chief Ammin's close advisors are dead."

"Your husband said nothing to you of alliances, or even promises of them?"

"He did not think I had the wit to understand."

Wick grunted, making a comment of it. "I suggest

we meet with Mistress Cunarda and Master Ivomagus. And then speak still more searchingly with the captive."

"Speak?" Verica repeated doubtfully.

Wick looked grim. "I do not believe in torture. But as we just agreed, we all do as we must."

****

The captive already looked lifeless. He lay in the small storage hut that had been converted to a prison, sprawled on his back with his arms flung wide, like a man in his death throes. Young Cintus, currently serving as guard, followed Wick and Verica inside, where they stood for a moment while Wick watched, trying to catch a movement of breath that would betray life.

There—the wounded man's chest moved in a shallow rise.

Verica made a strangled sound and slanted a look at Cintus. "Has Master Callorix been by to see him today?"

"He sent his assistant, Antius, this morning after I first came on shift. I suppose Master Callorix is too busy to come."

Too busy to tend a prisoner more than half dead, Wick thought unhappily. They would get little information from this man.

And just what did he hope to discover? Perhaps why, after a campaign that had lasted most of Wick's life, the Gaels pressed them so much harder this year? Why they'd failed to withdraw, as they had in other seasons, when winter came?

Whether there existed a magical charm or weapon that could make them withdraw for good?

"Leave us," he told Cintus, and the young man

slanted an inquiring look at Verica, who nodded, before he went out. As soon as he did, Wick drew the knife from his belt.

"What do you mean to do?" Verica asked in a flat voice that did not quite cover her alarm.

"Wake him up, first of all." If he could.

The following moments were neither pretty nor pleasant. Wick, squatted beside the prisoner with his knife still clutched in one hand, smacked the Gael across the face repeatedly until the fellow groaned and opened his eyes.

It took the prisoner a moment to focus on Wick and on Verica, standing above him. When he did, hate blossomed in his pale eyes, the way blood blooms at the site of a wound.

Wick had seen wild creatures look that way when trapped, mindless and unreasoning, just before…

He showed the captive the knife and, in a low rumble, said, "I know you can understand me. You've seized captives enough to comprehend bits of our tongue, and I will keep it simple. Do you want to live?"

He considered it a valid question. The man lay here with a wound in his guts so terrible it stank, and no hope of release. Could Wick, even with his knife, do anything to intimidate him?

The Gael bared his teeth, the hate in his eyes impossibly bright. "Where is my son?"

Ah, so the dead boy had indeed been this one's son. Did the fellow not know the lad had died during their journey? Indeed, and how could he? He'd barely been conscious when they arrived.

Not softening his tone, Wick replied, "Dead."

The man spat. All his grief lay in the vile gesture,

and his rage. "You killed him?"

Verica moved uneasily before she replied, "He died of his wounds. They were most dire, as are your own."

"Then let me die also." The Gael jerked his head at Wick's knife. "Do what you will with that. Do your worst, Blue Man."

Wick discovered, much to his dismay, he desperately wanted to. It went against everything his mother had ever taught him of mercy, deference to the will of the gods, and the love that lay at the heart of all. Yet even his mother's teaching could not make him dredge up any mercy for this man.

That, so it occurred to him, made a good reason to put away his knife and get out of the shed before he did something he'd regret as much as he regretted handing over leadership of his tribe to Brude.

Yet he continued glaring into the prisoner's face even as the man glared back; at that moment they were, in the flesh, the two factions warring over the land Wick loved.

Hate for the sake of love. He seemed to hear the words in his mother's voice. *Wick, my son, could it be more wrong?*

His body jerked, and he looked at the woman standing by his shoulder. Had she heard? But she merely returned his look with inquiry, and some distress.

To the Gael he said, "Tell me your name and the name of your clan."

Silence and an implacable glare of hate met him.

"Tell me of your importance to your chief. Will he negotiate for your release?"

"Negotiate?" The man sneered. "With what aim?"

"Peace," Wick heard himself say. "The setting of a boundary past which your kind will not come."

The Gael laughed, a painful sound that wheezed from between his lips and wrenched up from the gaping hole in his abdomen. "The Ard Ri of Dal Riada himself has not that much importance, Blue Man. You may as well go ahead and kill me."

Wick laid the blade of his knife close against the Gael's throat.

"Tell me," he repeated, "who sent you here? Who, in the west, directs this invasion?" The mad idea occurred to him that he might journey there. Oh, he would no doubt die in the process, but perhaps he was meant to sacrifice himself for this cause. For Caledonia.

"You want to stop it? No man can stop it. The gods cannot, now. One day we will own all this land, Blue Man. And those who live where once you lived will forget your very name."

Rage rose to Wick's head and exploded. He forgot where he was; for an instant he forgot who he was. Words issued from between his lips, quite possibly not his own. "You may well overrun this land, steal the last hillock, and burn the last hut. But if you think you can destroy us, you are wrong. We are Caledonia: our blood flows in the streams and our bones lie in the rock. So long as the spirit of this land endures, so do we."

"Then I piss upon your land," the Gael said shockingly. "I piss upon you all."

He seized Wick's wrist in both his hands, the strength of a madman in his grip. Before Wick could react, the Gael twisted and plunged the knife Wick held into the terrible wound at his abdomen; he threw himself down upon it in a violent motion, so it reached his heart.

Verica exclaimed. Blood, not quick and red but thick and viscous, crept across Wick's hands. He swore, called on the goddess, and backed away from the corpse, which still stared at him with hate in its eyes.

How to fight an enemy who would rather die than speak reason?

****

"Are you all right?" Verica asked as they walked to the meeting at the chief's hut. She looked at Wick with some concern. The scene inside the Gael's prison cell had shaken her and must have shaken Wick also, yet his face appeared emotionless as stone. She'd insisted they return to her hut so he might sponge away the blood—she'd lent him some of Morirex's clothing and attempted persuading him to speak of what had just happened. He merely cleaned the blade of his knife with meticulous care and refused to look at her.

They found the meeting at the chief's hut well attended. Cunarda was, of course, there, plus both her daughters, in addition to Ivomagus, Motius, and Callorix, who'd stolen a few moments from his other duties.

As soon as Verica and Wick entered, she took the healer aside. "The Gaelic captive," she told him in an undertone, "is dead."

When he turned surprised eyes on her, she added, "He perished under questioning." More or less true, if by the man's own hand.

Turning to the room at large, she raised her voice. "The Gaelic prisoner died moments ago during questioning. Can arrangements be made to dispose of his remains? Master Ivomagus, do you think any words need to be said?"

Ivomagus widened his eyes. His nose twitched in a fastidious manner as he considered Verica's question. Ordinarily the first among men to spend his compassion and speak of honor, he now shook his head decisively. "Disposal seems sufficient," he said.

Hectia asked, "But what happened? I thought we meant to try and use him as a hostage."

Verica glanced at Wick, whose expression remained shuttered, before she said, "As I am sure Master Callorix will tell you, the man bore a fatal wound in his gut and was very weak. Master Callorix?"

The healer nodded, and Verica swiftly pressed on.

"Meanwhile, we now know for certain the Gaels are gone and we have a reprieve—I would not squander it."

"But," objected Smerta unhappily, "what can we do? We struggle day by day merely to survive."

"I know. We are all tired and in need of healing. But it is no time to give up the fight. When the Gaels return, come spring, we must be ready."

Cunarda nodded. "The goddess has granted us this stay, as Mistress Verica says, in answer to our prayers. We dare not waste it."

Determinedly, Verica went on, "Master Wick has suggested we use this time to reach out to the other tribes around us and strive to make alliances with those who may be in similar dire straits. As you know, it is why he came north in the first place, to find assistance for his people."

From the corner of her eye she saw Wick twitch.

Before he could speak, Motius asked, "Can we not,

Master Wick, form an alliance with your tribe?"

"Yes." Wick glanced at Verica. "I feel an alliance between the Caerena and the Epidii already exists. But even joined, I doubt we have the strength to make it through another long season's fighting."

Verica took it up. "We need to locate Chief Ammin's allies and persuade them to make a stand with us. Does any among you know with whom he had the strongest ties?"

"The Ongust," Cunarda answered promptly, "and the Canvorst. But both of those tribes were hard pressed even before Ammin died."

Hectia, silent until now, contributed, "Father spoke sometimes of Chief Enestimus of the Dimitii."

"Yes," Cunarda conceded, "but only in frustration. Chief Enestimus has never been one to form alliances, and did not respond positively when Ammin reached out."

Wick asked, "Where lie all these tribes?"

Cunarda answered him. "They did lie to our north, the Ongust and the Cavorst closest. The goddess alone knows where they may be at this season." Her face turned bleak. "Destroyed, or driven eastward."

Softly, Wick said, "By now, this Chief Enestimus may well have changed his mind about joining forces. When is the last anyone heard from him?"

"I do not know," Cunarda replied. "A goodly while. After…after Ammin died, contact ceased. We were too busy, holding on and fighting to survive, to send messages."

Wick grunted. "That is what is happening everywhere among the Caledonii."

Ivomagus lamented, "It is a dark time upon our

land."

Cunarda turned to him. "Master Ivomagus, have you Seen how long this reprieve might last us?"

"No, Mistress. But the darkness, as I say, hangs over us like smoke."

With a rush of conviction, Verica said, "We need a rallying point." Wick, so she believed, must be that point, a hero sent to save them. Their last chance at survival. Her last chance, perhaps, to salvage her heart.

She loved him. Sitting there in the presence of the others, with concerned and frightened faces all around, she knew it for truth. But she could not tell him. She dared not so much as confide it when she lay in his arms, in the dark. Because love made a woman vulnerable and weak. It left her open to hurt.

If Morirex had hurt her, she could not imagine what losing Wick might do.

She said, "I suggest we send a delegation to locate Chief Enestimus of the Dimitii and speak with him about an alliance."

"It will take some persuading," Cunarda cautioned.

Ivomagus spoke suddenly. "Who will make up this delegation? We have few to spare."

Swiftly, Verica replied, "I believe Master Wick should go, along with Mistress Cunarda, acting as Chief Ammin's representative. And me."

Cunarda looked shocked. "Me? But I rarely travel, and I am needed here."

"We are all needed here," Verica returned. "But needs must."

A bit tightly, Ivomagus asked, "And, forgive me, are we all agreed that Master Wick should speak for our tribe?"

Verica stared at him in shock, as did everyone else present—everyone save Wick, who lowered his eyes and bent his gaze on his hands. Such words as these came unexpectedly from Ivomagus, a man who usually expressed himself with only kindness and deliberation.

But perhaps, Verica thought, meeting the shaman's gaze, Ivomagus had deliberated this opinion.

Fiercely she said, "I gather you are not so agreed?"

Ivomagus shot a single look at Wick, still silent, before he replied, "I confess to feeling uncertain."

Before Verica could speak, Wick said, "Master Ivomagus is right. I may not be the best man for this mission."

Everyone stared at him.

With a scowl, Ivomagus said, "Perhaps, Mistress, you and I might discuss this privately. You have taken my advice in the past; will you not listen to me once more?"

Verica's stomach muscles clenched, and dread—that sickeningly familiar emotion—flooded her body again. Ivomagus claimed he had not Seen the future. But did he know something she did not about Wick map Radoc?

Sudden conviction descended whole upon her. Wick would leave her. Despite what he had said, despite the passion they shared, despite all her desperate hope.

She would never survive it. Oh, what had she done by letting him into her heart?

Not quite steady, she said, "Certainly I will meet with you and listen to whatever you have to say. I respect both your advice and your judgment."

She shot a glance at Wick, who still refused to look

at her. Her heart thudded with misgiving.

"Come," she told Ivomagus, "back to my hut. We will speak together there."

Chapter Twenty-Eight

"It is not like you, Master Ivomagus, to speak in front of others words that might better be kept private," Verica said as soon as she and the shaman reached her hut. "Have you some objection to Master Wick's presence?"

Ivomagus eyed her, a dark look. A muscle jumped in his cheek. "Upon consideration, I find I have."

"But..." Verica sank down beside the fire, refusing to glance toward the bed where the furs still lay in disarray. She could not let herself think about what had happened there. She could not allow herself to dwell on how much she loved—no, needed—Wick, not if Ivomagus had dire information to share. "Not long since, you told me the gods"—here her lips twisted unpreventably—"sent a man, or a beast, on my behalf."

"I said he came for you. And so he has." Restlessly, Ivomagus took a turn around the room before he joined Verica beside the fire.

"Yet you are not at ease about it." Never one to dance around a subject, Verica demanded, "Have you Seen something more?"

Ivomagus looked at her. "I need not the Sight to see what goes on between the two of you."

"Well." Verica drew back. "Then let us speak of it honestly."

"I am always honest with you, Mistress. And in

this case, I fear you endanger yourself."

"How?"

Ivomagus swallowed convulsively before he said, "You have taken the man to your bed."

Ah, plain and frank talk indeed. Verica flushed. "What bearing has that on the matters at hand?"

"Every bearing." As if he could not help himself, Ivomagus did glance at the bed. "It makes me suspect his motives and, if I may say so, your discernment. Mistress, you are rarely a hasty woman, and yet—"

She interrupted him. "Master Ivomagus, I am indeed a hasty woman. I was hasty when I threw myself at Morirex and hasty when, in the midst of blood and loss, I took over leadership of this tribe. Both, as you know, have cost me dear."

"I do know that." Ivomagus's eyes warmed. "Especially the former. And I would not wish to see it happen again."

"I am aware of the risks, Ivomagus."

Intently, he said, "I cannot help but believe that makes it worse. To knowingly risk your wellbeing once again—"

Verica stared at the shaman in consternation. Did she hear her own doubts issuing from his mouth? Tersely she said, "I am able to look after myself."

"So I did believe," Ivomagus returned with some heat. "But to leap into bed with this man and moreover to take him into your trust so hastily—"

"That is not what I have done."

"It is; you merely cannot see it."

"I do see quite clearly."

"Tell me this, Mistress. Had I come to you a few years ago and warned you against marriage with

Morirex, would you have listened?"

Verica, as honest as he, had to shake her head. "Probably not. I was enthralled." More with the idea of belonging to the fierce war chief than by love—she knew, now, what she'd felt for Morirex had not been love. "But I was a girl then."

"One with faulty judgment."

"Yes."

"I tell you quite frankly, Mistress, I see no difference now."

"But," Verica reiterated, "you are the one who told me he was coming—and for me."

Now Ivomagus flushed with consternation. "I did, and now I am sorry for it. I did not mean for you to fall so readily under his spell. I will admit there is a magic about the man. It enfolds him like an invisible cloak. And you have, as I say, proven yourself susceptible in the past. Morirex also had a—a mystique, though not a magical one. He had power. You may not see what you think you see, Verica."

The use of her name added intimacy to the impact of the shaman's words. Yet Verica retorted, "Is this warning speaking, or jealousy?"

Ivomagus reared back; for an instant Verica thought he would refuse to answer. Honesty, though, won out.

"I am jealous, yes. You know I have feelings for you, Verica. I understand I cannot compete with a man like Wick map Radoc. I am no great warrior, no heir to a chief, no hero. But you can trust me to my dying breath."

"I do know that, and it counts for much. Explain to me, all jealousy aside, why you feel I should not trust

Wick." If Ivomagus had legitimate doubts, she must listen.

Ivomagus's eyes grew hazy, as if he gazed within. He said, "From the very first, there has been something about him—something I cannot quite See. It is wrapped in the magic he carries, and perhaps concealed by it. He is hiding something, some truth about himself. Ask him, Mistress. Ask him before you give him your heart and get hurt again."

Too late for that. But Verica agreed, "I will. And I promise, Ivomagus, I will be as careful as I can both with my emotions and the welfare of this tribe. But I must go north with him—you do see that? If the Gaels return and find us as we are, all but defenseless, wracked by illness and injury, we will go down to defeat. We cannot last another season on our own."

Ivomagus appeared to consider that and nodded. "I say only, before you put any more trust in this man, ask him for the truth."

"I will." She touched Ivomagus's shoulder lightly. "Thank you for your friendship and loyalty." Lost in her own thoughts, she almost did not see the agony in the shaman's eyes.

****

Wick looked up sharply when Verica reentered the chief's dwelling, trying to discern her mood. Lately it seemed he could feel what she felt, catch the ebb, flow, and essence of her thoughts even when she kept from expressing them. He knew where she wanted him to place his mouth when they lay together and where he should touch her with his hand. He knew when passion lit her, when joy—fleeting enough—lifted her. He could see the trouble that now rested on her, as she returned without the shaman.

Tension held her tight, and she did not so much as flick him a glance. The others had continued the discussion in her absence. They'd speculated over the possible success of a delegation, and Cunarda had reiterated her reluctance to go in Ammin's place. Her daughter, Hectia, volunteered to go instead.

They refrained from expressing their curiosity over Ivomagus's behavior, but Wick had few doubts the shaman had warned Verica against him. What had he Seen? Details of Wick's past? The shame he carried?

He did not blame Verica for failing to look at him.

Heat washed through him as he realized their relationship, the warmth that existed between them, must now end. He'd lost her regard, and only in losing it did he truly grasp what it meant to him.

His stomach heaved, and regret seized him. He should have been the one to tell her the truth; he should have done so before ever they lay together. But the pleasure of her company and the admiration in her eyes had been too much to risk.

Now, he'd lost all.

He stared at his hands while young Smerta at last asked the question no one else would.

"What is it, Mistress Verica? What did Ivomagus say to you?"

"Hush," Cunarda chided her daughter. "It may have been something personal and not to be aired before all." Cunarda glanced at Wick. Did his shame show upon him?

Verica gave a short shake of her head.

Wick surged to his feet, a confession nearly bursting from him. Verica did look at him then. Their gazes connected tangibly, and her eyes widened.

"I do not understand—" Smerta began.

"Hush," her mother interrupted again. "Verica, what has been decided about the delegation?"

Verica, releasing Wick from her attention, faced the chief's widow. "We will go. You, me, Motius, and Master Wick if he agrees to accompany us."

Cunarda told her, "If you go, I need to stay and oversee the tribe. Hectia has volunteered to go in my place and represent her father."

Verica gave the girl a sharp glance. "Well enough. The four of us, then—if, as I say, Master Wick is willing."

"I am willing," Wick, still on his feet, told her.

"Then we will leave in the morning."

Wick grunted. One night in which he must tell her the truth. And no doubt destroy her opinion of him.

****

"You are very quiet," Verica said as they prepared for bed some time later. Their goods lay packed for an early morning departure, weapons and as much food as the tribe could spare.

They'd shared a small supper beside Verica's fire, though Wick still felt too tense to eat much. His mind teemed with unexpressed words and questions. What had the shaman told Verica? What did it mean that, having listened to Ivomagus, she still asked him to accompany her on the journey?

Had her heart already changed toward him? Despite the affinity that had blossomed between them, he could not tell. Starkly, he said, "Ivomagus warned you about me, did he not?"

She turned in the act of drawing her tunic over her

head and faced him. Her unbound hair tumbled around her naked shoulders and caressed her small breasts. "Why should you say that?"

Wick swallowed hard. He forced himself to say, "I saw your expression when you came back in."

Her face tensed. She drew on a clean tunic and wrapped her arms around herself. "Wick, is there something you have failed to tell me?"

Meeting the challenge in her blue eyes, bright as a newly painted war shield, he knew he must speak the truth, now if ever—speak and quite possibly destroy all hope of happiness.

Chapter Twenty-Nine

"Tell me what the shaman said to you."

The last light of the day lingered outside Verica's hut. Inside, the fire burned up precious fuel—gathered arduously and at great cost—but lent Wick little comfort. Once before, in the past, he'd shattered his life with an ill-chosen decision. Now he must admit that decision and shatter it again.

Better to go home, face Brude down, demand the return of his tribe, and make things right. Yet how could he, unless he had something of value to offer them? Either the promise of an alliance or a leader worthy of their trust... He might assuage his own shame, but how would that benefit his tribe?

At least tell Verica the truth, he chastised himself. You owe her that, and more.

Yet now he held in his hands her happiness as well as his own. Therein lay the danger of bonding so deeply with someone—a man assumed responsibility for another person's wellbeing. A weight he could no longer bear.

She glanced at him and spread her fingers toward the fire as if seeking to warm them. "I did not tell you this, but Ivomagus foretold your coming."

"What?" Wick felt a chill.

She nodded. "He claimed you would come wrapped in magic and that you came for...for me."

Before Wick could speak, she went on, "Yet now that I've embraced your presence, he turns around and preaches caution. It is the way of the gods, to give with one hand and take with the other."

Ignoring the irony in her voice, Wick asked, "He preaches caution? Against me?"

Verica moved restlessly. She shot Wick another searching look and glanced away again. "He is jealous. He has long made his interest in me plain. But I...I swore never to take another man to my bed." A wry smile twisted her lips. "What do you think of that, Wick map Radoc?"

Wick thought many things. Even now, torn apart by doubt, he ached for her. Had he never had those nights in her bed, in her arms, he might not have survived. Yet he said, "Master Ivomagus is right to warn you against me. Verica, I have not told you everything about myself. There is much you should know." And it would change the way she looked at him, the way she felt about him. It would change everything.

She turned those bright, war-shield eyes on him, and her lips parted. "What is it? Just tell me, Wick. Tell me all. It is worse"—she swallowed convulsively—"worse not knowing."

Wick groaned and closed his eyes against the darkness. "I am not what you suppose, Verica. To begin with, I am no hero."

That hard resistance still bright in her eyes, she said, "But you are. I have seen you fight. I have felt your strength. Why would you deny it now?"

"Because..." Wick swallowed hard. "Because it is a lie. I wish I were a hero, Verica, if only for your sake. I should have told you the truth from the very beginning. But I did not imagine I would do aught save pass through here."

"The truth."

Wick squeezed his eyes closed as if he could shut away what must come. "The need to find help for my tribe is not what took me from home. It is an excuse I made for myself. I left because I could no longer face my lot. I broke, Verica—my will, and my courage."

"What?" Her gaze flew to his now, full on. "I do not understand."

"I abandoned my tribe and all those who depended on me. I fled my responsibilities. I abdicated from all I'd been taught to defend." He delivered the words brutally, so she would have no doubt.

"Abandoned?"

"Deserted my family, my tribe. When they needed me most. When they were pressed, hunted, beaten."

"That's not possible."

"It is."

"But you said you helped your father, the chief, when he was sore injured. You are chief after him."

"So I should have been. It is a duty, yes, a sacred duty, and one I forsook. There was a disagreement, questions about my father's past leadership and mine, how I might take the tribe forward. Instead of staying and facing down my challenger as my father—the bravest man I have ever known—would have done, I placed leadership of the tribe in the hands of him, my challenger, and went off into the wilderness. I went to lick my wounds like the craven excuse for a man that I am."

Verica said nothing. Her fingers curled into fists at her sides.

"You think you know me, Verica, but you do not. I am not worthy of you or of any good woman. You took me into your bed thinking me a valiant warrior, but I am not that, either."

Verica ignored those words. "Why would you…why would you abandon your tribe?"

Indeed, Wick thought, a woman of her mettle, one who had stepped up into her husband's place without thought for herself, would stick at that.

He got to his feet as if prodded by a spear; Verica remained where she sat.

"I doubted myself, my ability to lead. I believe I always had those doubts, even when my father was alive. You did not know my father so cannot imagine. Before his injury, he was strong and vigorous; the day came alive when he rose in the morning. His roar of laughter lit the world. He told me always I'd been born to take the place of chief after him, as his firstborn son, gifted by the god and goddess. But I knew I could never hope to fill such footsteps as his.

"Then—before I was ready, long before I was ready—he was taken down by a Gael's chariot. He very nearly died. Verica, I prayed—how I prayed he would survive. And he did survive, cursing and hollering and flailing against the pain and the damage to his flesh. My mother pulled him through with her faith and her magic. With her love. He survived but was never the same.

"Someone might have replaced him then, as chief. But his grip on the hearts of the tribesfolk remained too strong. They begged him to continue leading them, first from his bed and then from a litter. But…he could no longer perform the role of warrior."

"How old were you?" Verica asked.

"Just turned sixteen. Old enough, you might say. My brother, Taloc, is younger than that now, and he is strong. The goddess knows my sister, Barta, itches to lead."

"But not you?"

Wick shook his head. "Barta should have been a son and the first born. She is most like Father. They butted heads constantly. He and I did not. I acted as bidden."

"And grew into the place?" Verica prompted.

"I am certain folk believed that I did. I often heard them congratulate my father on having such a fine and dutiful son. I had the muscle for the place, yes. But not—not the heart."

Verica said nothing. She wrapped her arms around herself and held hard.

She is withdrawing from me. I can feel it. Grief washed over Wick in a wave. Doggedly, he went on. "I turned into a decent enough warrior. It was the other part of it that daunted me—the responsibility. Decisions I had to make had heavy consequences. I saw how the rash decisions my sister made played out. They cost the lives of people for whom we cared.

"And then came the attack that resulted in my parents' deaths and Tally's injury. The Gaels overran us. Fired many of the huts. My mother died, and my father—" Wick's voice broke. "He spent himself defending her despite his infirmities. His good hound, Bright, gave her life to protect Tally. That, Verica, is valiance." Turning back to the fire, he seized her arms and forced her to look at him. "Not what you see before you or what you supposed me to be."

She shuddered, as telling a reaction as Wick could imagine.

Pain hit him like a mortal wound. If he could change the past—change the man he was at that moment—he would. Yet he could only stand and stare into her shuttered face.

Fumbling for words, her lips moving silently before they came, she asked, "But what had that raid to do with you? Gaels attack ceaselessly. It is what they do, what they are."

"Who do you think it was had responsibility for protecting the settlement that night? Who set the guard? Who held the faith of those he loved, charged with defending them? Not my sister, whom I criticized so harshly. I gave the orders. I chose the men on watch."

In a harsh whisper she offered, "None of us is faultless."

"But do you not see, Verica, that is what a chief should—must—be? And I failed. I failed those I love more than I love my own life."

He never realized he wept until he felt the wetness on his cheeks. "All my life my parents taught me what a Caledonian chief should be, taught me not by lessons but by example: valiant and wise. Valiant like Father and wise like Mother. They would be bitterly ashamed of me."

He felt that shame for himself. Suddenly he could no longer remain beside this woman, she with the courageous heart. He turned from her, caught up his cloak, and moved toward the door.

"Wait," Verica said.

He froze. His heart shuddered on a thread of hope, even though he knew he had already lost her.

"You have not told the rest of it, how you came to leave your folk."

"I have told you. I handed over leadership of the tribe to Brude. I broke, Verica—and that is the truth of it."

"And that meant you had to leave?"

Wick smiled harshly. "You cannot fathom it, can you? My sister begged me to stay, but I had nothing left to offer my tribe, Verica. Nothing. I should have told you at once what I was: a sham, a lie, and not worthy of your regard. I should have left before ever I came to your bed."

"You tried." What did he hear in her voice? Irony? Disgust?

By the goddess, he could bear anything but her disgust.

"It was I who dragged you back," she admitted heavily. "I wanted what I wanted."

"And now you pay the price. I am sorry, Verica. You deserve better. You would fare better with the shaman—he is an honorable man."

Fully dressed at last, he left her sitting in the hut, there in the dark, and fled into the gray light of the gloaming.

Chapter Thirty

Verica sat perfectly still beside the fire after Wick left the hut. Not a sound disturbed the ensuing silence, no voices or footsteps could be heard outside, not so much as the distant wail of a child. Wick had disappeared as if he never existed.

But he did exist, this man she'd let into her heart like no other. If she closed her eyes, she could still feel his palm sliding up her thigh and the heat of him when he filled her. His scent lingered in the hut.

Everything else, though, had changed. She could not deny that it had. He'd arrived on a stream of magic, a hero and potential savior, a man finer than any she'd ever known.

Certainly better than Morirex, with his cruelty and his harsh sense of duty. Better than Ammin, with his single-mindedness. Or than Ivomagus with his mystical preoccupations. The other Caerena warriors and their willingness to let her lead. She'd believed Wick to be worthy of her heart.

And now by his own admission he declared himself unworthy. And her heart—her heart did not know what to feel.

She could sympathize with his tale of a young man struggling beneath the expectations of a father he idolized. They all struggled. She could even understand his desire to flee. Had she not experienced that desire also, especially when Morirex used her body so carelessly?

But Wick had gone through with it, turned his back on those who needed him, and not just to secure the help that might allow them to survive.

She heard his voice again, rough with distress. *I broke, Verica, and that is the truth of it.*

She felt her heart break also, shattering inside her chest. What was wrong with her that she made such disastrous choices in her men? Why did she look at a man—at Morirex and now at Wick—and see what was not there? An admirable warrior where lurked a cruel abuser, a savior where lurked a shirker?

She'd been so certain this time, sure even before she took Wick to her bed. She'd been convinced he'd come not only to save the Caerena but to save her. To set her alive, allow her to love after her terrible blunder of choosing Morirex.

Another blunder. But what of the way she'd healed since taking Wick to her bed? Her wounds had closed miraculously; new skin grew at an astounding rate, and she'd nearly forgotten she carried wounds.

She'd begun to forget the pain of both body and spirit.

Whether or not Wick map Radoc's honor remained bright, no one could deny he did carry a whisper of magic.

Tears came to her eyes then, on a wave of disappointment and regret. What to do with the ache that filled her? She rarely cried and had not shed a tear when Morirex died. Not since first they wed and she realized just what she'd taken on had she wept hot tears. Not even when Morirex forced her had she let herself break down.

She could not afford weakness; the tribe could not afford it. Not even when she'd chosen the wrong path—so disastrously—again.

And what now? She still had deep feelings for Wick; they had connected deeply and fiercely. She could no more dismiss that out of hand than stop breathing.

And they were meant to depart for the north together, come morning.

That thought got her out of bed, shivering in the cold pre-dawn. She moved to the door in Wick's wake and pushed the curtain aside.

Gray light filled the settlement, sifting through the bare branches of the trees overhead, darker in the west. No one stirred, save the guard. The ground, a slushy mess of footprints, gave no hint of which way Wick might have gone.

Yet the guard must have seen him go.

She turned her head, searching. One of their youngest men, Tamus, caught her eye from his station at the edge of the trees. Hastily she went to him.

"Tamus, did you see Master Wick pass by?"

Tamus's dark eyes searched her face curiously; she wondered what he saw there. "Yes, Mistress."

"Which way did he go?" Surely he hadn't left—run again? He'd taken his cloak, but his pack remained back at her hut.

Tamus shrugged. "The midden, perhaps?"

"Ah." And thence, where?

Tamus said nothing. Did he, like everyone else, know she'd taken Wick to her bed? Did he think they'd quarreled? She lacked the patience to feel humiliated.

She hunched her shoulders, feeling the weight of the young man's gaze follow her as she took the well-worn path through the trees. She'd stopped caring what folk thought of her, back when she took up Morirex's position. She could not let herself mind now.

Yet no tall, muscular figure lingered at the midden, and she saw him nowhere among the trees. As she had once before, she began walking the perimeter of the settlement, looking for tracks leading away, but saw only the marks of deer in the snow.

She tramped on, heart aching, and found herself mouthing words—praying, she who no longer believed. *Only let me find him. Do not let him disappear as mysteriously as he arrived.*

She spotted him at last in the very first place she should have looked—the same spot near the edge of the settlement where she'd caught up with him last time.

He stood motionless, his head raised as if he listened, dark auburn head bare and gleaming with red in the low light.

Hearing the crunch of her footsteps, he turned to look at her, but this time, for once, their gazes failed to reach, meet, and hold.

Instead he glanced at her mouth, at her throat and her breast, before he looked away.

Verica's heart broke into still smaller pieces. If I keep this up, she thought, it will be dust.

Anger rushed to fill the void. She marched up to him and demanded, "Were you going to go, leave without another word?"

He shook his head; his misery flowed out and engulfed her, knocking her anger down.

One did not seek to hurt where one loved. She still

loved him; that she could not deny.

Yet the pain had a tongue of its own. "We are supposed to leave on a journey come morning. Will you abandon that also? Will you abandon me?"

"Verica—" He got no farther before his voice cracked.

She stepped up to him. "Listen to me. Look at me."

He turned and faced her. His dark eyes—deep, magical eyes—did meet hers then, though she could feel his reluctance. What did she see there? Cursed if she could tell.

He said, "Let me go. I have hurt you enough."

Let me go. She didn't know if she could.

"Listen to me," she repeated. "I know you, Wick map Radoc, perhaps better than you know yourself. I have learned you since you came. I have stood beside you in battle. I know you for no coward."

He made a strangled sound. "Fighting in battle is easy. Taking wounds, shedding blood, that is nothing. Valiance, Verica, is all about sacrifice. You know that."

"Sacrifice, like your father's."

"Yes." Emotion flared in his eyes. "And like yours. We both know I am not worthy of you." He said again, "Let me go."

"To do what? Disappear into the forest? Wander on and on until you lose yourself completely?"

She reached out to touch him, thought better of it, and withdrew her hand. "And what of all that lies between us? You cannot deny there is a connection. I dare you to deny it."

"I cannot."

"It is deep and…and sustaining. I feel at peace in your company. You have healed my wounds—quite truly healed them. I trust you as no one else, ever."

"Trusted me," he corrected. "I have destroyed that now."

Had he? Despite her sense of betrayal, Verica still wanted to touch him, craved the sensation of warmth, the belonging that rushed over her when they made contact.

Raggedly she told him, "I don't claim to understand why you acted the way you did, why you let down those who trusted you. But I believe you will not do that now. I need you to go with me, Wick, and help me convince Chief Enestimus he should enter into an alliance with us. For the sake of all that we have shared, will you not at least remain with me long enough to fulfill that commitment?"

He raised his eyes to hers again. Beneath the misery—beneath the shame—she saw her answer, and she breathed again.

****

They barely spoke to one another during that journey. The four of them moved silently through the gray winter gloom of the forest, very like a small herd of deer. Even Hectia and Motius communicated but rarely and in whispers. Wick's grave, restrained mood touched them all.

They followed no trail save that of the deer, which seemed to lead in the required direction. Wick studied it with care before signaling the group on. After a day and a half's hard tramping, they came upon the first settlement, burned and lying in ruins.

"Wait." Wick's arm came out and barred Verica's way before she could push past him. "It may not be safe."

That said, he moved off soundlessly, spear drawn at the ready, while the rest of them paused and Verica's apprehension spiked. He endangered himself so readily, this man who denied all claim to courage.

Soon he reappeared and waved an arm for them to join him.

"No one here," he concluded. "No fresh tracks— only those of the deer that have skirted the place. And these marks of burning are old."

"This was the Ongust settlement," Hectia said. "Father had good relations with their chief at one time." She told Wick, "The Dimitii will be farther on, unless they have also been chased off."

"The Gaels lie all around us," Verica breathed. "They must have pushed in clear to the Moray. If Enestimus has fallen, we will have no choice but to move away east—now, while we can."

"This place gives me the willies," Motius shivered. "It feels dead. Let us move on."

Hectia nodded. "Chief Enestimus's lands should be due northeast."

Wick grunted. "Then it seems we must continue following the deer."

****

Verica dreamed. Wrapped alone in her skins and blanket, she imagined she lay instead in Wick's arms. Drowsy with warmth and comfort, she reached for his mouth; the glorious sensation of belonging that always found her in his company washed through her, slow and languorous.

Then all too suddenly the dream changed.

They ran. Wick pounded along beside her; she could feel his presence like a flash of light, just to her left. Emotions spiked inside her, distress and alarm. She felt the fluid throb of her muscles working, heat rising from her hide, the wild rhythm of her hooves striking the ground.

She was a deer pursued. And she ran.

She heard the hunters coming behind, crashing through the wood the way men always did, revealing themselves with careless disregard. Her nostrils flared; she could smell them, a raw, ugly scent.

They had already taken the other members of her herd—her family—one by one. So few now remained, only a small group of souls like points of light in darkness. He who made up the other half of her being—he without whom she could not live—remained at her side.

Her nostrils flared again. She smelled death on the wind. One of the pursuers loosed a bolt, the same kind of flying missile that had already taken down so many of her herd.

She leaped, knowing she must defend her partner, her mate. Nothing mattered at that moment but that he should continue to exist, to run free through the forest and through her spirit. But he leaped also, without thought for his own safety, and when the bolt found flesh the pain flashed so bright she could not tell into whose skin, bone, and muscle the arrowhead tore—his, or her own.

Chapter Thirty-One

They encountered members of the Dimitii guard well before they reached the settlement—a good sign, Verica thought. The two men who intercepted them were young, surely no older than Hectia, and when she explained the reason for the Caerena party's presence, they agreed to conduct them to their Dimitii chief.

"So the Caerena are holding on?" one of them asked as they moved through a group of structures that bore clear signs of attack. Several huts stood damaged, and the residents—few enough in number—gathered to stare as the Caerena group went by. "We did wonder."

The chief's house, when they reached it, bore marks of recent damage. Verica had seen Chief Enestimus but once, and that from a distance. The man who turned to face them now did not resemble him. Enestimus had been a broad man, well into his middle years, with a scowling, heavy face. This fellow, taller and of a narrower build, looked as young as the guards.

"Chief Enestimus?" Verica asked uncertainly.

The young man's face cleared. He had steady eyes of clear, light brown, not unlike Ivomagus's, and a handsome, heavily tattooed face.

"My father, Chief Enestimus, perished last spring." He grimaced. "I am his son, Caltram, chief of the Dimitii."

Verica bowed her head. "I am Verica, war chief

and acting leader of the Caerena. This is Hectia, daughter of our former chief, Ammin, along with one of our foremost warriors, called Motius, and this…is Wick map Radoc of the tribe Epidii."

"The Epidii?" Caltram raised his brows. "Master Wick, you are indeed far from home. But please to sit, all of you. Allow me to offer what hospitality I may. We have not much at this season, but all I possess is at your command."

A warm welcome, and no mistake. Verica wondered if they would have received as ready a reception from Chief Enestimus.

"So," she said when they had all settled beside the fire, "you are as hard-pressed here in the north as are the rest of us who hold the western doorway to Caledonia."

Caltram made a gesture with his hands as if to say, *What else, with these Gaels?* He studied each member of the party with his clever eyes before he said, "As you see."

A woman appeared from the rear of the dwelling; Chief Caltram introduced her as his mother, Maerta. She moved about preparing food and drink.

Chief Caltram settled his gaze on Hectia. "You have my condolences on the death of your father," he told her directly. "From all I ever heard, he was a strong leader and a good man."

Tears flooded Hectia's eyes. "We live with loss each day, Chief Caltram, and fight on. But we find we can no longer put up a good fight on our own. We are too fractured, too reduced in numbers and supplies. So we come to you, in hope of forming an alliance."

Caltram quirked an eyebrow and glanced at his

mother before he said, "An alliance, eh? I cannot say but I have considered seeking to make the same offer, could I but catch my breath long enough. My father never countenanced it, you understand. He was fiercely independent and insisted the Dimitii should keep to their own lands, and defend them." His lips tightened bitterly. "You can see how that has cost us."

Tentatively, Verica said, "You took his place upon his death?" She wondered what Wick made of that. This man, far younger than he, had stepped into formidable footprints indeed. She shot Wick a look, but he sat quietly, his eyes blank.

Caltram nodded. "There was no other choice. It was take a stand or flee eastward like frightened rabbits. You do realize all the other tribes around us have been chased off, this past season. The Gaels have made deeper strides into our territories than ever before. Does anyone remain standing between here and Caerena?"

Now Verica grimaced. "We encountered only ruin on our way north. And during the fighting season, as you say, we had no time to put out feelers and discover who survived."

"My father would never forgive us if we failed to stand. So we remain, even though the absence of the other tribes only makes the fight harder. Come spring, the Gaels will have fewer targets and will throw all their might against us."

His mother, pausing beside the group, asked, "And what then?"

"I fear," Hectia answered, "we may all perish. There will be nothing left of the tribes, save whispers and memories."

Caltram's look at her was frankly admiring. "We

cannot allow that to happen, can we, Mistress?"

"No."

"Mistress Hectia, you come clad like a warrior. Do you fight against the Gaels?"

"I do. Mistress Verica did learn the skills of combat from her husband; she taught me and my two sisters to stand with her. One of my sisters, Cinta, fell in a raid not two months since. Smerta and I remain."

"Most admirable. And you, Master Wick, have come north seeking to gain help from other Caledonian tribes?" Not waiting for Wick's acknowledgement, he went on, "It is a course we tribesmen have been all too reluctant to follow." Again he glanced at his mother. "Perhaps it is time for that to change. I will listen to what you have to say, and then, perhaps, we can see how to ransom the future."

****

Stars shone through the bare branches of the trees that enclosed the Dimitii settlement, looking like bright eyes peering down. Wick, standing alone and taking in deep breaths of air to steady himself, suddenly thought of his father's war hound, Bright, whose eyes had gleamed in just that way, with devotion.

Perhaps, he thought, it was devotion and not courage that he lacked. As he'd told Verica, risking harm to his flesh came easy. But a valiant man gave of both body and spirit, unstinting.

Like young Caltram. There, if ever Wick needed to see one, lay an example of what a Caledonian chief should be. Caltram seemed fully prepared to form an alliance with them, which meant the Caerena would receive the help they needed. Wick might even persuade them to extend it south to the Epidii, before he moved on.

If he secured help for his tribe, then perhaps he might persuade himself he'd achieved something of worth.

Would his mother then forgive him? Would his father—now far beyond this realm of pain and struggle—cease to be ashamed of him?

Would it be enough?

A shadow moved beside him, the merest suggestion of presence. It might have been anyone, a Dimitii tribe member or a spirit. He knew her by the way his body came to attention; his very skin prickled with awareness.

"Wick, are you all right?"

Was he? Far from it. But he could not deny things had come clear in his mind, as clear as these stars that shone down.

Instead of answering her, he said, "A good and profitable meeting with Chief Caltram this day."

"It was, yes. He proved so much more receptive than Enestimus might have." She paused, and Wick felt her consciousness probe his emotions in the dark. "He has some two score fighting men. Combined with ours and yours, we might well make a decent stand."

"Yes." How to tell her he would not be there when that happened? He felt he'd fulfilled his debt to the goddess—stayed with Verica long enough to heal her and secure the help her tribe needed. Now he must free her to find something—someone—better. Anyway, given what he'd told Verica of himself, he doubted she would want him with her any longer.

She mused on, "Did you see the way young Chief Caltram looked at Hectia?"

Laura Strickland

Wick had. "He admires her."

"He has no wife as yet. And marriage makes a good way to unite tribes, so long as love is also involved. I feel hopeful."

"I am glad of that."

"Wick? Wick, look at me." Her fingers closed on his wrist and she tugged him around to face her. "I've been aching all day to speak with you. I have done nothing but think since you—since you explained to me the circumstances of your departure from home. And I need to say the ties of love are not easily broken despite...despite what we perceive as failings. You have stumbled in dealing with your tribe, I see that. But I love you, Wick map Radoc. I love you. And love forgives."

The breath caught in Wick's lungs and pain blossomed as if a bolt had penetrated his heart. She did not understand, though he'd tried so hard to explain—he did not need her forgiveness, but his own.

And that he did not know how to attain.

With passionate intensity, she said, "Let us put the past behind us. Let us form this alliance, and you can go back—back to your tribe, bringing them the help they need."

"And become their savior? Their hero?"

"Yes."

"And yours? Tell me, Verica, what estimation will I hold in your heart and mind?"

"I cannot live without you." Her voice broke. "I do not want to."

Wick closed his eyes for an instant, shutting away her beautiful face and the anguish in her eyes.

"Did you hear nothing I told you? You deserve

better. You deserve a man worthy of your courage and honor."

"I heard. I heard all you said, and I admit it is a bitter draught to swallow. But Wick, you cannot deny this deep connection between us. I felt it from the very first, and it has strengthened each time we touch, each time we lie together. And I ask myself, why else would you stay with me but for the sake of love?"

"Why else?" The pain inside him now sharpened beyond that of any wound he'd ever carried—pain not for himself but for her. He knew how much he loved her, more than his own breath. But if he'd learned anything from his father, from Bright and all the others who'd gone before him, it was that love equaled sacrifice.

Let him, if ever, do one fine thing—and free her if he could.

He put an ironic edge in his voice when he said, "You thought I loved you? Just because I lay with you and let you keep me warm those few nights? Because our bodies fit well together and you imagined something beyond the pleasure of physical joining?"

"Because..." Her voice faltered. "Because when I asked it of you, you stayed with me. Does that not argue you love me, even as I love you?"

He could not look at her. He stared instead away into the distance and hardened his heart. "It does not," he told her starkly. "I stayed only because the goddess bade me do so, in order to repay a debt I owed her. That debt is now paid. And I declare myself free of you."

He felt her react as if he'd struck her hard; her hand fell from his arm, and her spirit flinched. He'd never before been deliberately cruel to anyone—but in this case he deemed it a kindness.

She took a decided step backward, staring at him as at a stranger.

He bared his lips in a terrible smile. "I must thank you, Mistress. Your favor was strong, and I enjoyed my time in your bed. But if you think that means I love you, you are sadly mistaken."

She hissed, a sound that struck at him out of the darkness. It contained no anger, only grief, and he felt that rush at him also, like the cuts from a thousand knives.

As for his own grief, deep and dark and terrifying, it was no more than he deserved.

Chapter Thirty-Two

"Chief Caltram is a fascinating man. We sat up together most of the night, even long after his mother retired to her bed and Motius went off to his, and we talked—just talked of so many things. His past and mine, the future and what we must do to survive."

Hectia rattled on to Verica as the two women washed and dressed themselves for the day, but Verica barely listened.

"I do think we are fortunate in dealing with him rather than Chief Enestimus. Not but I grieve for Caltram's loss of his father. We have all lost so much."

"We have." Verica thought of Wick standing in the starlight with a look such as she'd never seen before on his face. Her stomach roiled, and the pain in her head increased. How could she have bared her heart to him that way, only to discover he did not truly want her?

But she'd felt so certain about Wick. She'd felt safe with him, safe and cherished. How could her senses, her intuition, have lied to her so flagrantly?

"What is it, Mistress Verica? You look unwell."

"I feel unwell."

"Perhaps something you ate last night has disagreed with you," Hectia suggested.

"Perhaps." She'd half expected Wick would be gone when she rose this morning following a night spent tossing alone on her pallet. But she'd caught a

245

glimpse of him only moments ago on the far side of the settlement, speaking with Motius.

Her traitorous body had leaped in response; her blood rushed helplessly through her veins, and her palms itched with longing to touch him.

Which just proved what a fool she was.

No more. Had she no self-respect? He did not want her.

Just like Morirex. Once again she'd built up a lie in her mind, in her heart, and sold it to herself.

A mysterious man appears out of nowhere wrapped in magic, with dark eyes in which a woman could lose herself and a body to make her mouth water. She wondered why he'd been bidden to stay with her—a debt to the goddess, he claimed, though he hadn't said what kind. It had not been, as she'd supposed, to enjoy the pleasures of her bed, her mouth upon him everywhere.

His mouth on her.

"You do think it a good decision, this alliance?" Hectia's plaintive voice recalled Verica from her nauseating thoughts. She shook herself mentally and turned to the girl.

"I do. The Dimitii and the Caerena will be much stronger together than alone."

"And the Epidii? You and Master Wick will remain allied also?" Hectia blushed. "Caltram did mention when we spoke last night how firm a bond marriage might prove. If you and Master Wick were to form such a union…"

"That will not happen."

"But why not, Verica? I've seen the way you look at him, and I am happy for you, in truth I am. It was not right, the way Morirex treated you. You deserve better."

Did she? Ah, but perhaps the cruel goddess, on whom she'd turned her back, dealt her what she truly deserved.

"And," Hectia went on in a hushed tone, "everyone knows you and Master Wick have been sharing a bed since soon after he arrived."

Yes, and she knew they knew—and had not cared. Her passion for him burned too bright to allow for discretion.

Carefully she said, "I think Master Wick intends to leave us as soon as he can."

"To return to his people, you mean? Well, that is understandable. But it would be a terrible loss to us, should you choose to accompany him."

"I do not see myself accompanying him."

"Yes, well, many things we do not foresee may yet happen. When Nactovus died, I thought I'd never be happy again. Neither did I think I might form a marriage alliance with the son of Chief Enestimus, of all people. It is as Mother always says, we cannot know the future."

A blessing. Else, how would Verica be able to go on?

****

Wick glanced up precisely as if someone had called his name and caught Verica's gaze on him from across the clearing. Funny how he could feel her regard, like a call to his spirit. He shrugged his shoulders, trying to dismiss the sensation.

He'd paced the camp most of last night, making no attempt at sleep, while remorse and regret beleaguered him in equal measures. What they'd shared had not been a conversation so much as an attack, on his part. He'd set out to hurt her—to save her—and had succeeded. She would want nothing to do with him now. No kisses, no trusting glances, no rush of need. But he lied, for the need still rode him hard.

He had to get away. But for all his tramping last night and the suspicious looks from Caltram's guard, he had not been able to make himself take up his gear and go.

He'd appealed to the goddess, begged her even as he'd done before for help and advice. Every plea met with silence.

The goddess had not miraculously appeared and bidden him remain with Verica; neither had she bidden him go. It must, he knew, be his decision. And he'd proven to be miserably lacking, had he not, in making such decisions?

Now he and Motius stood beside the cook pots, where they'd been offered breakfast—a prospect that turned Wick's stomach, though Motius eagerly accepted his portion. Motius spent some moments joking with the pretty girl who tended the kettle before turning to Wick, grease still on his chin.

"What are Mistress Verica's plans, eh? Do you know how long we'll stay here?" He nudged Wick with an elbow. "I would not mind growing better acquainted with some of these folk."

"Chief Caltram has requested another meeting, to decide how best we may aid each other."

"Yet another meeting? When?"

"I do not know. You will need to speak with Mistress Verica."

"I will go ask her now. Coming?"

Wick shook his head and stood watching as Motius approached Verica, standing on the far side of the settlement near the hut where she'd slept. He choked down his breakfast, food being too precious to waste, and returned his bowl to the girl tending the pot.

He must attend this meeting, though he did not begin to know how he'd face Verica.

In the end, it proved less difficult than he feared; young Chief Caltram summoned them all back to his dwelling, where they sat in discussion with Caltram's mother and several of his elder advisors.

Many things were decided during that meeting, among them that the three remaining westernmost tribes of the Caledonii—the Caerena, the Dimitii, and the Epidii—would form an alliance to stand against the Gaels. That Caltram would journey south to Caerena lands and speak with Hectia's mother, making plans for the future. That a marriage alliance between the two tribes should be considered.

Through it all, Verica never so much as glanced at Wick. Indeed, the two of them sat on opposite sides of the fire like strangers. She let Caltram lead the discussion, speaking and contributing only when asked a direct question. Wick spoke not at all, but his silence allayed none of his discomfort. He could still feel Verica's tension and unhappiness.

Better, he told himself over and over again—better that he hurt her now, with a lie, than fail her later. Better he bore the pain of this wound than live with the change in her regard. For yes, she claimed she still loved him. But in his heart he knew love and shame made poor bedfellows.

After the meeting, Hectia remained with Caltram and his mother. The rest of them filed out in ones and twos. Wick found himself at Verica's side. "A word, Mistress, if you please."

"Another word?" She did look at him then, her deep blue eyes guarded. "Are you certain you can spare me that?"

Wick stared at his hands, at the ground. Coward, he flailed himself. But what more did he expect?

"I wanted to tell you, I mean to accompany the party back to Caerena, and make certain of the alliance on behalf of the Epidii. Then I will depart."

"Return home to your people?" she questioned.

He shook his head and gestured with a wide sweep of his arm. "Off. Away."

Her expression grew hard, and he fancied he glimpsed the disparagement he'd dreaded seeing. "Why not return to your tribe with news of the help they need? Will they not be happy to welcome you home?"

"I don't know." He swallowed with difficulty. "Brude has assumed leadership there. If the tribe has accepted a new chief, they will not wish me pushing my way back in."

She turned away. "Do as you will."

"Verica, wait. I would request a favor."

"A favor?" She swung back half way. "You dare ask that of me?"

"Not for my own sake, I promise you."

"Speak, then."

"If I do not return south, will you assure the alliance is carried to the Epidii, to Brude and my sister, Barta?"

Her chin came up in a fierce gesture. "Why should

I? You can carry your own alliance."

"Please, Verica. They are desperate for help, and it will serve all three tribes, the Caerena not least of all. Three are stronger than one."

"So are two," she retorted, "a fact you seem all too able to dismiss."

Chapter Thirty-Three

Later, Wick never remembered the start of that journey. He knew they traveled south and westward, a band of seven, Caltram having brought along two of his warriors. He knew the day sparked cold with the scent of snow on the wind and that, once again, Verica refused to look at him. A fog wrapped around his mind, one that did not serve to protect him from the pain.

Distraction, as his father had well taught him, always cost a warrior and cost him dear. He remembered Radoc railing at him over it, urging constant vigilance.

It certainly cost him now. The attack came at the end of their first day's travel, when weariness and discouragement rode him hard.

Caltram and Hectia had been chatting most the day, like the oldest of friends, while the rest of them walked in silence. Caltram's two men brought up the rear and were first to fall to the savage blades of their attackers.

Wick's long knife came instantly to his hand even as he counted the number of Gaels closing in upon them. He dimly registered the weapons they carried along with a bag of game—a hunting party they must be, that had picked up the Caledonians' trail.

His first thought after that was for Verica. Even as the foremost of the Gaelic warriors bore down on him, he spared her a glance where she spun, separated from him by the rest of their party. She had her weapon out, head up and nostrils flaring like those of a war pony.

He should be at her side. He should defend her even if it cost him his life.

Part of his mind noted that Caltram had also sprung to readiness and stepped out in front of Hectia. He saw Motius go down in a shower of blood, his head separated from his body, and then all reasoning thought fled.

His body knew what to do, how to battle, even if his heart strained only toward Verica. His muscles responded to the demands of instinct, as one of the Gaels—a tall man with wild eyes and yellow streaks in his brown hair—engaged him. Battle, as he'd told Verica, did not frighten him, but the consequences of losing did.

Would he ever see home again? Tally, Barta, his parents' graves…

He felled his opponent swiftly and turned to face another. He whispered a prayer to the goddess, not for himself.

Protect her.

His second opponent went down.

Did he fight his way toward Verica, or she to him? He saw only a red haze of blood, heard only cries of defiance and glee, but he could feel her spirit all the while, reaching, reaching for him.

And then everything stopped. He stood in the reddened snow, blood dripping down one arm and a bright warning crying aloud in his head.

Verica.

He blinked and his vision cleared. He saw her held fast in the arms of a Gaelic warrior with bared teeth—

captive—a bloodied blade drawn to her throat.

"Toss down your weapon, mighty Blue Man, or she dies."

Wick barely recognized the words spoken in his own tongue, so badly did the speaker mangle them. He stood arrested with the breath whooping in his lungs, trying desperately to assess the situation.

Motius lay dead on the ground, along with two of the Gaels, both killed by Wick's blade. Another Gael sprawled near where Verica had fought, nursing a badly slashed arm.

Of Caltram and Hectia, there was no sight. Had they too fallen? With narrowed eyes, Wick counted bodies again. No. Gone as if by magic.

He looked at Verica, held hard against her captor, straining so severely at the insistence of the Gael's blade that her head touched the man's shoulder. She bore a slash to one forearm and another to her cheek. Her gaze, unnaturally blue in the dying light, reached for Wick and her breast heaved.

Everything he did now—each move, each step— must be for her sake. Only her survival mattered. He had, in essence, ceased to exist.

"Well, now." Verica's captor spoke again, teeth flashing in a cruel grimace. "You never know what you will flush while out hunting."

He shouted at his men in their own tongue. The wounded man near Verica's feet struggled up, and the other two moved to his side. Two down, dead—where had the rest of the band gone?

The Gaels' leader gave orders Wick could not understand. The men moved in on him and roughly wrested his weapons away. His hands were bound behind his back, so tight the leather bit into the flesh, all while Verica watched, still with the filthy blade at her throat.

It would take nothing more than a twitch of that blade to end her life. And to steal all meaning from Wick's.

Goddess, please. He had never wanted anything so much, not since he'd cradled his mother's dead body in his arms.

He could not lose Verica, with her strength and passion, with her flagrant courage. *Anything else.*

One of the Gaels grunted and shoved Wick hard. It took no real comprehension to guess that he ordered them to move.

Wick turned his eyes on Motius's body, lying headless in the red snow; he searched the trees around them for the others, while trying to pretend he did not.

Captive. He cursed bitterly as Verica's weapons were also stripped from her and her wrists bound. The Gaels pushed her into line beside him. Had they any hope? Had Caltram and Hectia made it away? If so, might they follow and attempt to free Verica?

He, Wick map Radoc, might as well be abandoned as a lost cause. He had failed once again to protect what meant the world to him and so deserved nothing more.

****

Verica struggled to fight down the sickness that rose in her gut, to keep her legs from collapsing beneath her. It would be far too humiliating to show any weakness in front of these beasts.

But the reek coming off them did not help, nor did her terror or the pain from her wounds. Motius, dead. And Wick—how badly wounded was he?

She'd caught glimpses of him during the fight just past, battling like a man possessed and taking down two of their attackers in swift succession. He'd fought with absolutely no regard for himself. She'd never seen anyone battle so, not even Morirex.

Nor had she ever feared so for Morirex, feared for him and beseeched his preservation from a goddess in which she no longer believed...

She had never loved her husband as she did this man beside her.

The anger she'd felt toward Wick, the frustration and wild sense of betrayal—all that had evaporated, as if it never existed, in her terror for him. Now, herded by the Gaels at a cruel pace, bleeding and stumbling, the connection between them still held.

The love, as she'd tried to tell him back among the trees of the Dimitii settlement, remained.

Yet hope did not. Capture, as Verica well knew, made for a bad outcome, even worse than death. In the hands of their enemies, they might suffer any terrible fate. Would she have to watch Wick die? And what might they do to her, a woman robbed of the ability to fight back?

Rape, most probably. Rape followed by the lowest form of slavery. At the moment, stumbling over her own feet through the snow, she barely cared. If Wick died, it would no longer matter what happened to her.

She stole a look at him, hustled forward at sword point beside her, and marked the blood that trickled down his arm, down his face. She saw the grim line of his profile and felt her heart shudder within. So this was love. Not what she'd felt in the beginning for Morirex, not even for her parents, now gone—that had been, respectively, attraction and deep, abiding affection. This emotion possessed her, allowing no barriers and no excuses, caring for nothing save the welfare of this one man with all his faults, all his strengths and weaknesses. They might well be robbed of hope, but the love she felt for Wick would remain with her through every horror to come, strong as her heart's blood.

She stumbled again as the party suddenly halted. Two more Gaelic warriors appeared through the trees—the balance of the party now rejoined them. Where had they been? Verica shook her head and strained her ears to follow as they spoke rapidly in their own tongue. One of the men gestured to the forest behind him, and the Gaelic leader scowled heavily.

Verica's heart leaped. Had Hectia and Caltram got away? She remembered seeing Caltram thrust Hectia behind him during the fight. Then Caltram had battled—they had all battled, and Verica lost track of them. Wick had fought so hard after Motius went down, no one could get near. Had Caltram used that opportunity to get Hectia away? If so, could the pair of them do anything to help her and Wick?

Oh, traitorous heart that wanted to keep hoping, that longed even to pray to a deity who had never before taken her part!

The Gaelic leader railed at his men. In that moment's distraction, Wick turned his head and looked at Verica. She felt his gaze touch her torn cheek like a caress, and felt the sorrow and regret in his dark eyes as if they were her own.

Her lips formed a word. "Hectia?"

"Flown."

Someone pushed Verica from behind. She stumbled, barely catching herself from sprawling. They moved on.

And on.

How long the forced march lasted, she could not say. It became an exercise in endurance that required every shred of strength Verica had ever possessed. Her wounds bled, but she worried more about the blood still flowing down Wick's arm and over his bound hands, where it dripped from his clenched fists. They walked through unbroken snow toward a dying sun. When the light remained as only a streak of gold through the naked trees, Verica smelled smoke and sensed movement ahead.

Propelled by another shove between the shoulder blades, she plummeted forward and into the Gaels' encampment.

Her stunned, stunted senses fumbled in an effort to grasp what she saw. The camp, not large, sprawled like a dirty bruise beneath the trees, no more than three skin shelters amid a welter of stained and trampled snow. Surely nothing more than a hunting camp or, at most, a winter outpost.

The occupants came hurrying out, calling to one another and hollering in their ugly tongue. Verica and Wick were once more propelled forward forcefully.

Disgust turned her stomach, along with undeniable fear. She could feel Wick's anger—it burgeoned up through him accompanied by protest and frustration. Would these westerners kill him at once before using her as they willed? But if they'd meant to slaughter him, surely it would have happened back where Motius died.

The Gaels conversed rapidly among themselves, and Verica struggled to make sense of it. The man she'd thought to be their leader proved not—another, taller man with an air of authority listened to all he had to say and questioned him further, all while she strove desperately to understand something, anything.

Then the tall man sauntered forward to examine both Verica and Wick. He touched Verica on her torn cheek and ran a hand through her loosened hair. Wick twitched visibly, and the man looked at him.

"So," he said in a rough approximation of the Caledonian tongue, "my men say you are a great hero."

"No," Wick replied.

The man's eyebrows lifted. "Nay? But they say you felled two of our warriors quick as blinking and might have taken the rest, had they not seized the woman."

Wick said nothing. His face turned to stone; only his dark eyes showed any emotion, burning in his frozen face.

"Interesting." The Gael spat into the snow and jerked his head toward Verica. "She belongs to us now. What do you think of that?"

Still Wick did not speak, but Verica could feel his emotions. Protectiveness streamed from him and enfolded her like an invisible shield. Yet he did not move.

The Gael laughed, a low, ugly sound. "We shall see." He switched back to his own tongue, giving instructions to his men. One of the Gaels laid hold of Verica and dragged her bodily away from Wick. Ah, was she to be brutalized so soon?

Wick spun, and she saw again what lay in his eyes.

259

The intensity of it stole her breath.

I love you, she told him silently. *Now and forever*.

Chapter Thirty-Four

Wick fought desperately to master the emotions tearing through him. He felt anger—anger, yes, a flaming inferno of it—but at the moment, anger would do him no good. His father had used his anger wisely in battle and out of it, but had warned Wick against ever allowing it to overmaster him.

Already he teetered on the edge of losing control. He'd fought to break the thin leather thongs that bound his wrists, until his skin split, to no avail. He had no weapon, and he feared for Verica so much he could scarcely breathe.

What would his mother tell him, were she here with him now? What wisdom might she impart?

Save your strength. Watch for a chance. Take every opportunity to save Verica—her life matters far more than your own.

But had they any chance?

He watched Verica herded toward—and inside— one of the skin shelters. Sickness rose into the back of his throat.

No need to ask what would happen to her there. Yet the men in charge of her did not remain inside the shelter long enough to do what Wick feared.

"Blue Man. Blue Man," the Gaels' leader sang it like a taunt, summoning Wick's attention. "Do you have a name?"

Wick stared at him, striving to temper his hate with caution, and made no reply.

The man bared his teeth. "I am called Donhar MacAtholl, and I am in charge of this poor outpost—in return for the misdeeds of a past life, no doubt. You are responsible for the deaths of two of my men, both good friends. What should I do about it?"

A needless question. Wick already knew what the Gael would do about it, and so did the Gael: cause pain. His sort always sought to conquer, to destroy, and to cause pain.

Why did you bid me stay with Verica, goddess, if I could not protect her? Did you wish to show me my weakness once again?

Donhal MacAtholl nodded at the shelter wherein Verica had disappeared. "Is that your woman? Och, do not try to deny it. 'Tis visible all over your face."

Wick wanted to ask the man to let Verica go; he longed to make any sort of bargain, offer himself up for mutilation if it would buy her freedom. But he knew it would not, and he hesitated to beg.

Except…to spare Verica, perhaps he would beg. He would do whatever he must.

Mother, what shall I do?

Did he hear Essa's voice in the wind? No, only the rattle of the bare branches overhead, like the clash of stags' antlers.

If he, Wick, were a stag, then the Gaels' leader must be one also. And in the defense of the hind, the stag knew but one action.

Abruptly he said, "Fight me for her. For her freedom. If I win, you will let her go unharmed."

The man's eyebrows soared. He let his narrowed

blue gaze inspect Wick from the head downward, lingering on the old scars and the new wounds. "A true warrior among the Blue Men, are you?"

"Caledonii. We are Caledonii, and this is our land."

Donhal MacAtholl huffed a laugh. "Not for long, Master Caledonii. Your day is nearly done. Fight you, eh? And what do I get if I win?" He jerked his head toward the shelter. "A night's-long pleasure with her, eh?"

"You will do that either way."

"Me? I am a man of honor. Son of a chief in Dal Riada. Youngest son," he snorted, "which puts me in this drear and forsaken place, but son of a chief all the same. Are you, great Caledonii warrior, the son of a chief?"

Wick nodded.

"Well, ask me how I knew! That makes it right and proper, anyhow. We might fight out the ownership of this whole land here and now. If only 'twere so easy, eh? Then I might go home and find a warm bed with something other than a blue savage in it."

Savage. Wick did not betray his anger by so much as the twitch of a muscle.

Donhal MacAtholl snorted again. "You, Master Caledonii, might provide some entertainment in addition to that we wrest from your lass."

He jerked his head toward his fellows, most of whom stood watching them. "There are eight men in this camp—one of those sore wounded. That means seven men who can enjoy a woman or raise a weapon. Will you fight all of us for your lass's release?"

Wick, not sure he'd heard right, given the severe mangling of his tongue, scowled. "Say that again."

"Eh?"

"Your offer, if such it be. Speak it plainly so I may understand."

Donhal MacAtholl once more lifted his eyebrows. "My offer is this: provide us some amusement this cold night. Take all of us on, and if you best each and every one, I will release your woman."

"Face all of you? At once?"

"MacAtholl gave a great hoot. "Hear that, men? This braw warrior thinks he can take us all together. It is a grand fighter indeed! Nay, Master Caledonii, I meant but one at a time, in succession."

Swiftly, Wick assessed himself. A few of the men left here on guard had not been part of the hunting party and would be fresh. He himself felt anything but, and the wound on his forearm had cost him a great deal of blood.

"Seven of you," he repeated, stalling for time. "Do I need to kill you all?"

"Do you think you can? And is seven not enough? Need you take on every man in Del Riada?" Donhal MacAtholl sobered abruptly. "I do have two other men, but I have sent them out in pursuit of your companions. Aye, my man tells me two of your party—a man and another young woman—got away. Should they return with or without prisoners, you need not face them. Just we seven, here. What say you?"

"To the death?" Wick insisted again.

"Nay. You need only disarm your opponents."

Wick sucked in a breath. "How do I know I can trust you?" He would willingly give his life in exchange for Verica's freedom—he did not value it nearly as much as he valued her. But not for a lie.

"Have I not said I am a man of honor?"

"Honor." Wick wanted to spit then; his mouth, as he discovered, was far too dry.

"I give you my word, Blue Man."

"I have only your word that your word is worth a jot."

"Suspicious, are you not?"

Wick glared steadily at MacAtholl. "If I kill you first, how do I know these others will keep your bargain?"

MacAtholl huffed, but his eyes remained serious. "I will give them orders. And you shall face me last."

Wick hesitated, his thoughts racing wildly, looking for flaws in what seemed like the only option available to him.

Impatient, MacAtholl said, "Come, man. Is your lady's release not worth the price?"

"It is. What happens to her if I fall?" He could not allow himself to fall.

"She will travel back to Dal Riada, when next we go, as a slave."

After warming the bed of every man Wick failed to kill, for the goddess only knew how long. Verica would not break easily. But after her harsh treatment at Morirex's hands, such a fate might defeat even her bright spirit.

He could not fall. Whatever flesh and bone might endure and accomplish, he must do.

"I accept your bargain. And"—Wick looked MacAtholl in the eye—"may all your gods hold you to it."

MacAtholl hooted in what sounded like glee. Switching back to his own tongue, he gave a slew of orders, and his men scrambled. Someone cut the thong on Wick's wrists, roughly, from behind; he barely noticed the pain.

Help me, goddess, he begged again. He'd willingly die a thousand times over if it assured Verica's release.

The Gaelic warriors formed a rough circle such as Wick had seen often enough in the past during contests, most recently when his sister's companion, True, requested entry to the tribe and faced what should have been an insurmountable challenge.

Wick had himself fought the shaggy-haired incomer during that contest and been soundly defeated. The memory did nothing, now, for his confidence.

"Blue Man," MacAtholl sang out, "with what weapon would you fight?"

Wick thought about it. "Long knife."

"Good enough!"

His own long knife, wrested from him earlier, was presented to his hand. The hilt fitted between his fingers with blessed familiarity.

"Bring the woman," MacAtholl called.

"Eh?" Wick's head turned involuntarily.

"Why should she miss the entertainment?" MacAtholl bared his teeth. "Besides, it will remind you for what you fight."

As if he could forget.

"And it will impress her place upon her, watching you overthrown."

Wick grunted and fitted his fingers still more securely around the hilt of his weapon, grateful the steadily bleeding gash marked his left arm rather than his right. Blood, as he knew, made for a treacherous grip.

He turned his head again as Verica was hauled bodily from the skin tent. Eyes wide and wrists still bound, her gaze fixed on him and did not waver, though she stumbled as she was pushed forward. He sensed her bewilderment as she was shoved into place in the rough ring, and he felt it the instant comprehension seized her.

"No." Her lips formed the word, but no one heard.

"Come, men!" MacAtholl called, still in Wick's tongue. "Who will be first to face the great Caledonian champion and teach him of what we are made? Och, now, if one of us cannot easily defeat a single Blue Man, how will we ever take hold of this great land?"

Easy, did they think this would be? Wick experienced a fierce rush of rage. He could most certainly assure they would not find him easy to defeat.

Chapter Thirty-Five

Verica shuddered as her stunned mind sought to accept the scene before her eyes. It could not be what it seemed. Could not. For it looked like a contest, and Wick stood free and unfettered with a weapon in his hands.

No, not unfettered. He was penned inside a rough circle made up of wild-eyed, shaggy-haired Gaels. Verica's terror—not for herself so much as for him—threatened to trip her up again. She knew the formula of a contest at arms. But that could not be what happened here.

Wick looked at her, and in his dark eyes she saw...a whisper of the magic that had cloaked him at his arrival back in Caerena. The memory of the first time they'd kissed and of every night they'd spent in one another's arms. Heat and longing and tenderness. Love, so much love.

Sacrifice.

She saw the truth of it then—he intended to sacrifice himself for her. But to what avail? Even if he defeated his opponent, would she not still be a prisoner?

A hopeless endeavor. There must be a way she could spare him. Might Hectia and Caltram find a way to return and free them? Might she, Verica, somehow secure a weapon while these men stood distracted, and rush to Wick's defense? But her hands remained bound, and the man beside her stood so near the reek of him turned her stomach.

She turned her gaze on the man who must be the Gaels' leader, not the same who had captured them. This man, surely no older than Wick, had cunning eyes and a reckless grin, and hair streaked liberally with yellow dye. He spoke her tongue, but so badly she could barely understand what he said.

All thought fled then as one of the Gaels, holding a long knife, stepped into the ring. It expanded to afford him room; the circle also encompassed the camp fire— an added danger, just like the slush beneath Wick's worn hide boots.

The Gaels' leader emitted a cry—an order?—and the combat began. Wick hurled himself at his opponent, knife raised between his hands and face set in a rictus of determination. He appeared to have no heed whatsoever for his own safety.

The breath froze in Verica's throat; her heart stuttered in her chest. Once, twice, thrice did the Gael raise his weapon and try to press the attack upon Wick. But Wick continued to force the man back and back in a circle until, with a fierce push and a vicious kick, he tumbled his opponent into the fire.

The Gael screamed as his hair and clothing took light. His fellows hauled him out and beat down the flames with more haste than concern.

Verica gasped. Had Wick won? But no, for stepping into the ring, so swiftly, came a second opponent. Only then did Verica grasp the truth, and her heart sank sickeningly.

They expected him to face them all. No, no, no!

She sucked in a desperate breath and looked at

Wick through new eyes. She knew his strength, had felt the bulge of muscle beneath her hands in the dark, had stood beside him in battle. Yet now he looked worn, weakened by loss of blood and the previous skirmish. His shoulders bunched beneath a tangle of auburn hair, his left arm—still bleeding—hung limp at his side, and a sheen of sweat coated his skin.

He could not possibly endure, could not possibly win.

Verica wanted to scream. She wanted to decry the Gaels' courage—seven men facing one—to shame them. She wanted to protest, to leap into the ring and stop this vile contest. Anything rather than stand here watching…watching the man she loved die by hacks and slashes.

Yet when the second opponent gave a wild bellow and leaped in upon Wick, he held his own. Fiercely, half-crouching, the two men circled one another before Wick leaped, wasting no breath in a cry of warning. He took out his opponent with three well-placed slashes—shoulder, chest, hand. The Gael dropped his weapon with a roar.

The rest of the Gaels, so verbose only a moment before, muttered. Wick stood with his weapon dangling from stiff fingers, blood running down his left hand.

Verica spoke up. "Master Gael, allow me to bandage that wound on his arm."

"Eh?" All heads spun to her, including Wick's. She supposed he would have preferred her to stay silent and keep from drawing attention to herself.

She had not the strength to remain silent.

"What is that?" demanded the Gaels' leader.

She tipped up her chin. "It is only fair. Your men

have tied up their wounds. Do you possess too little honor to allow your opponent the same courtesy?"

The man's nostrils flared. "What do you, a savage, know of honor?" His hard eyes raked her. "A woman who fights like a man."

"I suppose your women lack the courage to stand at your side."

"They fight, some of them."

"Let me tend him," Verica argued, thinking at least to afford Wick a moment's respite.

The leader eyed Wick and jerked his head. The fellow beside Verica—her guard?—hauled her around and cut the thong at her wrists.

Pain flooded her fingers as the blood returned to her hands. She gritted her teeth and ignored it, her one thought for the man who stood at the center of the circle. Watched by everyone there, she stepped up to him and gazed into his eyes.

"What are you doing?" she asked, barely a breath.

"If I can defeat them all, the leader swears he will let you go. Try and catch up with Hectia—"

Verica bit her lip savagely. Did he think she would flee, leave him behind? She drew a cloth from inside her tunic and used it to bind the slash on his arm. No hope of washing it or providing anything but the rudest treatment, but if she stopped the bleeding he might retain some strength.

With her fingers lingering on his skin, she once more raised her eyes to his. Her heart pounded impossibly, and she wondered if this, here before their enemies, might be the last time she would touch him.

She could see his concern—all for her—his determination, and his love. How could this man claim to be anything but valiant? At that moment he represented to Verica everything that had ever been strong, courageous, and fine. Any doubt of him she'd felt fled in the face of it, swallowed by intense longing.

"Verica," he gasped, "I did not mean what I said. I—"

She finished the statement for him, "I love you. *I know*."

"Enough!" The Gaels' leader roared the objection and roughly waved her back. She took her place in the circle, feigning obedience she certainly did not feel, glorying in what she saw in Wick's eyes.

And in the fact that no one remembered to bind her hands.

She clasped her fingers behind her back and clenched hard as another of the Gaels—this one short and burly—bulled his way into the circle to face Wick.

What followed caused Verica physical pain. She felt every slash and blow—felt each howl of approbation when Wick took a wound. She felt the strength drain steadily from him, the way the blood had, felt his limbs grow heavy and the breath burn in his lungs. He sweated heavily and, after five opponents, had lost any lightness of movement. Yet so far he had succeeded in disarming them, one by one.

Give him my strength, Verica whispered in a prayer—she who had given up all ability for praying. *Burn me up on his behalf. I do not want to live without him.*

He looked at her then, even as his sixth opponent stepped into the circle. Had he heard her? No—he but touched on her presence, as one might on a battle charm.

New and livid wounds had now joined those he'd taken earlier—plenty of them. Blood flowed from a cut across his forehead; he blinked furiously to keep it out of his eyes.

"Chief," Verica called desperately, "you must allow me to—"

The Gaelic leader, apparently no longer amused, shook his head at her brusquely. "Let us finish this."

Wick's sixth opponent, a mere lad, should have given him little difficulty. The fact that the boy got Wick down on his back testified to Wick's obvious exhaustion. Wick threw him off with a groan and stepped on his knife hand before kicking the weapon away.

He looked then at the Gaels' leader and drew a great, shuddering breath.

"Just you left," he growled.

The man stared. He did not appear so much frightened as cautious, but Verica could not blame him if he were taken aback. A swirl of magic surrounded Wick, and as the leader moved to take up his weapon, a wind rose, rattling the bare branches of the trees overhead, making them clatter.

The Gaelic chief flexed his shoulders like a bull, raised his weapon, and stepped into the rough circle.

Verica never forgot what she saw next. It seemed to happen so quickly yet to last forever, a moment spanning many moments and stretching impossibly. The tiny encampment in the winter forest became a place apart from the world; only the handful of them inhabited it, and the two men circling, circling—staring at each other like adders poised to strike, the snow turned to ugly slush beneath their feet and the wind rattling, rattling above.

The Gaels' leader attacked first, a blistering onslaught that drove Wick to the very edge of the circle and had the breath up hard in Verica's throat. Every line of the Gael's body expressed his intent—he wanted this thing done and he wanted victory in the eyes of his men. He, like everyone there, must feel Wick's exhaustion. Yet Wick fought his way back from the edge determinedly, teeth gritted, and step by step pressed the Gael leader in turn.

At the edge of the fire, unable to step back, the Gaels' leader lifted his head and roared at his opponent. Crying words in his own tongue, he launched a crashing blow that Wick barely caught with his blade. Wick went down to his knees in the slush.

No. *No!* Verica screamed the word in her mind. Desperate, raw with a fear she could not contain, she forgot all her past hurts, all her past skepticism, and reached for belief long left behind.

Goddess, please! Goddess, hear me! I will give anything.

Head cocked back and dark eyes slits of suffering, Wick strained every muscle. The Gael withdrew his weapon and swung a blow meant to take Wick's head.

Verica sobbed. She cried out her agony, and on a surge of sheer faith transcended the woman she'd been. Without hesitation she leaped forward, willing to sacrifice herself rather than see the blade connect with Wick's flesh.

But before she could substitute her body for his, Wick changed.

It happened in a blur that befuddled Verica's vision, making her misjudge what she saw. Amid a shower of magic, Wick's limbs lengthened, his back arched and his torso grew. The brown hide of his tunic and leggings came alive, and his weapon dropped into the slush. The branches of the trees overhead seemed to bend low and take root on his head.

A man no more…

Verica screamed. So did the men who formed the circle; they broke apart and scattered, all except Wick's opponent, who stood as one mesmerized. The Gael shied from the creature that faced him, steam rising from its hide.

No longer a man but a stag.

The Gael hollered unintelligible words—a curse? a prayer?—and dropped his weapon. Verica knew he saw what she saw, what she thought she saw. He staggered back a step, and the animal reared on its back legs, a gesture of challenge. Its front hooves took the Gael in the center of his chest and struck him down.

Crushed? Dead? Verica could not tell. Her overwrought mind still doubted the evidence of her eyes. Such a thing as this could not occur.

Perhaps she—and Wick—had both died.

Seeing their leader go down, the Gaels yelped and hollered; they goggled at the great stag in their midst and raised their weapons. A gang of hunters could bring down a deer, and terror possessed Verica's heart once again.

The stag turned from the downed man to face its would-be attackers. It—*he*—shook his antlers, and a shower of enchantment erupted around him, like snowflakes. He looked at Verica with Wick's fathomless dark eyes, and she heard his voice in her mind: *Run.*

She did not know that she could. Challenging the knot of Gaels who seemed prepared to attack him, Wick snorted. She heard his voice echo inside her head still more loudly. *Verica, run!*

Her paralysis broke the way ice shatters. She darted forward and snatched up Wick's long knife from beneath his hooves.

And she ran.

All part of the magic, she told herself as she darted between the naked boles of the trees and set a wild course away. She had dreamed of running like this. She might still be dreaming. Surely it could not truly be happening. Yet it sounded, if not felt, real; a howl of pursuit rose behind her, and stealing one desperate look over her shoulder, she saw that a dark form followed close on her heels.

The hart.

Wick.

Feet pounding, and with his knife thrust through the loop at her belt, she ran on, gasping. And ran. She still heard the Gaels coming after and the swift rushing flight of the animal just behind her. Breath soon threatened to fail her, and her legs went weak as boiled leather. Her vision blurred so she could barely see what lay ahead.

Through the dying afternoon's gloom came— what? Two men. The Gaels sent out by their leader to pursue Hectia and Caltram? Verica checked, she stumbled and went down to one knee in deep, unbroken snow.

The hart very nearly overran her. She felt the heat of his body as he loomed above, trembling. The two men halted also, facing them—Verica saw them staring.

She heard the cries of those coming behind.

Trapped. Could she and Wick—the hart—break through? Even if they did, their pursuers might shoot him down like any other deer sighted during the hunt. But no—it could not happen. He had fought too hard. He deserved to live.

Please, she prayed with all her heart, with all her being. *Goddess. Not for me, but for him.*

Wick blew a great breath over her like a shower of magic. The trees clashed overhead so loudly she could no longer hear the cries of their pursuers.

Wick spoke in her ear and bade her, *Run with me.*

Chapter Thirty-Six

They ran, Verica with the great stag now just ahead of her, a flash of russet in her blurred sight. She followed him more by instinct than otherwise— followed the sense of him, bidden and held by their deep connection. The breath surged in her lungs, and her limbs stretched out impossibly. She looked down at herself and saw…

Her legs were not her legs but the front limbs of a deer, ending in hooves. White.

Verica knew enough to remember that when it came to the gods' creatures, white equated enchantment. Yet Wick—who must surely encompass all magic—possessed an ordinary, russet-colored hide.

Verica did not understand. But she ran, following him as if tugged along by his great energy.

Arrows came at them from behind, just a few bolts, which they swiftly outdistanced even as they outdistanced the pursuers themselves. At length, nothing surrounded them but silence and the wind still rattling the branches far overhead.

Wick decreased his pace and came to a gradual halt, breathing hard and puffing visible steam. Unbroken snow stretched ahead of them and on either side.

Wick's ears twitched; he listened. Verica also strained her heightened senses but could hear no further sounds of pursuit.

Wick turned, and she stared into his eyes. Yes, his gaze remained the same—Wick's gaze—dark, mysterious. Loving.

A sob broke from Verica's throat, and she collapsed into the snow, a woman again.

She lay with the breath pumping in her lungs, the cold snow burning one cheek, wondering what had happened, and how. After a moment, gentle hands seized her. Strong arms lifted her and turned her around. She fell forward against Wick's chest.

He was a man, and clothed. They both stood clothed, he in the hide leggings, boots, and tunic that matched the russet hue of the hart's hide. Deer hide clothing, she realized. Her own clothing, once very similar to his, had now paled to a color only a shade deeper than that of the snow.

She contemplated it while they clutched each other, her arms clamped tight around his body, her cheek smashed against his shoulder. His breath stirred her hair and warmed one ear. Their hearts calmed and at length beat in time.

"What just happened?" Verica asked then.

"I am not certain." He swallowed. "Deer. We were deer."

"How?"

"I do not know that either. It has happened to me before."

She drew far enough away to study him. The wound across his forehead had dripped blood all down his face. He looked exhausted, but his eyes—those deep, dark eyes—remained steady.

"When our hunters shot you," she said in wonder.

"When you were first brought in—it had happened then?"

He nodded. "My mother would call it an enchantment."

"So might anyone." Verica reached up and touched his cheek in wonder. "You saved me. Back there, you would have given your life for me. I have never seen anyone so brave."

He started to shake his head, but she trapped his face between her hands and prevented him.

"You cannot deny you would have sacrificed your safety over and over again in exchange for mine."

Emotion flooded his eyes. Hoarsely he said, "It is what a man does for someone he loves."

As simple and as profound as that. Was there more to be said? If so, Verica did not possess the words.

Instead she kissed him, a soft brush of lips on lips, mouth on mouth, one she meant as a pledge. When it ended, tears stood in her eyes.

"Say you will stay with me, Wick map Radoc. No"—she placed her fingers on his lips—"I do not care what happened in the past. I don't even care why. This is not about choice but about need. Stay with me, or let me stay with you. Else I will need to follow you all over Caledonia."

"You would not."

"I would," she assured him. "Would you not follow after your heart?"

He lowered his forehead until it touched hers. "You deserve someone better."

"There is no one better."

"Ah, Verica—"

"Wick, I might search the world and not hope to

find a finer man than you. Let us dismiss the past and begin new from this moment. Yes?"

She felt it the instant he acquiesced. A small smile quirked one side of his mouth. "Yes."

Peace crashed over Verica in a wave. "Come," she told him, "let us tie up the rest of your wounds, else the Gaels will be able to track us by the blood. I do not think they will, though. Once our trail changes from hoofprints to footprints, they may well lose their courage."

Wick nodded. Verica stepped away from him reluctantly.

"Wick, I want you to know—after I wedded Morirex, I lost the ability to pray. I think I felt betrayed by the goddess when life with him turned so hard. But"—she cast a look at the man standing bloodied and torn beneath the bare trees—"when I thought I would lose you, I *prayed*."

He did smile then. "And you were answered."

"Yes. What do you think it means?"

"There is a kind of belief that goes straight from our hearts to the gods' ears."

"Imagine that—yet another gift you have given me."

****

Verica tore her undertunic to pieces and used the soiled fabric to tie up Wick's wounds. Not the best bandaging, he acknowledged, but they possessed nothing else, having lost both packs. His own clothing proved too shredded and blood-soaked to serve.

A curious thing, but he barely remembered the men he'd faced when standing against the Gaels and he hadn't felt any of the blows or cuts he'd sustained.

Those moments seemed hazy and indistinct, like something from a mad dream.

In retrospect, even the flight with Verica, their hooves pounding the ground and sending up great gouts of snow, seemed impossible. But the moment when he took Verica into his arms, when they kissed, would endure with him forever.

She loved him. As he loved her—to the core of his spirit and beyond. Could she save him? Might such a love be enough to redeem him from the past?

She said she wanted to dismiss the past, wished to start new from that moment they came together. He did not think it would be so easy for him.

They moved on slowly, leaving but two sets of boot prints in the snow, Wick's blood-stained. They talked in whispers, and the cold dark closed around them. Wick could hear no sounds of pursuit—nor could he feel any danger playing along the threads of his consciousness. But that did not make him relax; a man, as he had learned, might lose much through carelessness.

What might the Gaels make of what had occurred, back there? He shook his head, and Verica, intensely aware of him, murmured, "What is it?"

"Nothing. Do you think Hectia and Caltram got clean away?"

"I do. The men the Gaels' leader sent out after them came back empty-handed."

"Donhal MacAtholl. He said that was his name. I wonder shall we hear of him again."

"I devoutly hope not. If I never see another Gael, it will be too soon."

"Do you think Hectia will head back to Caerena?"

"Yes, unless she has lost her way."

"I hope," Wick said, heartfelt, "we do not." The impetus of the battle had faded, and he hurt from the head downward.

Verica touched his hand. "No, Wick; I suspect we have found it."

Reality faded for him after that. There remained only the determined taking of one step after another, the cold and dark, the pain. And his connection with Verica—that upheld him, lent strength every time she so much as brushed against him. He could feel her thoughts even when she did not speak them aloud.

For a time, he fancied his father walked beside him, barely seen in the dark. But how could that be? Radoc had lost the ability to walk, and after all, he'd perished when his hut burned, back during the raid.

On the night Wick had failed him.

Son, keep walking. It is not long until morning.

"I am walking."

"I know you are," Verica replied.

Wick, focused on the man at his side, disregarded her.

"How is it you are able to walk?"

Radoc gave one of his deep, rumbling laughs. *All it takes, here where I am, is believing. All anything takes, son—even where you linger—is believing. Do you understand that?*

"No." Wick dredged up the pain from deep inside him and presented it to his father unstintingly. "You must be so ashamed of me."

Radoc grunted. *I could not be more proud.*

That made Wick stare. For the first time in years he looked at his father and truly saw him. Radoc's dark hair, liberally streaked by gray, gleamed with health. He moved with the strong confidence Wick remembered from his youth. But how had Wick failed to notice he overtopped his father's broad, powerful figure in height? Ah—he'd finished growing after Radoc's injury. He'd been but a lad when life changed so drastically.

"Why do you say that?" he questioned. "I broke, Father—I crumbled the night you and Mother died. I abandoned our tribe; I handed leadership over to Brude. After all the years you fought and struggled to hold the place of chief, I merely passed it to your harshest critic, and fled."

Your Mother insists you needed to find yourself. You always possessed valiance—you had to find your wisdom.

"Mother?" Wick's heart faltered. "You see her still?"

See her? She is inside me. Inside you too, if you could but sense it. She is everywhere. As are we all.

"I wish I could see her, be with her."

Then look. It is something I failed at when I was alive, and something at which your mother always excelled. I battled hard, yes.

"Harder than anyone I've ever known."

Yes, and where did the strength lie, at the end of it all? In love. Your mother kept our strength always at her heart.

Radoc nodded toward Verica. *The love of a woman makes a man; it completes him. The whole is stronger than the half. She is a good woman.*

"Yes." Wick's overwrought mind struggled with all of it, his father here, whole and not burned in the fire. His strength and reassurance.

"Father, are you saying you forgive me?"

There is nothing to forgive.

"But I abandoned my place in the tribe, our tribe."

Radoc turned his head; their eyes met. In his father's eyes Wick beheld all strength and all courage, tempered by his mother's kindness.

Yes, son. And now you will go home and take it up again.

Chapter Thirty-Seven

"I must go back. I need to return home."

Wick repeated the words, not for the first time. Urgency gripped him, warring with his weakness, which reached all the way to his bones.

He opened his eyes and blinked furiously at the faces all around him. Callorix the healer—how was that possible? He and Verica remained somewhere out in the forest. And there, the shaman, Ivomagus. And yes, Verica herself—he'd been certain he sensed her presence.

He must be dreaming once again, just like when he thought he walked and spoke with his father. Surely that had been a dream?

"He keeps saying that," Ivomagus remarked.

"He is out of his head," the healer pronounced.

"You will go back." Verica touched his brow. "Hush now and rest."

Darkness descended like a blow, rendering him senseless.

When he again awoke, it was to see red eyes gleaming at him through the darkness. He lay quietly, just breathing, and counted them. One, two, five, seven eyes…did they belong to the Gaels he'd battled? To wolves? Were he and Verica back out in the snowy forest?

He fumbled for his long knife and instead

encountered soft flesh, part of it twined around him. An arm lay clamped across his chest. He traced it to a shoulder and then the softness of a naked breast.

Verica.

He lay wrapped in her arms, warm in her bed. And the glowing eyes of the encroaching wolves could only be embers in the dying fire.

The deep comfort of Verica's presence sounded through him like a bell. He lay just breathing; his thoughts stirred to life.

Had he truly walked with his father? No, as the healer said, he'd been raving, out on his feet.

Did it matter if it had truly happened?

No. Magic blended with reality; the dead were everywhere, never lost. Men and women turned into deer and back again.

The one enduring truth was love.

Ah, he'd been fighting too hard, struggling too hard, doubting too much. Meanwhile the goddess had brought to him a gift of love, all his heart—or arms—could hold.

He turned his head and kissed Verica's cheek, there in the dark. As soon as he stirred, his body screamed in protest. But the body didn't matter, not so long as the spirit endured.

Mother, are you here?

The dark seemed to close in around him, to brush his face with feathered fingers. Comfort flooded through him. She listened.

"I must go back."

Verica failed to rouse at the sound of his voice; she too slept the deep slumber of exhaustion. It didn't matter; he knew in his heart that she heard.

All will be well. His mother's voice, soft and musical, came from all around him. *You have learned an important lesson, son: there is no such thing as death.*

"Only…only parting?"

A smile lit Essa's voice, the kind that used to turn her mist-gray eyes bright. *Not even parting. Your father and I are part of this land, we flow with the water. We dance across the moors, we run with the deer.* She paused while the significance of that penetrated Wick's mind. *Wick, my darling, we are Caledonia, and it will endure forever.*

"Yes, Mother." He stirred again, in wonder, and started to ask, "But—"

What can there be, son, except joy?

"Joy," Wick repeated, "and magic. You knew that, always."

Verica did stir then, moving in his arms. Or did his arms merely tighten around her? Lying twined together so tightly, he could not tell.

She touched his chest, a feather-light touch, and then his face. She whispered, "Wick? Are you all right?"

"I am well." Very well. He'd been given a gift. *Joy.*

"And," Verica whispered, "all is right between us?"

How could it be otherwise? She was part of him, spirit and flesh. "Oh, yes."

"Good." She snuggled closer. "Good, because I love you. So much."

"And I love you, Verica."

She kissed him softly, without demand. Comfort

streamed from her lips and flowed throughout his body, easing his pain.

When the kiss ended, Verica sighed. "Do you remember healing me?"

"Eh?"

"Because you did, when we slept together. You mended my wounds and the pain in my heart. I will do the same for you now, my brave warrior. And then you will return to the Epidii and heal them also."

"Will you go with me, back to my tribe?"

"If I am wanted."

"You are wanted."

"Tell me something, Wick. Tell me, did we truly turn into deer back there, in the forest?"

"Yes."

"And run faster than the wind for a very great distance?"

"We did."

"How?"

"Magic—a gift from the goddess, the very best kind."

"I hope the magic stays with us all our days."

"I believe so, Verica. I do believe it will."

****

The new day dawned with a soft sky and a breath of warm air from the south, hinting at spring. Wick emerged from Verica's hut wearing a wealth of bandages and stood for a moment scenting the wind like the hart he had been. Home lay in that breeze. Did the very air beckon him?

He tried to imagine returning home, and his mind shied. What could he say to them, those on whom he'd turned his back? That he'd had a change of heart? Put his doubts behind him and meant now to take up his place?

But his place had been given to another. Brude had stepped into it weeks ago and might now lead with an iron hand. No weakling, Brude, to be pushed aside and expected to stay there.

Verica emerged from her hut behind him and paused, eyes clear blue in the morning light, black hair hanging loose over her shoulders. She looked so beautiful, Wick caught his breath.

"A soft day," she observed.

"So it is."

"You should not be up on your feet, soft day or otherwise."

He shrugged. "You cannot expect me to lie abed when there are things to be done."

She quirked an eyebrow, and to forestall further objections, he went on, "I never had a chance to ask—did Hectia and Caltram make it back safely?"

Grief flooded her eyes, and she shook her head. Before she could complete the motion, a furor broke out, cries and calls—not of alarm but what sounded like gladness.

Verica dashed forward, only to be intercepted by Cunarda, who darted out from the chief's house.

"I heard my daughter's voice—Hectia!"

A weary and footsore pair appeared from the trees and stumbled into the settlement hand in hand. Wick, following Verica more slowly, arrived in time to watch Cunarda enfold Hectia in her arms, with Smerta close alongside.

The rest of the tribe crowded around, exclaiming excitedly.

"I thought you lost!" Cunarda wept. "Oh, what happened to you?"

Hectia, struggling not to weep also, said, "We tracked too far west before finding our way and heading home. Almost stumbled upon yet another Gaelic settlement. Mother, this is Caltram map Enestimus, chief of tribe Dimitii. He and I—we have forged an alliance to stand and fight together."

"Have you?" Cunarda turned amazed eyes on Caltram. "Son of Enestimus, yes—I have heard your name. My husband, Ammin, never did succeed in forging an alliance with your father."

Caltram, who looked exhausted and nursed a livid wound of his own across one shoulder, answered her forthrightly, "Yes, Mistress. My father believed in his heart that each tribe should stand on its own. But I am not my father. Times change, as do our needs."

"You have brought my daughter home to me; that is all that matters now."

"Mother—" Hectia's eyes filled with tears. "It is not all that matters. I bring grave news. Motius is dead."

"I know, Daughter. Verica told us."

"Verica!" Hectia, looking up, located Verica and Wick near the rear of the crowd. Astonishment widened her eyes. "But we thought them captured, lost! Caltram, they are here! How, Mistress Verica, are you here ahead of us? Mother, when we fled, we feared they would not get away."

"We nearly did not." Verica pressed forward and the tribesfolk allowed both her and Wick to pass.

Hectia seized her hands. "Then, by what miracle are you—?"

Verica glanced at Wick before she replied, "Master Wick fought for our freedom. Then we…we too fled."

Caltram reached out and clasped Wick's arm. "I am grateful you found your way free, Master Wick," he said with admiration in his eyes. "I hope you will not think harshly of me for choosing flight. I needed to get Mistress Hectia safe away at any cost."

Wick smiled. "I am the last man to condemn anyone for his actions. We are all safe now. Let us concentrate on the future, and forging strong alliances."

Caltram nodded, but he did not look satisfied.

Chapter Thirty-Eight

"A word with you, Master Wick, if you do not mind."

Wick, sitting alone outside Verica's hut, looked up to find Caltram standing over him in the evening gloom.

It had been a good day, a hopeful one. Spirits ran high in the Caerena settlement; now evening came with the same soft breath from the south that seemed to beckon Wick homeward.

What he might find there, he still did not know, but his heart felt ready to find out.

He got to his feet, and Caltram extended his hand; they clasped arms heartily.

Wick liked the young man, steady and forthright. If the Caledonii succeeded in standing against the Gaels, it would be thanks to young people like Caltram, Hectia, Smerta, and his own brother, Tally.

"Please sit," he invited and indicated the stoop he'd occupied. "Let us speak together."

They sat; for several moments though, Caltram failed to break the silence.

At last he ventured, "It is peaceful. Such times are few and far between."

"My mother used to say that if you kept quiet at nightfall, you could hear the heartbeat of the world."

"Your mother used to say?" Caltram repeated with

an inquiring look.

"She was killed in a raid."

"Ah—you have my sympathy. I have to say, Master Wick, I am curious about you. I hear little but praise of you from everyone I have met here at Caerena."

"Oh?"

"The great hero from out of the south. It's whispered you wear an invisible cloak of magic."

"Do not believe all your ears may hear."

"No?" Caltram gave him a frank look through clear eyes. "Then answer me this: how did you manage to fight your way free of all those Gaelic warriors?"

"I made a bargain with their leader and then faced them, one by one."

Caltram shook his head. "That is more or less what I did hear. You must be a very great warrior."

"No. But I have fought against the Gaels most of my life."

"Still, there were how many of them?"

"I faced seven, including their leader."

Caltram studied him closely. "I must admit, you carry wounds enough to prove it. What made you undertake such a feat?"

"It was the only available choice."

"Still, I cannot imagine the courage I would need to have, nor the confidence to think I could win, had I been in your place. I feel abashed."

"Abashed?" Wick bent a look on the young man. "Why?"

"I had an instant to choose whether I should stay and continue to fight or get Mistress Hectia away. I thought only of her. Just as it seems you, in turn, thought only of Mistress Verica."

"I told you before, we all do as we must. You got the girl safe home, did you not? That is what matters."

"It is generous of you to say so. I must admit, my heart rather than my head made the choice. But I can only imagine what a man of your ilk must think of me."

"Master Caltram..." Wick closed his eyes for an instant, feeling in full the irony of the moment. This young man's remorse echoed his own so closely it made him ache. At that instant he knew he had come full circle on a hard road. There in the soft dark, he wondered about it all—at his impulse to leave home, the goddess bidding him stay and heal Verica, the magic of their flight.

Would that magic ever come to him again? Did it matter?

"I see," Caltram said heavily, "you cannot so much as look at me. I do not blame you. I am ashamed of myself."

"Do not be."

"But..."

"Do not." Wick opened his eyes and looked full into the young man's face. "I do not doubt your courage," he said. "You took your father's place and stood to fight the Gaels—no mean feat, as I can attest. And you followed your instinct to protect Mistress Hectia; it was a good instinct."

"Yet it left you to face those savages alone. You might have died, and Mistress Verica taken into slavery."

"Chief Caltram, I have learned that men fight in many ways, sometimes invisible battles. You know what you've heard of me, but not all. I have stood where you stand, been asked to take on leadership of a tribe before I was ready. I did not do half so fine a job as you."

"I find that difficult to believe."

"It is true. I hope you will dismiss any remorse from your mind. I will be honored to form an alliance between the Epidii and the Dimitii."

"Hectia told me you were kind as well as brave. I would have to add merciful to your attributes," Caltram said ruefully.

"A strong man can afford mercy. Have you told Mistress Cunarda that you and Hectia mean to wed?"

Caltram's face lit. "Yes."

"And when will the handfasting take place?"

"Soon. Hectia would like Mistress Verica to be present, so it should take place before you leave and return to your tribe. You must be anxious, indeed, to reach home."

He was. And again, he was not. At the thought of presenting himself there, his stomach flipped in a slow roll.

"I shall have to find them first. They were on the move and falling back eastward when I left." Brude would not be happy to see him. The news that Wick meant to reassume his father's place would rouse his every instinct to battle.

What if it came to a fight, a war between Wick and his old friend?

Ah, then he would fight with everything he had.

To Caltram he said, "Remain here with the Caerena in my absence, if you will. Join with Hectia and lend her your strength. We are like points of light, Chief Caltram, shining against a great darkness. Whatever may happen, do not permit your light to go out."

****

"I hear you've been to see the healer."

Verica spun from her task of organizing supplies for the journey south when Ivomagus spoke directly behind her.

"And now"—his quick gaze marked the goods lined up in front of her—"you prepare to leave us again. Tell me, Mistress Verica, do you intend to return?"

A good question. Verica considered it, and not for the first time. This was her tribe, anchored to her spirit, and always would be. But her heart had fastened itself to Wick; wherever he went, she wanted to be also.

"I do not know," she told Ivomagus frankly. "We combine tribes and will be stronger together; I cannot say where the bulk of us will end up. But I did think it a mark of good faith to take some supplies with us, what little we can spare. We have yet a bounty of ale and these weapons we stole from the Gaels. The Caerena may be in dire straits, but listening to Master Wick, it is plain the Epidii have lost nearly everything."

Ivomagus spared no glance for the goods she had gathered, but focused on her face. She wondered if, with his affinity for magic, he could perceive the deep spell that had ridden her while she ran as a hind through the forest. A white hind... Did some tendrils of enchantment linger around her still?

A curious expression came into the shaman's eyes.

"Mistress Hectia has requested I speak words of handfasting over her and Chief Caltram map Enestimus. She would like them said tonight, so you may be there. She tells me you will leave at first light."

"Yes."

"I wondered…" Here Ivomagus faltered. "I wondered whether you and Master Wick also wish such words spoken."

"Ah."

And what had it taken for Ivomagus to come and ask that question so forthrightly?

Impulsively she laid a hand on his forearm. "There will be no handfasting for me and Master Wick before we depart. None of us knows what may happen in the days to come—unless you have Seen?"

"Glimpses of things, I have. There is to be a rallying point in the south, a great tower. An enduring light shines there."

Verica's brows lifted. "Good—that is good."

Ivomagus nodded, but she saw the grief in his eyes.

Wishing to leave no doubt or false hope in his mind, she added softly, "Even though Wick and I do not join now, my heart rests securely in his keeping."

From somewhere, the shaman summoned a smile and bowed his head. "Then, Mistress, what can I do but wish you every happiness?"

Chapter Thirty-Nine

"Are you feeling anxious about returning home?" Verica asked Wick the question as they prepared their packs for departure the next morning. He glanced at her and wondered how to reply.

Had she felt his turmoil as he tossed and turned all last night? Even after they made love, his mind refused to release him to the solace of sleep.

Now, in the clear, cold morning, she laid aside the bundle she'd just tied shut and came to stand directly in front of him, very nearly in his arms.

She searched his eyes before saying, "I know you have doubts about how your family may receive you. But surely you do not doubt this is the right thing to do?"

He smiled tightly and shook his head. He felt as if he'd weathered a raging storm since leaving home, one that had dealt with him harshly but changed him, like metal in the fire.

He said, "None of us—Caerena, Dimitii, or Epidii—may be strong enough to stand alone. But together we might yet hope to hold this land we love."

"It is all about love."

Wick made no reply. No doubt interpreting the expression in his eyes, Verica whispered, "They will welcome you."

"I hope so. You bring them supplies they no doubt

need desperately. It is uncommonly generous of the Caerena to offer so much."

"A sign of good faith, as I told Ivomagus."

"Ivomagus?" Wick experienced a spike of uneasiness amid his sea of doubt.

"He came to me last night and asked if I'd be returning from the Epidii lands after we offer the alliance."

"What did you tell him?"

"That I did not know. Will I be returning here, Master Wick?"

He took her in his arms, drew her against him and gazed into her eyes. Forever lay there, and the greater measure of his strength.

"I hope that wherever I may be, there you may be."

"That is my wish, also."

She kissed him, offering herself up in that wondrous manner she had, glad and unstinting. Wick's doubts fled, and he felt healing spiral through him in ripples pure and strong.

"What did I ever do to deserve you?" he wondered aloud when their lips parted. "You have become my strength and my guiding light."

"The light is all inside you," she declared. "I saw it from the first, even when you did not."

"Now," he vowed devoutly, "I must strive to be worthy of the faith you have in me."

"You will succeed, Wick map Radoc. I have no doubt at all."

****

The journey proved long and hard. A score of times, Wick despaired of locating his tribe amid the snow and threat of attack by overwintering Gaels. It made him wonder—after such a long and troubled journey, was he not meant to return home after all? He felt a fool, with a train of Caerena tribesfolk, including Smerta, following behind him, unable to find his own people.

Throughout it all, Verica remained his solace and his strength. She slept in his arms on the trail at night and never once questioned his choice of direction.

Yet he knew he could not lead her and others of her folk unendingly through the winter forest. At last, footsore and weary, he turned to Verica, who sat beside their evening fire.

The others, save one man on patrol, had already fallen asleep, victims of their weariness. He and Verica were as good as alone.

Softly he said, "I fear I have lost my way." Again. "We have traveled too far east along the path my folk should have taken." Bleakly, he concluded, "Either they have all been killed or they have given up the fight and scattered."

That, too, would be his fault, laid squarely at his feet. How could he ever forgive himself?

Verica covered his hand with hers. "Let us get a night's good sleep; it will look far better come morning."

Wick shook his head. "In the morning I must make a choice. It may be best for us to turn for home—your home." And he would need to accept the fact that he truly had failed his people.

Verica's blue gaze remained steady on his. "Save that decision for morning."

But he had difficulty sleeping, took a turn at watch, and never returned to his place in the blankets beside

Verica until near dawn.

The dream came upon him abruptly, so it felt as if he tumbled into it. A deer once more, he led a herd of others all running before a band of hunters. Like a flock of birds, they all changed direction as one, connected by instinct far deeper than reason. West—he needed to turn west.

In his ear, his mother's voice sounded. *Son, come home.*

He ran. The breath surged in his lungs and freedom flooded through him, leaving no room for doubt, grief, or remorse. The land spoke to him and called as his mother had.

Up ahead he saw a tower rising into the air, amid the branches of the trees—a symbol of strength.

He awoke suddenly and lay breathing into the new dawn, his heart pounding. The sun had already risen on a soft day, for midwinter. The other members of his party stirred around him; Verica sat up in their shared blankets, her black hair tumbled over her shoulders.

He reached out and caressed it, let it slide through his fingers like black rain. The Vision of the broch lingered in his mind.

She turned her head to look at him, a question in her eyes.

He told her, "I know where to look now, Verica." *Home.* "We will try the old place."

"The old place?" she repeated.

"Where my parents died. A miracle may have occurred and allowed them to retake it."

A smile invaded her eyes. "Good. Me, I no longer have trouble believing in miracles."

****

"How much farther?" Smerta asked as they moved steadily south and west, with the soft morning shimmering around them. Dangerous country, this. Brude must have set himself up as a bold leader indeed, if he'd taken the tribe back so far toward territory the Gaels had seized.

And Wick would now need to challenge Brude. Yet he felt no doubt, only a sense of destiny, humble as it was strong. With each step he took, he felt more clearly the pull of home.

No surprise when, just before midday, they caught the faint scent of wood smoke on the still air. Or when, not long after, they crossed what must be the Epidii patrol line and encountered two men on watch.

Wick knew them both, of course, and they knew him. Staring in astonishment at Wick and the party behind him, they immediately lowered their weapons.

"Chief Wick!" exclaimed the younger of the two, a contemporary of Wick's brother, Tally.

A good sign that the boy still called him Chief. An even better sign that both men regarded him with what looked like unqualified gladness.

"You have retaken our home ground?" he asked them. "When, and how?"

The second man, called Pollix, answered him proudly, "We drove the Gaels out in a series of fierce raids. Young Tally says we will build a grand tower here—a sign of our strength."

A tower. Wick grinned. "Imagine that."

"And now that you have returned," the man continued, "all must come right." He eyed the Caerena warriors in Wick's train. "Have you brought us more men?"

"I have, Pollix."

"The goddess be praised! But come, everyone will be so happy to see you."

Wick exchanged one speaking look with Verica before he followed the two guards through the trees, the rest of his party trailing him with new energy in their steps. Both men called ahead, and folk came streaming, alarm and then disbelief in their faces.

Foremost among them Wick saw his young brother, Tally, who came at him in a run, arms spread and a smile wreathing his face.

His brother Tally, who had his mother's eyes.

Wick knew, then, he had indeed come home.

Chapter Forty

"It has been a joyful day, and no mistake." Verica lay in Wick's arms within the newly constructed hut they'd been granted. An honor, she gathered the gift of the hut to be. A visible mark of respect she suspected Wick had trouble believing he deserved.

They'd spent a long time sitting beside the fire with his family and other members of his tribe, speaking of the immediate past and making plans for the future. Even now she could feel Wick's excitement and wonder. She doubted he'd be able to sleep anytime soon.

Well enough; left alone with this man, she could readily think of any number of things to do besides sleep.

She wiggled closer and slid her fingers inside his tunic, which she'd already loosened.

"Well?" she whispered.

"Well?" he returned with a smile in his voice. Wondrous, how she could feel all the emotions burgeoning inside him and the strength of his affection for her.

No, not affection: love.

"At least, Wick map Radoc, you can no longer deny your family was glad to see you. Your sister is overjoyed at having you back. And even your friend Brude seems willing to place the leadership of the

Epidii back into your hands."

"You are right." A miracle, that. Brude did seem ready to pass the place of chief back where he felt it belonged, a thing Wick could scarcely fathom. "They have forgiven me. I cannot imagine why."

"I can. They know you, Wick, and they sense the same things inside you I do. Your brother, Tally, insists he knew you would return. Is he a Seer, or did he just judge you more shrewdly than you judged yourself?"

"Tally has my mother's gift. He will achieve great things some day and be a man among thousands."

"That sounds very like a prediction."

Wick mused on, in an other-worldly voice. "Tally possesses Mother's magic and Barta has Father's stubborn strength. Why did I not see that back when I so hastily condemned her? Through them, my parents live on."

"Through them," Verica agreed softly, "and through you. I believe you have taken the best of both your parents, and made your own way."

Wick grunted, a sound that denoted dissatisfaction.

"Let me put it more plainly." Verica placed her lips a mere whisper from his ear. "You are the best of the Caledonii because you have strength tempered with understanding."

"Ah, Verica, I fear it will take me some time to accept that." He cupped her face between his hands. "And, beautiful warrior maiden, what of the question my sister asked, and the answer you gave? Would you truly be willing to handfast with me?"

Verica replied, unstinting, "In my mind, in my heart, the bonds are already tied. But if you want the answer spoken out, Wick, then I say yes. It would give me great joy to become your wife."

"I do not know what the future may hold, Verica. I can only promise to give myself wholly to it, and to you."

She told him, "Ah, but I do know what the future holds."

He smiled. "Just like Tally?"

"No, not like Tally. Like a woman who believes in the man who holds her heart securely in his strong hands. Days filled with hope, Wick. Nights filled with laughter and belonging. A wealth of love."

"How can you be so certain?"

"I have felt your spirit, Wick map Radoc. When we ran through the forest together, it joined most surely with mine. I carry part of you inside me now. Yours is the very soul of Caledonia—embattled but never defeated."

She pressed her lips to his and whispered the words into his mind on a breath of pure magic. "You, my love, are living proof: Caledonian hearts are both valiant and wise."

A word about the author...

Award-winning author Laura Strickland delights in time traveling to the past and searching out settings for her books, be they Historical Romance, Steampunk, or something in between.

Born and raised in Western New York, she's pursued lifelong interests in lore, legend, magic, and music, all reflected in her writing. Although she enjoys travel, she's usually happiest at home not far from Lake Ontario, with her husband and her "fur" child, a rescue dog.

Author of numerous Historical and Contemporary Romances, she is the creator of the Buffalo Steampunk Adventure series set in her native city. *Valiant and Wise* is the second book in her new historical Hearts of Caledonia series.